A
HOPELESS
CASE

K. K. Beck

A HOPELESS CASE

a mystery novel

THE MYSTERIOUS PRESS
New York · Tokyo · Sweden · Milan
Published by Warner Books

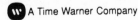 A Time Warner Company

CS
F
M
BECK

 Mysterious Press books are published by
Warner Books, Inc., 1271 Avenue of the Americas,
New York, NY 10020.
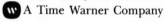 A Time Warner Company

The Mysterious Press name and logo are trademarks of
Warner Books, Inc.
Printed in the United States of America

First Printing: March 1992

10 9 8 7 6 5 4 3 2 1

Library of Congress Cataloging in Publication Data

Beck, K. K.
    A hopeless case / K.K. Beck.
        p.   cm.
    ISBN 0-89296-479-0
    I. Title.
    PS3552.E248H6   1992
    813'.54--dc20   91-58023

For Molly Friedrich
with thanks

Chapter 1

Jane wondered if she looked as stupid as she felt. She was slouching in front of a piano, one hand wrapped languorously around a microphone, in a tall, narrow house built in 1688 and overlooking a canal in Amsterdam, now serving as a restaurant with a smoky little bar on the first floor.

She shook out her brown hair, a practiced movement that also emphasized the way her dress curved around her breasts and hips. Then there was the studied bow of the head and the flexing of the mike cord, as if she were composing herself, before a brief nod to her accompanist. All these moves, which she had picked up from old movies since girlhood, and which she had once found reasonably amusing to execute, now seemed hopelessly corny. Maybe even—although she suppressed the thought —a little pathetic.

Jane, who felt that she had been born into an age glaringly devoid of charm and elegance, had tried to make her act a gentle homage to a classier era. But perhaps, she was beginning to think, it was just shabbily retro.

She was pleased to see that the preppy American, with whom she had established meaningful eye contact in the past, was here again tonight, but this time without his friends. She tilted her head back lazily, then brought it forward again, timed so her face ended up level with the microphone just as she began to sing in a husky but melodious voice, giving a world-weary air to "Just One of Those Things."

The noise level in the bar lowered briefly, but, she noted with irritation, rose again as she plunged through the lyrics. Fortunately, however, an exuberant female shriek from the corner of the room drowned her out when she went flat on "a trip to the moon on gossamer wings."

She glanced at the American. He seemed to be watching her with appreciation, and even glared menacingly at some noisy people at a table nearby. She rewarded him with lowered eyelids and the merest suggestion of a smile. He was rather attractive, with wavy hair, intelligent eyes, an athletic body. He looked younger than Jane. Lately, a lot of the attractive men around her looked younger.

It had come to that rather sooner than she had expected it would. If she hadn't been in mid-phrase, Jane would have sighed wistfully. He wore a Brooks Brothers summer suit, and a tie with little blips on it, which she hoped were not mallard ducks in flight. Moneyed, traditional East Coast Americans, if they were the hearty, expansive, check-grabbing type who chummed up to headwaiters and sang along at the opera, were okay. But she had a West Coast aversion to wardrobes that looked as if they were assembled primarily from Maine catalogs.

Really, she admonished herself, I must stop this tacky habit of flirting with the customers. If I don't look out, I'll turn into some predatory old harridan, leering at wholesome young American boys. She transferred her gaze from the man in the Brooks Brothers suit to an Amstel beer poster on the opposite wall.

When the song ended, she turned briefly to her accompanist, an irritable conservatory student with bad skin and an unwieldy Dutch name, Bouwdewijn Overdijk. He was giving her a nasty sneer, no doubt because she'd gone flat. Big deal. She could still sell a song, even if she wasn't always on key. And his timing was rotten anyway. Europeans couldn't syncopate worth a damn, no matter how musical they were. When she'd brought that up earlier in the evening, he'd had the nerve to tell her he thought the pewter dress she was wearing looked a bit tarty.

In the past, she might have laughed that off. Tonight, however, she was annoyed. She'd been annoyed a lot lately. Restless, impatient, and annoyed. In an act of defiance, Jane ended her set with "Begin the Beguine," just to aggravate Bouwdewijn. He could never get the rhythm right, and he knew it. And what the hell, she thought, why shouldn't I flirt with the customers? She gazed soulfully for a second too long at the young American, and raised one eyebrow, so she wasn't surprised when, after she'd finished to scattered applause, he approached her. He was probably going to ask her if he could buy her a drink. It might be nice to talk to an American for a while.

"Excuse me," he said eagerly. "Mrs. da Silva?"

She was curious. He'd called her "Mrs." Her framed black-and-white photograph on the sidewalk, at street level above the rather sinister stone stairs that led to this basement, just said "Jane da Silva." He must know who she was.

He pressed a card into her hand. "Hamilton Carruthers. From the embassy."

She looked down at the card. "Cultural section?"

"That's right."

"Don't tell me you're asking me to lay off Cole Porter in the interests of the exportation of American culture," she said with a sideways smile. She examined his tie. The little blips were crossed squash rackets, which probably meant he was in pretty good shape.

"I'm crazy about Cole Porter," he said, smiling. "And, frankly, Mrs. da Silva, I think you do him credit. No, I'm here because they're looking for you at the embassy. And while it's not exactly in my line, I volunteered to come find you."

"Oh," she said, casting a nervous eye on Bouwdewijn, who was shuffling through his sheet music in a surly way and scowling at her. He hated it when the customers came up and spoke to her, neglecting him.

"I knew who you were because I've been here before," Hamilton Carruthers continued. "I'm kind of a fan, actually. Perhaps you remember me," he added, raising an eyebrow.

"Perhaps I do," she said, giving him a level gaze. "Why are you looking for me at the embassy?" Maybe they wanted her to sing at some function. She hoped it wasn't the damned IRS again.

He clasped his hands together. "You have a message from home."

"From home?" With a start, she realized she didn't really have a home. She hadn't had one for years.

"From Seattle," he said.

"But I haven't lived there since I went on my junior year abroad," she said. "I've hardly ever been back." The last time had been for her cousin's wedding.

"You are from Seattle. You must be the right Jane da Silva. Seattle's a great town, they say."

"It's okay," Jane said cautiously. "I understand it's become kind of fashionable lately."

"Let's sit down and have a drink," Hamilton Carruthers suggested. "I'll explain everything."

He ushered her to his table and she asked for a cognac.

"They had a hard time finding you," Hamilton Carruthers said. "You're supposed to register with the embassy or consulate when you're abroad."

She waved her hand impatiently. "I know, but I travel a lot."

"I'm sorry to have to tell you," he said, now assuming a grave air, "that your uncle is dead." Hamilton Carruthers was, apparently, the genuine article—a true gentleman diplomat. No lower-middle-class "passed away" for him.

"Uncle Harold?" she said, her eyes widening.

"Yes. I have a letter here from a firm of lawyers in Seattle. They've been trying to track you down for weeks." He reached inside his jacket and pulled out an envelope.

Jane took a sip of her cognac and opened it. "Poor Uncle Harold," she said. "He was such a nice man. Kind of a do-gooder type." She found herself misting up just a little. Uncle Harold *had* been a nice man. Suddenly, she felt very melancholy. "He always liked me," she said, sniffing.

"I am so sorry," said Hamilton Carruthers, handing her an immaculate handkerchief as a tear rolled through her mascara and smudgily onto her cheek.

"Thank you. I'll be all right in a second. I haven't seen the old boy in years. We wrote, though."

He patted her hand. "It's difficult when one is abroad," he said.

She blew her nose. "Well, I wonder what the lawyers have to say. Maybe he left me a little something." She cheered up somewhat at this thought. God knows she could use a little something right now.

The letter was quite short.

Dear Mrs. da Silva,
　　Your uncle, the late Harold Mortensen, has named you in his will to continue his life's work by means of a testamentary trust. If you carry out the work of the trust to the satisfaction of the trustees, you will receive an income during

your lifetime, for as long as you satisfy the requirements laid out by your uncle.

The nature of your duties is sufficiently complex that I think it preferable that you meet with the trustees personally to learn of the exact nature and scope of the work.

If you are not willing to undertake the tasks outlined for you, the trust will be terminated and the assets distributed to charities named by your uncle.

Please contact us at your earliest convenience to discuss this matter.

Sincerely,

George W. Montcrieff

"How bizarre," said Jane.

Hamilton Carruthers coughed delicately, and gazed into his own cognac. It was clear he was too well bred to ask about the letter, but it was also clear that he wished she would confide in him.

She thought she might as well. After all, a certain degree of intimacy had been established by her snuffling into his handkerchief. She reflected briefly that she must remember to launder it properly and mail it to the embassy at The Hague.

"My uncle Harold's left me his money," she said. "But it sounds like I have to run his weird enterprise. It was always very mysterious, and everybody kidded Uncle Harold about it. My mother used to call it the Bureau of Hopeless Cases. But he called it the Foundation for Righting Wrongs."

Hamilton Carruthers's eyebrows rose.

"I know," she said. "It does sound a little ambitious, doesn't it? It was sort of a nonprofit detective agency. He had a grim little office in the Arctic Building, I remember," Jane continued. "A big old building with marble walrus heads decorating the outside.

"When I grew up I assumed it was some kind of a tax dodge." She frowned. "But Uncle Harold, I realize now, wouldn't have dodged his taxes. He was a real straight shooter."

"Do you want to do it?" said Hamilton Carruthers. "Right wrongs?"

"It might be fun," she answered.

"I love your singing," Hamilton Carruthers said suddenly. "How long have you been performing? Why aren't you famous?"

Jane laughed. "Probably because I'm not good enough," she said. "It started as sort of a joke. I was at a party in Brussels and I had a few drinks and sang 'Ten Cents a Dance,' and someone offered me a job. That was five years ago."

"I sort of assumed you'd always been a singer," Hamilton said.

"No. Just another splotch on my résumé," said Jane. She had been a governess, a hand model, a simultaneous translator (which gave her migraines), an aerobics instructor (which gave her shin splints), the editor of a shopping guide for tourists in Rome, and part owner of a small shop that sold baskets, sachets, and paperweights and folded in six months.

"To tell you the truth, I've been feeling rather sorry for myself, and put out with myself too, for having led such a raffish life when I am basically a very sensible person." She didn't add that she would be forty in three years, and on her thirty-seventh birthday she had made a vow not to be broke anymore after forty.

"And then this comes along. Uncle Harold. It's really kind of overwhelming." She sighed. "It's nice to talk to an American. You can get all personal and tell everything, and it doesn't make them nervous. I miss that sometimes."

"And your dress matches your eyes," Hamilton said.

"I know," said Jane, too preoccupied to take much notice of his non sequitur. "I planned it that way. I hate to break it to you, Hamilton, but all that kind of stuff is planned."

She paused. "The Bureau of Hopeless Cases," she said slowly. "Of course it depends on how much money there is, too."

Chapter 2

Exactly how much money are we talking about?"
Jane, wearing a Chanel suit Bernardo had given her years
ago, was sitting opposite George Montcrieff, an elegant,
elderly gentleman and a senior partner in the firm of
Carlson, Throckmorton, Osgood, Stubbins, and Montcrieff.
Jane hoped she looked like a deserving heiress.

She was talking not so much *to* Mr. Montcrieff as *at*
him. He seemed preoccupied, gazing out of the window
in the long pauses between his sentences.

"Mmmm," he replied. "There is a great deal of money
at stake here." He clammed up again and stared out of
the window some more.

Jane had been startled by the number of high-rise
buildings that had sprung up in Seattle since her last visit
ten years ago. This one, a looming tower of black glass,
had a magnificent view out over Puget Sound to Bainbridge
Island, dark with Douglas firs. A green-and-white Washington State ferry cut through the blue-gray water, leaving a ruffled white wake.

"Fantastic view," said Jane. "I had forgotten what a
beautiful city this is. You were saying, Mr. Montcrieff?"

"A lot of money." His gaze drifted back to her. "Your
uncle left his affairs in a very strange state, if I do say so,"
he said, frowning as if it were somehow her fault. "Quite

unorthodox. But he was adamant. Absolutely refused to set up a purely charitable trust. Said he didn't want the state attorney general or the IRS poking around. It left him in horrible shape, tax-wise. But he had plenty of cash, so he forked it out when he wrote the will. Still, the whole thing is peculiar." He eyed her as if she didn't deserve one dime of Uncle Harold's money, and as if the government would probably confiscate the whole estate anyway because Uncle Harold was so eccentric.

"Well," Jane replied tartly, "it is my understanding that you drew up the will, so I am sure you will agree that it is a perfectly sound document. I would like a copy, by the way."

"Of course," he said, placing his fingertips together. "Harold quaintly called his enterprise the Foundation for Righting Wrongs.

"Its chief asset was Harold and his desire to set things right. But there is also the house. You knew about his house? Under the will you may live there as long as you want if you are doing the work of the Foundation for Righting Wrongs. If you fail, the trustees will expect you to vacate within thirty days. Of course, it's only yours during your lifetime.

"You do understand, Mrs. da Silva, that you are perfectly free to choose not to carry on your uncle's, er, work. In that case, I'll simply ask you to sign a statement to that effect and the funds can be distributed to the specified charities. All very worthy ones, I might add.

"I understand you are some kind of a chanteuse." He paused, and allowed a dubious look to cross his features. "You would then be free to return to Europe and pursue your career."

Jane was tempted to ask him whether he was crazy, or whether he just thought she was. Instead, she said, "Mr. Montcrieff, let me be frank. My present career leaves a lot to be desired. It is not steady, the pay is not very good, and while it used to be fun, it isn't anymore. When I was widowed, my husband left me in bad financial shape, and I am afraid I was unprepared to make much of a living for myself." She left out all the tedious details of Bernardo's crooked manager, the disastrous devaluation of the Brazilian peso, and the fact that, as an American, getting a work permit had always been difficult in Europe.

He would have asked why she hadn't come home, and she wasn't really sure, now that she thought about it, except that coming home had always seemed to represent defeat. After all, she'd left when she was nineteen with a view to leading an interesting life, never coming home. Sort of Jean Seberg in Godard's *Breathless*, a savvy ex-patriate.

She'd remembered Seattle as a relentlessly dull town, far away from anything else; but, walking to Montcrieff's office this morning, she'd found it quite charming, full of espresso carts and window boxes with flowers and nice old architecture lovingly restored and interesting-looking people on the streets, and the *New York Times* on sale. Had she changed, or had Seattle changed? Both, she supposed.

"I am here to find out exactly what Uncle Harold's work is and how much money there is."

"Well into six figures, I'd say," he replied. "Of course, it all depends on how it is invested and so forth. Should you choose to participate, you will receive the interest—after taxes and a few minor expenses."

"I see. How much return can I expect on it?"

"Well into six figures," repeated the lawyer. "I was speaking of the interest, Mrs. da Silva. Not the principle."

Jane nodded silently and tried not to look absolutely overjoyed. It wouldn't do to clutch Mr. Montcrieff's lapels, jump up and down, and shriek like some game-show contestant. "I would like to learn more about the Foundation for Righting Wrongs and what would be expected of me," she said gravely.

For that kind of money, she'd do anything. Well, practically anything. She imagined it meant getting on the phone and untangling little old ladies' utility bills or finding out why the mail order merchandise they'd sent for hadn't arrived. If she worked it right, it shouldn't take more then twenty hours a week, max.

"Very well," said Mr. Montcrieff, opening his desk drawer. He produced a pair of binoculars and peered out the window.

"I see a bird of prey out there. A hawk perhaps. Very interesting." He strode eagerly over to the window. "It's circling over the city. How fascinating." Mr. Montcrieff's face became animated for the first time since she had met him. "What prey has it spotted?" He put the binoculars to his eyes.

"To think that, little over a century ago, downtown Seattle was teeming with wildlife. Deer of course, and raccoons and so forth. Otter. The beaver, its fur prized in Europe for the making of hats."

Jane walked over to him. "Tell me," she said firmly, "what I have to do to get that money."

"I'm a little vague on that point."

Jane had already assumed that vagueness was Mr. Montcrieff's habitual state. "How can we find out?" she said. "Someone must know."

"The trustees. They're very anxious to meet you. I'll turn you over to my nephew Bucky. He'll handle this for you." He squinted into the binoculars and rotated his head, presumably tracking the hawk in its flight.

"Fine," said Jane, grabbing her purse. "I'll have your secretary arrange that, shall I?"

"Good idea," said Mr. Montcrieff, now leaning far to one side of the window. "It's a red-tailed hawk if I'm not mistaken. Forgive me if I seem distracted, Mrs. da Silva."

She let herself out of his office, glancing over her shoulder to see him still plastered against the glass. Montcrieff's eccentricity had given her pause. If he had drawn up the will, wasn't it possible that it wouldn't hold up? What if those charities contested the will? It sounded as though there was enough money to make it worthwhile to some nonprofit group. And after all, a lot of those organizations didn't really do that much good. Just put on parties so all the women could make their husbands wear black tie.

In the outer office, an efficient-looking secretary blitzed away on a keyboard. "Mr. Montcrieff wants me to meet with his nephew," Jane explained.

"Yes, I thought he would. I'll take you to his office. He's expecting you." This sounded promising, Jane thought. As they left, she heard an intercom crackle. "Miriam, get me the Audubon Society on the line, would you?" Miriam rolled her eyes and kept walking.

Bucky, whose name according to his door was actually George W. Montcrieff II, was a well-groomed, tanned, angular man in his thirties. He wore a very unlawyerly Italian suit and silk shirt. His slightly sharklike smile indicated that if his nickname had had anything to do with prominent teeth, orthodontia had corrected the problem.

"Well hello," he said, taking her hand and clasping it enthusiastically. He looked her up and down thoughtfully, then glanced at his wafer-thin wristwatch. "You know," he said, "perhaps we could discuss this over lunch. There's a great seafood place right on the corner. They're usually crowded, but I'm sure they'll have a table for me. Miriam, would you call down and tell them I'm on my way?"

He took Jane's elbow and glided her along to the reception area, where he leaned over to a young girl there. "Listen sweetheart, I'm expecting Calvin Mason in about twenty minutes. Send him down to McCormick's, will you?"

The girl nodded and they entered the elevator. As they went down to the lobby, Jane noticed Bucky's expensive but overpowering cologne. The whole elevator smelled like a new issue of *Vanity Fair*.

Seated in the restaurant, Bucky, unlike his uncle, came to the point and stayed there. "Well," he said. "I imagine you're anxious to find out just what the Foundation for Righting Wrongs does, and what part you are expected to play."

"Exactly," she said. "I'd also like a copy of the will, which it seems to me I should have received by now, and some kind of a list of what Uncle Harold had. I'd like to know how much money there is and how it is invested." Maybe the whole deal was crazy, but there was no point acting less than serious about it at this point. After all, there was all that fabulous money at stake.

He nodded. "I'm so sorry we didn't get you a copy of the will sooner. I'll have my secretary get you copies of everything. For now, here's a copy of a letter your uncle left you to read after his death."

She opened the envelope with a table knife and read:

Dear Jane,

I'm not sure you want to take on the task I've prepared for you, so I've made it worth your while. I feel you are well suited to continue my work after I am gone.

I also believe, my dear (and I don't mean to be presumptuous, but as I am not only your uncle, but your deceased uncle), that you ought to respect my views, that this work would be good for you and give you a sense of higher purpose that may have been lacking in your life.

Since childhood, you have displayed a natural altruism with a native cleverness, and these qualities can be brought together to good purpose if you carry on the work of the Foundation for Righting Wrongs.

My instructions to the trustees are very specific. The tasks you undertake must be difficult ones, for there is no real satisfaction, I have discovered, in anything that is too easy.

I have chosen to indulge your love of luxury, another of your traits, Jane, and perhaps a less commendable one, in order that you will choose to take on the work; so that you will not be distracted from it by the need to earn a living; and because of my affection for you.

I have no doubt that you will earn every cent of it, and that, if you discharge your duties faithfully, someday we may both be reunited in a world in which there is no Wrong, only Right.

Love,
Uncle Harold

A hell of a deal, Jane thought rather tenderly. Big bucks, and my soul gets saved too. Uncle Harold had thought of everything. It was quite touching.

She folded up the letter and said, "I hope to be worthy of the confidence my uncle has placed in me."

"I've met with the trustees," said Bucky, "and it is my impression that they will hold you to your uncle's high standards."

"You mean you think they will be difficult to please?"

"Your uncle's little enterprise," Bucky said, with a smirk that seemed to indicate he thought Harold Mortenson was a fool, "is based on the idea that sometimes injustice must be overcome by herculean efforts."

"There is no real satisfaction," quoted Jane, "in anything that is too easy."

"I suppose so," he said dubiously.

"Well I'm going to do my damnedest to make this thing work," said Jane, half to herself.

He looked at her thoughtfully. "I sure would. The

income attached to it is pretty hefty. You could have a very pleasant life."

Jane smiled at his frankness. She also wondered what motivated it. Was he trying to let her know he was on her side? Or trying to get her to admit she was only after the money?

"Anyway," said Bucky, smiling back, then glancing at the wine list, "your biggest problem will be finding cases. Hopeless stuff. Nothing that can be solved by simple legal action or a letter to the newspapers."

So much for her theory that she'd be tracking down lost social security checks or missing pets.

"I see," she said.

"I'll set up a meeting for you with the trustees. If you'd like, I'll go with you."

"I'm anxious to meet them as soon as possible," she said. She didn't really think she needed to take an overperfumed lawyer with her. She'd rather tackle the trustees alone.

The waiter came over, and she put her elbows on the table and leaned toward Bucky, smiling. "Why don't you order for me?" she said, managing to convey by her tone that she had complete confidence in his savoir faire.

Until she had her hands on that money, signed, sealed and delivered, she'd be nice to everyone. The lawyers, the board, and whoever else was involved. After her position was secure, she looked forward to the most satisfying aspect of being rich: the ability to tell people, very nicely of course, for Jane believed in the old-fashioned virtue of civility, to fuck off whenever it pleased her.

Chapter 3

Calvin Mason walked into McCormick's and scowled into the dim corner where Bucky was sitting. Calvin was in his mid-thirties, with untidy curly dark hair and horn-rimmed glasses. He had a purposeful but rather shambling gait, his body hanging from wide shoulders. He wore jeans and a light blue work shirt, and he carried a manila envelope and a black plastic videocassette box.

Typical of Bucky, he thought to himself irritably. Makes me take the damned elevator all the way up to the seventieth floor for nothing. Two elevators, actually, because you had to transfer on the thirtieth floor, and listen to a snotty disembodied female voice call out the floor numbers accompanied by electronic chimes. And all the while, Bucky is sitting down here drinking white wine and eating oysters with some babe.

He brushed aside the maître d' and strode over to the table.

"Oh, hello Cal," said Bucky, smiling up at him. "What have you got for me?"

"Just what you ordered." Calvin looked at Bucky's companion with curiosity. A little older and classier than Bucky's usual type, she was wearing some kind of a nubby suit with gold buttons. It looked expensive and

17

feminine. Probably some rich client he was hoping to lure into matrimony.

Maybe she was the client in the divorce case he was working for Bucky. In that case, the contents of the tape he was delivering would be of real interest to her. It featured an amorous airline pilot and a saucy little flight attendant bouncing around on a creaking brass bed in a quaint little Victorian bed-and-breakfast in the San Juan Islands.

Calvin was normally discreet, but Bucky had irritated him by not apologizing for making him take that elevator ride while the Toyota was parked next to a fire hydrant. And Bucky *had* said, "What have you got for me?" So Calvin expanded on his answer.

"The place had those flimsy white curtains, so I only got them in silhouette, but the heavy panting on the audio comes through loud and clear, and we ID'd him all right. She calls out his name a couple of times. He just says 'Oh, baby.'" He smirked. "On top of which, the dope parked his Z car right in front of the place. I got stills of it."

The lady's eyebrows rose and she sipped her wine hastily, a maneuver that made him wonder if she wasn't suppressing a laugh. Calvin smiled at her in a rather cocky, man-of-the-world way. If she was the client, it was clear she was more concerned with adding some big bucks to her settlement than with her husband's low-budget fling in some mildewing Victorian pile in Friday Harbor.

Bucky gave him a sharp look. "Thanks," he said, snatching the cassette box. "I'll call you."

Calvin flung the envelope down on the white table-cloth. "My report, the stills, and the invoice are here. Prompt remittance is appreciated."

He turned and left, brushing the maître d' aside again on the way out.

"A private detective we use sometimes," said Bucky airily. "Unfortunately, we need someone like Calvin around once in a while when we're obliged to take a more unsavory route in the practice of family law." He frowned.

"Yes, I'm sure you rely on the unsavory route only with the greatest reluctance," she replied, smiling charmingly. "He certainly is colorful." She glanced in the departing man's direction."

"Kind of a sad case, really," said Bucky, an expression of sympathy crossing his smooth brow. "He's a lawyer. A sole practitioner who can't make a go of it. He's got a grungy little office with a Murphy bed and a framed diploma from Matchbook U." Bucky shook his head sadly. "He fleshes out his meager collection of pathetic cases with some investigative work for respectable firms.

"A good investigator, but not, as you might have noticed, very couth." He gave a condescending chuckle and touched the knot of his paisley silk tie. "Still, he manages to make a respectable appearance in court when I need him to testify.

"But enough about poor old Calvin Mason. I was filling you in on the details. The trustees have arranged for you to get an advance. You can use it to live on while you get settled in the work—should you choose to tackle it, of course."

"I do choose," she said, slithering an oyster into her mouth.

"Yes. Well, they've also decided you can stay in his house while you settle in. Should you come to an arrangement with the board, the house is part of the package. It's an asset of the foundation."

She remembered the place, an old gloomy Craftsman-style house in a tangled garden up on Capitol Hill. There was a lot of dark woodwork inside, and leaded glass windows. Outside, it had the broad porch and deeply overhanging eaves that were standard for rainy Seattle.

She wondered how much the advance was. She was anxious to get her Jaguar out of storage and have it shipped from London. It was all that was left of the life she'd had with Bernardo. The car was a classic. No matter how bad things got, she'd always managed to pay the storage fees.

If the trustees decided she wasn't up to Uncle Harold's standards and wanted the advance back later, let them sue her for it. Maybe she could get a few good cashmere sweaters in basic colors—black, gray, and red. And white— white could always look dressy—and a Burberry trench, too, to set her up for the next ten years.

"When can you give me the keys?" she said.

"Right away. If you'd like, I'll help you move in or whatever."

"That's very kind of you, but it won't be necessary," she said, noting with disapproval that he'd eaten four of the half dozen oysters they'd ordered. What a jerk. She grabbed the last one on the plate hastily. "And I would appreciate it if you could arrange that board meeting as soon as possible."

"No problem. I'll set it up for tomorrow. The old darlings haven't got much else to do, as far as I can tell. They're all well on in years."

"Oh really?"

"Yes. All retired. Contemporaries of your uncle. Judge Potter and Professor Grunewald and the bishop."

"Bishop?"

"Yes, an Episcopal bishop. Name of Barton."

"Oh. He christened me," she said. "And he must have been ancient then. Practically dropped me, they tell me."

"If it was after lunch, the explanation is simple," said Bucky, gazing significantly at his wineglass.

"I see," said Jane.

"And my uncle, of course," added Bucky. "He's an ex officio member."

"I've already met him too," said Jane with a forced smile. "Well, I certainly look forward to meeting the others."

After the waiter arrived with plates of salmon and then withdrew, Bucky leaned confidentially over the table. "The word is," he said, "that the old boys plan to give you six weeks to come up with a really juicy case. They don't think you can do it."

Jane couldn't help but notice a certain relish in his tone. She decided to tackle him head-on. "You sound as if you think they want me to fail," she said, with a smile designed to be disarming.

Bucky smirked a little. "They're very conservative and set in their ways. They'd never admit to themselves they'd want you to fail; but, let's face it, a bunch of old guys like that, used to their old pal, Harold, well, they just aren't going to take you as seriously. You're female and comparatively young. And you're new. Harold's up and dying and your replacing him is bound to shake up their comfortable routine."

"I see," said Jane.

"But I certainly want you to succeed," said Bucky, looking just a little too sincere to be sincere.

After lunch, Jane went back to the offices of Carlson, Throckmorton, Osgood, Stubbins, and Montcrieff, where she received a copy of the will, a check for three thousand dollars, and a key to Uncle Harold's house on Federal Avenue East.

Thanking him effusively for lunch, she fended off Bucky's attempts to offer her any further assistance and went to a bank on the corner. There she opened a checking account with her advance, using her passport for identification (and hoping they wouldn't check the status of her accounts at the Crédit Lyonnais and the Algemene Bank of the Netherlands, or her current status with Visa; they didn't).

She cashed the last of her traveler's checks and bought an international money order to send to Jean-Pierre, her last serious lover. He had probably forgotten about the five thousand francs Jane owed him, but she hadn't.

Jean-Pierre had been a turning point. He was sleek and handsome in an older, silver fox sort of way, and he'd been crazy about her. And he was so rich. But near the end, when she realized he'd just become a pleasant habit, she made herself stop taking money from him.

"Don't be ridiculous," he'd said. "I have plenty and you don't and if we're going to be together I want to be comfortable."

"But it makes me feel like a rich man's mistress," she'd said. And he'd replied, astonished, "But of course. That's what you are. Do you want to get married? Would that make it different? We could get married." He'd said it with the air of a puzzled aristocrat, indulging some bourgeois whim of a straitlaced American.

She'd borrowed that last five thousand francs to get herself to Amsterdam, because she knew she didn't want to marry him, and she couldn't give him up and stay in Paris. And the unhappy reason she couldn't give him up, beyond missing the comfortable life they had developed together, was that she was afraid of starving to death in some grim little flat. She was also faintly horrified to find herself casting around for someone else to take her on.

Here in Seattle, all that seemed ridiculous. Like something from a Henry James novel.

She hadn't driven for a while, and she was rather startled by the high-tech gadgets on the rental Chevy: digital clock, alarms that sounded when the key was in, a seat belt that loomed at her when she closed the door, a scanner on the radio. She felt disoriented, and vaguely ashamed that she had somehow let the world pass her by.

She thought she could navigate from downtown Seattle up to Capitol Hill, but downtown looked entirely different, with lots of new buildings, festively encrusted with postmodern details and plazas dotted with concrete tubs bursting with flowers. The simple, rigid grid pattern of serious buildings had been glitzed up so that she was completely lost. Besides the new topography, there seemed to be many more one-way streets.

Instead of getting out the map that came with the car and plotting out a route to her destination, Jane drove up and down the streets, looking around. Even the people looked different. When she was a girl, downtown used to mean white men in business suits and white women dressed up to go shopping or to work in offices. Now there was more of a bazaarlike quality—more blacks and Asians, more aggressively chic young people, and—something she'd never seen before in Seattle—mad-looking, apparently homeless people, carrying their belongings with them, or hunkered down on street corners.

One thing hadn't changed. Pedestrians waited politely on the curb for the light to change, and motorists waited politely for them to cross. Nobody jaywalked, and nobody leaned on the horn. In all her travels, especially to Latin countries, Jane had made the necessary adaptation to chaos and learned to break the rules to keep the flow going. But she had always felt guilty, as if she were betraying the pleasant orderliness with which she had grown up.

When she did get herself across the freeway and up to Capitol Hill, she realized that Uncle Harold's quiet neighborhood of big, boxy houses built in the first decade of the century hadn't changed much at all. The house, however, was bigger than she had remembered, almost what you'd call a villa in Europe. But then everything back home seemed bigger than she remembered, after years of living in hotel suites with Bernardo and later in a series of small European apartments.

It had begun to rain, and as she stood on the porch

fiddling with the key, she listened to raindrops splashing on the shiny leaves of the overgrown camellias that flanked the porch. She opened the door and went inside with the slight sadness one feels when entering a house that isn't lived in.

Inside, there was a musty smell, probably from Uncle Harold's cigars. The place would need a general airing out and a good cleaning. She set her suitcase in the hall, then wandered, rather dazed, through the rooms. Could she actually use all this space? There were good-sized rooms with dark beams running along the ceiling and built-in bookcases and sideboards and niches of various kinds. With new paint and better lighting it wouldn't be gloomy at all. Pruning back the overgrown camellias would help, too.

There was some dusty-looking mohair furniture around, and some very decent but worn Orientals on the floors. The kitchen had apparently not been remodeled since the fifties. The refrigerator had rounded corners, and there was a lot of pink Formica. Upstairs were a couple of bedrooms, charming rooms with coved ceilings, yellowed wallpaper, diamond-paned windows, and window seats.

It was a comfortable house, well made and a good example of turn-of-the-century reaction to Victorian excess. And besides, she felt rather close to Uncle Harold here. She wanted to feel close to him. He had—it seemed so far, anyway—saved her. In a way, she thought grimly, she had been feeling like a pretty hopeless case herself.

She sat down heavily on one of the mohair sofas and gazed over at the tiled fireplace. Hanging over the mantel was a big etching in a dark wooden frame. Saint George, with a resolute expression and flowing hair, was inserting a lance purposefully into the flank of a twisting dragon.

Hopeless cases. Funny how that phrase kept coming up. Her mother used it when she talked about Uncle Harold's foundation. And then, Bucky had used it. It was apparently what the board wanted her to come up with in the next six weeks.

Or had Bucky used it? No. He'd used "pathetic" cases. But he'd used it in another context. What was it? She concentrated, then remembered. It was how he'd described that seedy investigator's legal cases. What was the guy's name? Calvin. A very upright kind of name for someone prowling outside of a hotel room with a video recorder. His last name was Dixon. No, Mason. Calvin Mason.

Chapter 4

The trustees met the following evening at a restaurant in downtown Seattle. Jane remembered the restaurant from when she was a girl. It was the sort of place, that, although open to the public, managed to resemble the dining room of a private club. The furnishings were dark and respectable, and there were plenty of heavy draperies and carpeting to muffle the sound. The menu ran to roast beef, Yorkshire pudding, and lamb chops. The waiters were elderly and never introduced themselves by name or recited additional selections that had not been printed on the menu.

When she arrived, she had been surprised to learn that the actual meeting would take place in a private room. The restaurant itself seemed private enough—dim and quiet in a way modern restaurants never even tried to be. The place was empty except for two old ladies eating Caesar salads in silence; a family party with several twentyish children; and, tucked behind a potted palm, a couple in their forties with the intense, furtive look of middle-class adulterers.

Jane followed the maître d' to a long windowless room, overheated and giving the impression that it needed dusting. There, six white-haired gentleman rose courteously.

One of them was George Montcrieff, who introduced the others.

Bishop Barton was recognizable by his dog collar and the gleam of Episcopal purple beneath his black suit. Judge Potter wore a white carnation in his lapel. Professor Grunewald, beaky and square-jawed, hunched over and peered at her through trifocals. There was also Franklin Glendinning, a retired banker with a wintry look in his blue eyes, and Commander Kincaid, a retired navy man with ramrod-straight posture and an engaging way of talking out of the side of his mouth, as if every remark were a wisecrack.

"Really amazing," continued George Montcrieff as they all scraped their chairs and sat, continuing to gaze at her with well-bred curiosity. "Mrs. da Silva and I spotted a red-tailed hawk from my office window the other day."

They all ignored him.

"It was circling its prey," Montcrieff persisted.

"Nature red in tooth and claw," said the bishop, waving vaguely, then reaching for his highball glass with a gnarled hand. "Something to drink, my dear?"

"Yes, thank you," said Jane. "A sherry, please."

It seemed the proper drink for a gathering like this. "I am so glad to meet you all," she continued, vaguely aware of the schoolgirlish tone to her voice. "I look forward to working with you."

And, she thought to herself, you'd better not give me any trouble, either. Powerful old men, she thought to herself. All civic leaders with long, distinguished careers behind them. And they had absolute power over her future and her money.

Powerful old men, she had noticed, often had an irritating vagueness and cautiousness. It made you wonder how they had ever made it to the top. Only the navy man, Commander Kincaid, looked decisive. The rest had that dithery quality, and Glendinning, the banker, looked like big trouble. He was watching her carefully, his small mean mouth in a little frown.

When her sherry came, she raised her glass, and said "Please join me in a toast to Uncle Harold."

"To righting wrongs," said the bishop. "Your uncle's customary toast at these gatherings." He brought his glass to his lips with a trembling hand, ice cubes rattling furiously.

"How much," the bishop continued, "do you know about your uncle Harold and his work?"

"He was always rather secretive," said Jane. "In the family, we always thought of him, I suppose, as quiet and conservative, and with a terrific sense of noblesse oblige. He was too modest to talk much about his work. But I know he helped people." They were looking at her expectantly, so she continued.

"Mother told me so. Her hairdresser had a problem once. Something about a husband who'd disappeared and left her to raise her kids alone. Uncle Harold found him for her. He'd been living bigamously in California. Mother said Uncle Harold found the guy and managed to get him to pay a ton of money in back child support, and then he got her a decent divorce so she could remarry."

"Precisely," said the bishop. "Now if that hairdresser had only had the money, she could have hired a crack private investigator to ferret out the absconding husband. But she didn't, so your uncle Harold took on the job.

"It all began," he went on, "with a rather simple case, much like the one you describe. Harold's housekeeper had a son who was arrested for a crime he didn't commit. The boy may well have committed other, similar crimes, but Harold was convinced he hadn't committed this particular offense. It was a matter of finding a missing witness. Harold pulled it off, and the boy was saved. The experience convinced him there was an unmet need for investigative work to benefit those who couldn't afford it, or, whose cases seemed too daunting or dicey for a regular private investigator."

Professor Grunewald chuckled. "Like that business with the Boeing janitor and the glamorous female Russian spy."

Jane raised her eyebrows. This sounded rather promising.

"She wasn't really a glamorous Russian spy," countered the bishop, waving his hand impatiently. "The poor fellow just thought she was. Actually, she was a Swedish dental assistant."

"With thick legs," added Commander Kincaid. "She had him running around town dropping off secrets for a while, before she told him she'd just as soon have the cash. Your uncle managed to get him out of her clutches and gather up all the secret papers and destroy them."

The bishop laughed. "The secret papers were things like vacuuming schedules and requisitions for industrial cleaning preparations, but she had him scared, all right. Harold got him a job somewhere else, anyway, just to be sure."

Jane wished the bishop hadn't laughed at the besotted janitor. She imagined how desperate he must have felt. "I think it's wonderful that Uncle Harold helped these people," she said.

"Harold loved the work. He liked poking around, finding things out," said Judge Potter. "Claimed it gave him a sense of adventure. The rest of his life was pretty straightforward. Not like his father's."

Uncle Harold's father, Jane's great-grandfather, had made a lot of money in Alaska. He'd outfitted miners in the gold rush, selling them pickaxes and hard tack, and later he'd racketed around up there himself, running a saloon in Skagway, which Jane had always suspected might also have been a brothel. What was certain, though, was that the beer he served was a loss leader. He made a lot of his money off the poker games. He had died many years before Jane was born, but tales of his ability to recite interminable verses of the poetry of Robert W. Service had been passed down in family lore.

Jane's great-grandfather had two sons late in life. Uncle Harold, and Jane's own grandfather, Victor. The latter had run through his inheritance back in the twenties, spending a small fortune on bathtub gin and the flat-chested floozies of the period. Not having inherited his father's skill at the gaming table, he lost the balance of his estate one afternoon in Monte Carlo, thereby managing to get a leg up on everyone else by starting out the Depression flat broke.

Victor returned to Seattle, married a gentle spinster, fathered Jane's mother, and lived out the rest of his days in a maroon silk monogrammed bathrobe, while his wife eked out a living giving piano lessons and sight reading popular songs at Woolworth's for customers contemplating buying sheet music.

Jane had a dim memory of him in the famous bathrobe, playing solitaire and humming.

His brother, Harold, however, had set himself up in the office supply and typewriter repair business, avoiding the stock market because he thought it was really just gambling, of which he didn't approve. Years of selling accordion files, three-by-five cards, filing cabinets, rubber thumb protectors for file clerks, bottles of ink, and reams of paper, did convince Harold, however, that in the future, office procedures could be simplified with modern technology. It became clear to him sooner than to almost everybody else, it seemed, that buying stock in International Business Machines might be a good investment.

Judge Potter spoke up winsomely. "Let me say that it is a little unusual for us to be meeting here with an attractive young girl. It will take some getting used to, don't you think, gentlemen?"

"I'm not really young," she protested. "I'm thirty-seven." Jane was embarrassed by her generation's tendency to persist in thinking itself young well into middle age, and often conducting itself like a bunch of whiny adolescents as a result.

"That's young," Commander Kincaid said firmly.

Jane, in an effort to impress the board with her seriousness, thought of pointing out that two times thirty-seven was seventy-four, and as such she might as well be considered middle-aged. After all, she was sure that when they were thirty-seven they considered themselves at the height of their powers. It was a safe bet they had assumed serious responsibilities, and, like her own father at that age, wore gray suits and felt hats and acted completely grown up. But she decided not to point all that out. It wouldn't be tactful to remind them of their own actuarial status.

"Tell me what is expected of me," she said instead. "Mr. Montcrieff has given me the basics." She managed to look a little helpless, trying to convey that it was his fault if she was ignorant of her new duties. "And your description of some of Uncle Harold's cases has given me a better idea."

"You are expected," said the judge, "to find cases of injustice requiring investigative skills. Cases which cannot be solved by ordinary means or regular methods, because the facts have been obscured."

"Cases in which the laws of men have proven to be inadequate," said the bishop.

"Cases in which only quick action and persistence bring justice to bear," added the commander. "Finding 'em yourself is half the battle. Harold had a real nose for people's troubles. Why, I remember he got involved in that missing baby thing eavesdropping on the bus! Harold was a real snooper."

Jane brightened a little. So was she. She'd been known

to change a seat in an airport lounge to overhear what looked to be a promising conversation.

"Missing baby?" she asked.

"Harold got it back. A berserk hospital nurse managed to spirit away half of a pair of twins, fool around with the records. Amazing deal. The mother was anesthetized during the birth. Didn't even know she'd had twins!"

"So I'd be running a kind of nonprofit detective agency," said Jane, rather astounded at the mystery of the missing twin. She imagined Uncle Harold restoring the bundled-up infant to its mother on the doorstep, and its mother setting it gently next to its identical sibling. The picture practically brought tears to her eyes.

"That's right," said Glendinning. "The only funds involved are the funds which you will receive as income, should you choose to take up the work, and should we approve of your cases and your handling of them."

There. It was out. They'd mentioned money. She smiled. "I'm very much looking forward to it," she said. "What are your criteria for suitable cases? And for proper handling of them?"

"Simple enough," said the commander, as the waiter passed around plates of cream of asparagus soup. "It's got to be some kind of mess that needs fixing. Life is pretty messy, you know. And you have to find the messes yourself. Show initiative."

"It must be," said the bishop, raising a bony finger, "a problem that mere money cannot solve. I mean, you've got to use your wits."

"Although," interjected Mr. Glendinning, "you are expected to use your own funds for any incidental expenses."

"And," said the professor, "it must be handled by strictly ethical means. No sloppy situation ethics."

"In addition," the judge added solemnly, "the letter of the law must be followed. Sometimes Harold managed to bend the spirit of it a little," he added with a twinkle, "but he never did anything illegal." She thought of the janitor. She supposed, strictly speaking, he should have been turned in to Boeing security or the FBI or something.

Jane nodded solemnly. She'd had time to go over the financial report Bucky had given her. Whatever these old geezers wanted, she would do. It all sounded like one of her beloved old blue-bound Nancy Drew novels.

"Is there some written record of Uncle Harold's cases?" she said.

"No," said Mr. Glendinning. He seemed to enjoy saying no. Probably useful in a banker. "And we all promised complete secrecy. No publicity. Ever. That's very important. Those we benefit are guaranteed strict confidentiality."

Mr. Montcrieff coughed. "Gentlemen, I've told you before, and I will repeat my concern. Without a written record the residual legatees—those charities, could cause trouble."

The commander waved a hand. "Forget it, Montcrieff. We don't want a lot of paperwork. And we want privacy."

"There's also a very practical consideration," explained the bishop. "You wouldn't want a lot of people coming to you with their problems, many of which, sad to say, would be inconsequential and better solved by good old-fashioned Christian fortitude.

"But also," he continued with a smile, "Harold felt that it was better to do good works without drawing attention to oneself. The sin of pride can so easily corrupt the most meritorious undertaking. Once these cases are solved, we never speak of them again."

"I see," said Jane. The main course, veal cutlets, was served, and the men all began sawing away at their plates with interest.

She surveyed their six white heads bent over their places, a seventh white head, the waiter's, moving artfully among them. For now, these half dozen old men were the most important men in her life. They had the power to give her the freedom she wanted. She had to be able to handle them.

She cleared her throat. "All right, let me get this straight." Jane thought it was time to summarize. "I'm supposed to find a mess that needs fixing, and set it right. Then I'm to come to you for your approval."

The trustees nodded.

"If I can't find a case, or you don't approve of what I've done—"

"Then the money goes to charity," said George Montcrieff.

"And if I do succeed?"

"Then you will receive half of the annual income that goes with the trust. We'll expect another case in six months," said Mr. Glendinning. "Two a year."

"And if, at any time, you don't approve of my efforts?"

"The principal will be distributed to charity," said Mr. Montcrieff, "and the Foundation for Righting Wrongs will be a thing only of memory."

And I'll see you clowns in court, she thought to herself.

"Thank you," she said pleasantly. She wondered how new trustees were to be appointed as this crew died out. It was probably a self-perpetuating board, and there were tons of other cantankerous old fossils waiting to take the place of the present collection.

She turned to George Montcrieff. "Did he give you any written instructions, other than what was in the will? It would be handy to have a specific criteria for cases."

He flapped his napkin at her. "Harold left it nice and vague. You needn't worry about that. Everything's at the trustees' discretion."

Chapter 5

All right, all right," said Calvin Mason irritably. "We can trade it out. But Jesus, Kenny, I can't trade out everything. I need cash to put gas in my car. And buy the occasional cup of decaf cappuccino."

"Ideally, you could trade everything out. In a perfect world," said Kenny Martin dreamily. He was dressed in paint-and-plaster-spattered work clothes.

Next to him, Kenny's dark-haired daughter, Leonora, whose own paint-spattered T-shirt read ROOSEVELT HIGH SCHOOL, clicked her tongue in derision. She shifted her weight from one foot to another, the way teenage girls do, and tilted her head to one side, eyeing the world at a wary slant.

"The kid's right," said Calvin Mason. "There's nothing wrong with a cash economy. If only you and I could hook into it somehow. So what did you have in mind?"

"Well, this place could use a little sprucing up," Kenny remarked, gazing around Calvin's office, which was actually an apartment in the Compton Apartments, a three-story squat brick building constructed in 1928. It had a gloomy tiled lobby and ten units. A Hong Kong Chinese lady in suburban Mercer Island owned it; Calvin Mason managed this building and a few others that belonged to her, in exchange for free rent on his unit.

On his letterhead, Calvin's office was called Suite 7, but actually it was apartment number seven. The living room served as an office, with an old desk, some army surplus file cabinets, a telephone answering machine, a nice old fireplace, and a sofa for the clients.

Calvin lived in the bedroom beyond; he forced himself to make his bed every day, just in case a client needed to use the bathroom, which was situated off the bedroom.

"Okay, okay." He looked around. The walls did look as if a large, greasy animal had rubbed its body along them over a long period of time. Maybe he could get Mrs. Liu to repay him in cash. The lobby needed work, too. And the ground-floor unit was going to be vacant soon. It probably hadn't been painted in ten years.

Calvin had represented Kenny in a long, drawn-out suit against a customer who claimed Kenny had ruined his house with a bad paint job, and later, in a matter involving some cement work—a retaining wall had collapsed. That case had become complicated because the retaining wall was on a property line and there were two angry property owners involved, and because Kenny had sued the guy who sold him the load of cement. There was also a further complication, involving the tenacious root structure of some creeping Saint-John's-wort, which one party had inadvisedly planted over the crumbling remains. Both cases had dragged on for some time, and Kenny owed Calvin about seven hundred dollars.

"Leonora here's helping me out," said Kenny. "She's a real good trim painter."

"Yeah, and I make sure he gets paid, too," she said tartly.

"Well, take a look around, give me an estimate," said Calvin. He handed Kenny a bunch of keys. "This apartment and the lobby. Plus unit one, right off the lobby before you get to the laundry room. But I'm not coming up with cash for the paint. You want to trade, trade out the paint, too."

"We've got some nice white latex left over from another job," said Leonora. "We could add a little color to it if you wanted."

"We'll let you figure it in at cost. No mark-up," said Kenny. "Seeing as I'm stuck with it and all."

"Dad," moaned Leonora, burying her face in her long slim hands in exasperation. "What am I going to do with you?"

Just then, there was a harsh buzz from the door. Calvin went over and returned the buzz, wondering who it could be. He didn't have any more appointments this afternoon.

A moment later, there was a firm rap on his own door. When he opened it, it took him a moment before he recognized the woman. She'd been having lunch with Bucky a few days ago. Now, though, she was wearing jeans and a sweater and she didn't look like a party to an upscale divorce at all.

"I'm sorry I didn't call for an appointment," she said. "My name is Jane da Silva, and I met you—well, almost met you—the other day."

"Yeah, Bucky didn't bother to introduce us," said Calvin. "Come in. What can I do for you?" Maybe Bucky was too high-priced for her, and she wanted to hire him as a lawyer, he thought optimistically. He gestured to the sofa, and she sat down.

"Kenny and Leonora here are painting contractors," he explained. "Why don't you guys look around and give me that estimate."

Kenny and Leonora disappeared into the kitchen, and Calvin Mason seated himself behind the desk.

Jane had rehearsed several tactful ways of approaching her subject, but they all hinged on the fact that Mason's clients were losers, and his cases pathetic, and that Bucky had said so. She had finally decided to wait until she was face-to-face with him and then improvise. That was why she hadn't made an appointment; she'd been afraid he'd ask her on the phone what she wanted to talk about.

Her eyes flickered over the room. To someone like Bucky, it was no doubt a pathetic excuse for a law office. She imagined it had been witness to many a hopeless case, but still, it was a comfortable room with character. It needed a coat of paint, though.

She caught his eye again. He had a slightly defensive expression on his face. She wondered if he thought she was put off by his office. She didn't know quite where to begin.

Finally, he spoke up. "Did Bucky send you here?"

"Well in a way." She took a deep breath. "I'm looking for a hopeless case. To help. It sounds absurd, I know—"

"A hopeless case?" He looked wary.

She took a deep breath and began again. "I recently became involved with a trust—I suppose you could call it a charity—and I need to find—"

"And Bucky said I was a hopeless case!" Calvin Mason's wary expression flashed into anger. "That jerk. The only reason he's on the seventieth floor with a corner office is because his uncle was too far gone not to keep him out of the family firm. Otherwise, he'd probably be selling magazine subscriptions over the phone."

Jane smiled.

He smiled back. "I'm sorry," he said. "Bucky's an okay guy, I guess. Just a little patronizing."

"No, no," she said. "I don't think *you're* a hopeless case. I just wondered if, in your work as a lawyer, you haven't run across some cases that seem hopeless. Cases of injustice. Perhaps," she hazarded, "someone accused of a crime he didn't commit. That kind of thing."

He looked at her with a look that said, *Someone here is crazy and I don't think it's me.*

"The point is, Mr. Mason," she said with a sigh, "I

stand to inherit a lot of money if I can come up with some hopeless case to solve."

Calvin Mason perked up. "A lot of money?"

"Yes. But I can't touch a dime if I don't come up with a hopeless case to solve. I know it sounds bizarre. It *is* bizarre. You see, Mr. Montcrieff, Bucky's uncle, drew up the trust and the will and—"

"In that case, *bizarre* is likely to be the operative word," Calvin interrupted thoughtfully.

"This is all privileged information, isn't it?" she said, mindful of the board's admonition to avoid any publicity.

"Absolutely," said Mason.

Quickly, she outlined the criteria the board had set. "I'm supposed to find the cases myself," she said. "And I just thought I might start here. Bucky gave me the impression that you took on some difficult cases."

He leaned back a little in his chair. "I do a great deal of pro bono work," he said. "I find it hard to turn down a needy case." Probably because he didn't get any other kind, Jane mused.

He gestured around his office. A large orange cat entered an open window, bounced off an old radiator with rust showing through the paint, and dropped itself on his desk, curling up in a nest of papers. "I don't worry about a fancy overhead or anything. I didn't go to law school just to make a lot of money."

"Exactly," she said. "Do you think you can help me?"

He flipped through a Rolodex file on his desk, and the two people who'd disappeared into the kitchen reappeared. The man looked like an old hippie, with thinning hair and a gingery walrus mustache. The young girl with him was thin and dark and gave Jane an inquisitive look as she trooped by. Jane read her T-shirt.

"We'll check out unit number one now," said the man, rattling some keys.

"The tenant's probably not there. Knock first, then go

ahead in," said Calvin. He resumed pawing through his Rolodex file.

"I went to Roosevelt," Jane said after a pause, slightly bemused. "I can't believe I'm back home."

"You grew up here, huh?" said Calvin. "I went to Ballard myself. He frowned at his Rolodex. "I may have to think about this," he said. "It's sort of an unusual request." He paused. "And you say there is a lot of money involved?"

Jane sighed impatiently. "Yes, there is. And to be perfectly honest, I can sure use it. Naturally I would compensate you if you came up with a suitable case. A finder's fee. But I think it would be best if we kept it confidential," she added. She sounded so stilted sitting here talking to him, she thought as her words hung in the air. Was it because she'd spent all those years speaking French, which, literally translated, came out sounding like stilted English? "I mean, it's got to make sense for you, financially," she said.

"Fine," said Calvin Mason, looking suddenly cheerier. He sat back in his chair. "Give me a little time on this, will you, Miss da Silva."

"Mrs.," she said. "I'm a widow." A look of sympathy flitted across his face, which Jane found rather charming. "But please call me Jane."

"All right. But you don't look like a Jane. Where can I reach you?"

She gave him her address and phone number, and he rose and saw her to the door. She paused for a moment, to ask him what she did look like, if she didn't look like a Jane, but she just gave him her hand to shake instead. It was a nice firm American handshake. She realized she'd become accustomed to limp French handshakes.

"Roosevelt, huh?" he said. "Did you grow up in Laurelhurst?"

"That's right," she said. Laurelhurst was a comfortable

upper-middle-class neighborhood full of perfect gardens and big square brick or Tudor houses. When she was a kid she'd been embarrassed to admit she came from there. People thought she was a snob. Which, in fact, she was, she supposed. She remembered her impression of Ballard High School, just a few miles away, in a lower-middle-class Scandinavian neighborhood. It had a rough reputation.

"When did you leave Seattle, and where did you go?" Calvin Mason asked, lingering in the doorway.

"I went to Europe soon after Roosevelt," she said. "When I was in college. Twenty-some years ago now."

"Why did you leave?" he asked her.

She shrugged. "Laurelhurst seemed pretty boring."

"It still is," said Calvin Mason. "But pleasant. Not the kind of place where the neighbors let you have junker cars in the front yard or anything."

"Definitely not," she said.

"Well, welcome home," he said. "The place has changed a lot."

"Thanks for your help," she said. On her way through the gloomy corridor to the lobby, she wondered if she hadn't made a mistake. Would Calvin Mason have attracted some poor wretch with a noble cause to his practice? Or would he simply have a tedious and predictable string of crummy divorce cases and acrimonious landlord-tenant disputes?

No, she thought, there wasn't any tedium here. Failure, perhaps, but not tedium. There was something about Calvin Mason that she recognized, with a painful twinge, as being part of her own make-up. Calvin Mason was one of those people who lived on the edge, often by their wits. One of those people who had never really achieved security, and wasn't quite sure why, but whose life was never dull.

When she reached the lobby, which was dominated by a

large, defiant-looking aspidistra in a glazed ceramic container, she was startled to hear piano music. A Chopin étude. The piano seemed a little out of tune. Without thinking about it much, she drifted in the direction of the sound. It came from an open door with a brass numeral "1" hanging crookedly from a screw.

She stepped into the doorframe and saw the paint-spattered young girl at an old upright, head bent in concentration, fingers curled over the keyboard, while the man stood back, stroking his chin thoughtfully and gazing at the walls.

She waited until the girl had finished, and then she said quietly: "Brava."

The girl turned to her and blushed. "Oh, I hope whoever owns this apartment doesn't mind my using the piano."

Kenny turned to the door. "Isn't she great?" he said. "Great little fingers."

"It's not just her fingers," said Jane. "It's the phrasing, the expression, the interpretation. All very sophisticated, but fresh and young, too. As if the piece is writing itself as it's being played. Great stuff."

The girl beamed.

"Excuse me," said Jane, "for just bursting in here. I'm Jane da Silva."

"Kenny Martin," said the man, waving. "And Leonora, my daughter."

"I just had to see who was playing so beautifully," said Jane. "Keep up with your lessons."

"Lessons?" said Kenny. "I don't see why she needs more lessons. Her teacher says she can't teach her much more. You should see the awards she's won."

Jane and Leonora looked at each other for a moment with understanding. She needed to keep studying, now more than ever, if she was ever to become a mature pianist. Jane liked the look of the girl. Serious and intelligent but still charmingly unfledged.

A moment later, as Jane stood at the curb, opening the door to her rental car, the girl, slightly out of breath, ran up to her. "Can I talk to you?" she said. "I was listening when you were telling Cal what you were looking for. Dad doesn't like to talk about it—doesn't want to believe it—but I'm a pretty hopeless case. Do you think you can help me?"

Chapter 6

I don't remember my mother at all, okay. So you don't need to say I'm sorry, or anything like that." Leonora curled her long fingers around the teacup and lowered her head as she drank, so that a screen of dark hair fell in front of her face. She was sitting opposite Jane in Uncle Harold's gloomy parlor.

"She died when I was a baby. Sixteen months. I've always been with my dad, and he doesn't like to talk about her. Or her money."

"Her money?" Jane heard herself say. It was disgusting. She was becoming obsessed with money. Or maybe she was finally waking up and smelling the coffee. Money was what made everything else fall into place.

"My mother was rich. For about a week. She came into a big inheritance on her twenty-first birthday. Just before she died." Leonora looked up from her tea. "I need that money now. I need it to go to Juilliard. My teacher at school says I might be good enough. Maybe not Juilliard, but somewhere good. He can, like, arrange an audition. But I can't do it without money."

"What happened to it?" said Jane, wondering if Kenny had somehow frittered it away on sprout sandwiches and sandalwood incense.

"My mother gave it away. She had known it was coming

ever since she was about fifteen. But by the time it arrived, she was mixed up with this cult, and gave it all to them. She and Dad were like hippies. Her parents disowned her, but she always knew she'd be getting this money from her grandmother."

That knowledge, thought Jane, would have made it easier for Leonora's mother to kick back and groove.

"Then, she got totally involved with the Fellowship."

"The Fellowship?"

"Yeah." Leonora laughed a little bitterly. "The Fellowship of the Flame. Sounds really dumb, huh?"

"Yeah," Jane agreed with a sigh. She wondered what anyone could do after all these years. Presumably, the transaction was completely legal. "Did your dad try to get the money back?"

"No. He thought about it. A few years ago, he told Calvin Mason about it, but Cal said it would be too hard. For one thing, Mom and Dad weren't really married. They went through some ceremony on a mountaintop somewhere. I'm the one who should have inherited.

"And, after all these years, we don't even know if these people exist, or who they were. But Dad's always said it was fraud. They got that money from her with a lot of lies. They made her kind of crazy.

"Mom's parents, my grandparents, they tried to get it back. They couldn't even find the Fellowship of the Flame. They were like a supersecret group. It was back a long time ago. Sixteen years."

"How did she die?" said Jane, imagining a drug overdose.

"She drowned. They found her in Lake Union."

Jane was silent for a moment. It sounded hopeless all right. And it sounded like a wrong that needed to be righted. The Fellowship of the Flame, whatever it was, sounded unworthy. The name alone—slightly reminiscent of some boys' adventure book of an earlier era—was suspect. It also sounded harsher than other mushy cults.

"How much money did they get?" Jane asked.

"A quarter of a million dollars," said Leonora.

"God. That was a lot of money back then. It still is."

"I know. I could have enough to go to Juilliard and still not worry about Dad when I was gone."

"How old is your father?" Jane asked sharply.

"Forty-one," said Leonora.

"Well, he's old enough to take care of himself," she said. "You have to start thinking about your own life."

Leonora sighed. "He can't really take care of himself. He can't handle anything. He's just an old sixties person. If I went off and tried to put myself through school, who knows what would happen to him."

"What about your grandparents? You said they tried to get your mother's money. Don't they have some money? Couldn't they help you get to Juilliard?"

"They haven't seen me since I was a baby. They're kind of nuts, to tell you the truth. They hate Dad. They blame him for everything that happened to her. They act like he's after their money, or something. Dad says we don't need them. And Dad blames them for the way my mom turned out. She started going to shrinks when she was about thirteen. I guess she was just really screwed up."

Leonora's eyes, thought Jane, were too old for her face. They had a steely, resigned, wary glint to them, a knowing look too mature for a young girl.

"How old are you, Leonora?"

"Seventeen. I'm a senior at Roosevelt."

"Really? That's where I went to high school." About the time this girl's parents were running around in a psychedelic VW van somewhere, she thought. It occurred to Jane that they were a little out of it. The summer of love had already become history sixteen years ago.

"Listen," said Leonora now, standing and thrusting her hands into the pockets of her jeans. "This is really dumb.

There's nothing you can do. I know that. It's just that, after I heard what you said at Cal's office, I thought maybe..."

Were there the seeds of a suitably hopeless case here? Would the board care about Leonora's ambitions or about what her silly mother did sixteen years ago? All her life, Jane had made decisions based on two simple criteria. Was the situation interesting, and were the people involved likable? Lately, she'd been wondering if she wouldn't have been better off if she'd made choices based on more cold-blooded logic. She was curious about Leonora's mother and the Fellowship of the Flame, and she liked Leonora. She felt attracted to the situation, but she promised herself to get out fast if the case didn't shape up as suitably hopeless. After all, this was business, and Jane had decided that now, more than ever, was a time to be businesslike.

"Let me see what I can do," said Jane, after a pause. "I suppose the way to start is to get as much background as possible. I'd better talk to people who knew your mother, like your father and your grandparents. Maybe we can find out where your money went. It might be all gone and irretrievable."

She reached over and patted the girl's hand. "If it is, we have to think of another way to finance your musical education." Why had she said that? She reminded herself that her job was to find a hopeless case, not get bogged down in other people's problems.

"I don't think my mom was a bad person," said Leonora, a little defensively. "Just confused."

• • •

Two days later, Jane sat on the sofa at Kenny and Leonora's house, looking at a photograph of Leonora's mother. She didn't look confused, thought Jane, so much as she looked too open. A wide, broad-planed, slightly foolish face, with Leonora's eyes. The expression in them, though, was entirely different. There was no wariness there. They were big pale eyes with a fanatic's glaze to them. Her hair, dark like Leonora's, was parted in the middle and hung straight down to her shoulders. It was a studio portrait, with shadowy lighting. Leonora's mother wore a black sweater and pearls. It looked like a yearbook picture.

"That's what Linda looked like in high school," said Kenny uncomfortably. "That's what she looked like when I met her." He glanced quickly over at his daughter, as if to gauge her pain. Leonora was examining the picture coolly, dark brows knit together in concentration.

Leonora had called earlier that morning and asked Jane to come and talk to her and to her father. "I made him see," she had said, "that it's time to deal with this."

•   •   •

A small lake a little north of downtown Seattle, Lake Union was fringed by festive houseboats, sailboat moorages, maritime businesses, boatyards, wharves, and restaurants with views of the water and seafood on the menu. It was also, thought Jane with a shiver, where Leonora's mother had been drowned.

Kenny and Leonora lived on the east side of the lake, up a few blocks from the water's edge, in a little house on a dead-end street; the house looked like a neglected turn-of-the-century beach cottage.

The stand of bamboo separating it from the street gave it a bohemian look, and inside it was full of rough-hewn furniture and clutter.

Even though it was summer, and there was no fire in the cast-iron stove, there was a smoky tang to the air, and a dark, closed feeling from the weathered, silvery wood that lined the interior.

Kenny had produced a box, and from it, he was handing her, one by one, pictures and documents.

"I was going to save this stuff until Leonora was grown up," he said. "But I guess she is grown up. Pretty much, anyway."

There were more pictures. Leonora's mother and Kenny on their wedding day, he in a pirate's blouse and flared velvet trousers, she in a dress put together with yards of sheer muslin and elastic at arms and wrists. There were rhododendron blossoms in her hair.

"But it wasn't a legal marriage?" said Jane, thinking of her own wedding a few years later in Paris. She had worn a beige silk dress and a straw hat, and they had had lunch afterward at the Ritz with about ten friends, before leaving for Rio where she met the numerous da Silvas and learned the samba. She smiled nostalgically.

"Well sort of," said Kenny. "Linda and I had this friend do it. He was a Universal Life minister, I mean he sent away for the license to perform marriages and all that. But he never signed a certificate or anything, and he kind of disappeared. In fact, we never saw him after the ceremony. His name was Carrot. I don't know why."

Leonora rolled her eyes. As well she might, thought Jane. She was willing to bet money that the ceremony had included quotations from Kahlil Gibran, vows including bail-out clauses and woozy pledges of devotion long on metaphor and short on taste.

There were a few more pictures, Linda in jeans and a peasant blouse curled up on a sofa with a cat, staring into the camera. Linda from the waist up, her arms around a group of friends, tilting her head back laughing, in a sylvan setting. Everybody was nude. Much easier to spontaneously shed your clothes out in the woods when you were in your twenties, thought Jane. Linda had pretty breasts and smooth skin, with the long dark hair running over her shoulders like veiling.

"There were these things, too," said Kenny. "Her notebooks." Jane accepted the spiral notebooks in bright colors, and opened one of them. *I feel so close to the heart of the universe,* she read.

> *When I walk in bare feet across the grass, it's as if the grass itself were growing up into the soles of my feet. All living things are connected, and I know it with my whole self, not just with my linear little brain—the weakest part of us.*

Jane's own youthful journal had been much different. *I've got to get out of Seattle,* she had written, with a row of exclamation points. *And meet some really exciting people.*

"May I borrow these?" Jane asked. "They might help."

"Just what is it you're doing, anyway?" Kenny said gently. "Leonora says you want to help her get her money back. I don't see how you can do that."

"I don't know either," said Jane. "But I want to look into it for you."

"Why?" said Kenny.

"It's my job," said Jane, managing to put conviction into her voice.

Anybody else but Kenny might have said, "Get a real job," at this point, but he just nodded and said, "I have to tell you, those Fellowship guys were pretty scary. Evil. They were actually evil. They'd plugged right into the dark side, you know?"

"I know," said Jane. "I believe in evil." She savored the snobbish thought that her own belief was founded on more sophisticated theological principles than Kenny's, who apparently had developed a cosmic view based on the outer space movies of George Lucas. A lot of the evil Jane believed in sprung from passivity and foolishness and sloppy thinking, but it had blossomed into full-blown evil and taken on a life of its own nevertheless. "Tell me what you know about them."

"They were everything Linda was looking for. That was the horrible part." He sighed. "And then, they killed her."

"Drove her to suicide?" said Jane, darting a look at Leonora.

"No," said Kenny, shifting uncomfortably. "I think they killed the person she was. After the Fellowship, Linda became a stranger to me."

Jane didn't believe him. Or rather, she did believe his first, spontaneous statement before he'd backtracked. Kenny, she felt, really did think his wife had been killed.

Chapter 7

What exactly did happen to Linda?" Jane asked.

"I don't know. She drowned. They found her body. Floating." He glanced over at Leonora. "I had to identify the body."

They were all silent for a moment.

"I tried to stop her," he said. There was a defensive edge to his voice. "I tried to get her away from those people but I couldn't reason with her. You see, at first, they seemed okay. She hadn't been happy. She had never been happy, and they seemed to be helping her get centered.

"But then she got weirder and weirder. She kept secrets from me. She told me I wasn't spiritual enough to be told the secrets of the universe."

"I don't understand," said Jane. "You think if you'd been able to get her away from the cult she wouldn't have died?"

"Yeah, that's right."

"Do you think she killed herself?"

"No. She was happier right before she drowned than she'd ever been. She acted like she had all the answers. She was smug, I guess you'd say."

"So you think her death was an accident?"

"It must have been. But it's hard to believe. You see,

Linda hated the water. Why was she even there? She couldn't swim."

"I never knew that," said Leonora.

"If you don't believe it was suicide or an accident, then you must think it was murder," said Jane.

"There weren't any marks on her," said Kenny. "The death certificate said accidental drowning."

"Did you ever wonder if it was murder?" said Jane.

"Of course I did," said Kenny angrily. "But what could I prove? I talked to the police about it at the time. They told me I wasn't her next of kin, because we weren't really married."

"I don't see what that would have to do with it," said Jane.

"You didn't find out?" said Leonora. "She was my mother, and you didn't find out?"

"Hey, I did what I could, okay? The police weren't interested." Jane thought he sounded ashamed.

"She was my mother," Leonora repeated. The girl had more control than most adults. She barely raised her voice. Jane waited for an adolescent outburst but it never came. Leonora just stared at him with what seemed like resignation.

Jane wanted to know more. She decided to press on, hoping that using a matter-of-fact, uncritical tone would keep Kenny's defenses at bay. "What made you think she was murdered?" And why *hadn't* he pursued it? Jane tried to imagine him talking to the police. Back then, the cops had crewcuts, and the young people had long hair and mustaches. Now it was the other way around. There was a lot of animosity back then, too, between cops and hippies. And she doubted Kenny would have made a good impression. It occurred to Jane that the police, if they suspected murder, might even have considered him a suspect. Weren't spouses, legal or otherwise, the usual suspects?

"Nothing specific made me think it was murder," Kenny said. "That's it, don't you see? I didn't have anything to go on, really." The edge of shame still clung to his voice, and he glanced over at his daughter. She had turned away from him, and Jane saw her in profile, her jaw clenched tight, her pale face like a mask.

"There must have been something," said Jane. "Something that made you think she was killed."

"No one ever knew what happened during the last hours of her life. I never found out and I don't think I ever will. There's no point going into it now."

He leaned back and pushed his hair off his forehead. He had reddish, freckled skin and springy gingery hair with gray running through it.

Leonora turned back to look at her father. "I didn't know she didn't like the water," she said, slightly accusing. "There's a lot I don't know about her."

"I don't think I knew much about her myself," he said. The edge had gone from his voice. Now he just sounded tired. "We were in love. We hated our parents. We wanted to be free." He closed his eyes and tipped his head back, resting it against the top of the sofa. "If you want to know the truth, she could have been anybody."

Except, you fool, she was the mother of your daughter, Jane thought. There was entirely too much unfinished business here. "I'd like to start with the family," she said decisively, plunging on ahead, even though she wondered how wise it was to commit herself to a full-fledged investigation. "Her parents. Any siblings. Can you give me their names?"

•   •   •

It was too easy to say no on the phone, so Jane drove over to Bellevue. Once a small town with strawberry fields across the lake from Seattle, it was now a sprawling suburb with its own high-rises and four lanes of traffic snarled between downtown malls.

The house was easy enough to find. Jane pulled up next to the driveway. The mailbox sat on a rigid length of chain, the links welded together so they curved up like a snake charmer's cobra, a rather heavy-handed sight gag. The name was stenciled neatly on the box: DONNELLY.

The house was of postwar vintage, a low roman brick rambler, partially concealed by thirty years' worth of landscaping: prickly pyracanthus along the fence, lots of rhododendrons and camellias, a clump of birches. Everything was overpruned—the hedges too square, the tree limbs too short for the thickness of their trunks.

She walked up the drive. It seemed less intrusive than parking right in front of the door. She'd worn her Chanel suit and low-heeled shoes, so she'd look like a respectable young Bellevue matron.

Mrs. Donnelly answered the door.

Jane gave her a friendly smile. "Mrs. Donnelly?"

"Yes?" said the woman a little nervously. Mrs. Donnelly looked like someone who'd just had a magazine make-over. She was wearing an expensive, gaudy sweater, hand-knit and encrusted with orange butterflies embroidered in angora and outlined with black sequins. Her black trousers were probably wool gabardine but managed somehow to look like polyester. Her frosted blond hair was tightly permed. Her fingernails (probably acrylic) and mouth were exactly the same shade of orange as the sweater. But beneath the gloss, Mrs. Donnelly had a tired, worn little face out of a Depression-era photograph. It was the face of someone in a limp housedress and dirty scuff slippers.

Jane introduced herself briskly, and plunged right into the pitch. "I wonder if I could talk to you about your daughter, Linda. I'm a friend of Leonora's."

"Leonora?" Mrs. Donnelly said blankly. "Who's Leonora?"

"Linda's daughter. Your granddaughter," said Jane, trying not to sound astonished.

"Oh. You mean Lullaby."

"Lullaby?"

Mrs. Donnelly wrinkled up her nose. "That's what they named her. Has she changed it?"

"Yes," said Jane, trying to sound in full possession of the facts. "May I come in?"

"Well, my granddaughter is coming over pretty soon," the woman answered doubtfully.

"Leonora's your granddaughter too, Mrs. Donnelly."

"We haven't seen so much of her lately," she replied with incredible understatement. "But I guess I could talk to you." She stepped aside and motioned for Jane to come in.

They went through a slate-tiled entry hall into the living room. Jane took in the decor. Beige walls and carpets. Chocolate brown furniture sitting like islands. A bookshelf dominated by the *Encyclopædia Britannica*. A landscape over the sofa—autumn foliage and a barn—just a little better than the kind advertised as "sofa paintings" on TV. Some octagonal side tables with oversized lamps and icy-looking glass objects. The yellowish brick fireplace looked unused because of the immaculate brass fan-shaped screen in front of it.

Mrs. Donnelly sat down on the edge of the chair, touching her unyielding coiffure with her orange-tipped nails in a tense little gesture.

"You see," began Jane, sitting opposite her, "Leonora is a young woman now, and she is curious about her mother."

"Well, we can't see her. My husband wouldn't like it," she said. "It would be awkward. We never cared for Linda's husband, Kenny," she said by way of explanation. And then she smiled.

"I see," said Jane. "Actually, Leonora has never expressed an interest in meeting you," she said. Mrs. Donnelly smiled again. "But she is interested in recovering her mother's money. Money that went to a cult, as I understand it."

"My husband tried to do something about it at the time," she said. "I don't remember much about it."

"But weren't you concerned?" said Jane, rather exasperated. "This was your family's money."

"No," said Mrs. Donnelly. "It was Linda's real father's family. It had nothing to do with us."

"Linda's father?"

"Well, my husband legally adopted her. Gave her a good home. He married me when she was two. My first husband, Linda's father, left me. He was irresponsible, and I'm afraid Linda was, too. Such a shame. I never had any trouble with my other children." She smiled again. "My only satisfaction is that we did everything we could. Even when we'd given up on her, we still kept paying for a psychiatrist, hoping she'd come around, but Linda was always a problem child."

"Can you tell me anything about the cult?" said Jane. "The people who got her money?"

Mrs. Donnelly sighed. "She gave it to some people who had something to do with fire. Keepers of the Flame or something."

Jane just nodded and stopped speaking for a while, looking at Linda's mother expectantly. The silence finally got to Mrs. Donnelly. She spoke up. "Maybe if we'd had any religious faith of our own. Linda never went to Sunday school or anything. We were never church people." She looked doubtful. "I just don't know what happened."

"It was a difficult time to raise children," said Jane.

"My younger ones turned out just fine," said Mrs. Donnelly, an edge of defensiveness creeping into her voice. "My daughter's bringing her baby over in just a few minutes, while she does some shopping. Maybe you'd better go."

"Well, thank you for your time," said Jane, rising.

Mrs. Donnelly's eyes widened, and her head jerked back just a fraction. "The other kids don't know much about their sister. I don't want them upset. It's better to forget about it. I know my husband feels that way. There's no point dwelling on it."

Jane thanked Mrs. Donnelly, who saw her to the door. Once Jane was on the porch, Mrs. Donnelly locked the screen door. "You understand, don't you," she said through the mesh. "My husband would be upset if Lullaby wanted to see us or anything."

Then she closed the other door. Jane found herself wanting to shake Mrs. Donnelly, or maybe even slap her to get some kind of honest emotion out of the woman. Her genteel, high-pitched voice sounded restrained and under control. Her husband sounded even more grim. If Uncle Harold's work meant hanging out with more Mrs. Donnellys, Jane was ready to pack it in.

A psychedelic van, some old paisley bedspreads and lovebeads, and the scent of patchouli oil would have had quite an attraction for anyone who grew up here, thought Jane, sighing.

In the driveway, a brown-haired young woman was bending over the backseat of a blue Toyota, unbuckling a baby from its car seat. "Yes, you're a darling girl," she was saying.

Over her mother's shoulder, the baby tracked Jane with big brown eyes and sucked on her fingers thoughtfully. She was mostly bald with soft fuzz on her head.

The young woman picked up the baby and turned around, coming face-to-face with Jane. "Oh," she said, obviously startled. Jane smiled at her and said hello, then admired the baby, who regarded her with solemn curiosity, her plump arms resting serenely on her mother's shoulders.

Jane walked down the driveway. When the woman and her baby went into the house, Jane copied down the license plate number of their car.

· · ·

Calvin Mason had a nasty abrasion on one side of his face, and the flesh around his eye appeared purplish with yellow highlights. He sat behind his desk, trying unsuccessfully to look dignified, when Jane came into his office.

"My god," she said. "What happened to you?"

He waved a hand in the air and looked nonchalant. "Ran into a little trouble serving a summons," he said. He tilted his head back cockily. "Goes with the territory."

"I see," she said.

"What can I do for you?" he said, fidgeting with some papers in front of him.

"Well," she said. "I found what might turn out to be a hopeless case, and I'm pursuing it. I hope I'm not spinning my wheels."

"Oh, really?" He frowned, then winced as the gesture seemed to hurt his face.

"Yes. And while I'm handling the bulk of it, I thought maybe you could help me out on some of the details. As an investigator."

He leaned back in his chair. "I see. Don't you think you should put me in the big picture?"

Jane bit her lip. "For now, I just need a name and address to go with a license plate." She would have liked to confide in him, but the thought occurred to her that he'd think Leonora's problems weren't sufficiently hopeless, and that he'd try to talk her out of it. Or that he'd think she was an idiot who didn't know what she was doing, which had occurred to Jane herself.

"No problem. Fifty bucks."

"Fine." She handed him the paper with the license number.

"And I'd also like some background on a cult. They're called the Fellowship of the Flame."

"Uh-oh," he said.

"What do you mean?"

"Well, I had some dealings with them once. A custody thing."

"Oh, really?"

"In the sixties they went around in flame-colored robes, and devoted themselves to sex, drugs, and rock and roll. But by the seventies they'd cleaned up their act and looked like those Mormons that go door to door, you know? Neat haircuts, dark suits, black plastic glasses. But the word was if they thought you were crossing them, they could come on heavy. Anyway, I was followed for a while afterward. No big deal, but I've heard of worse stories. Scary phone calls. And my client was threatened by a couple of goons when he was trying to get his minor child out of there. There've been other allegations too. I can't remember all of it. I'm not sure they still exist."

"I'd like to find out."

"All right. I've got a little time right now," he said. "Have you got a budget on this thing?"

"Tell me when you hit a thousand dollars," she said.

Behind his wounds, Calvin Mason's face took on a sort of radiance. "Right!" he said.

"And, um, make sure I get an itemized billing," she added.

Chapter 8

The next morning, Jane drifted in twilight sleep, conscious that she was waking. But before she opened her eyes, she began to feel a familiar and not unpleasant panic. She didn't know where she was.

When she did open her eyes, the feeling became more intense. She was in an old-fashioned bedroom with a coved ceiling and some dark furniture. She felt physically comfortable under a light, cozy, down comforter, but she was conscious of the floating feeling of being nowhere familiar.

A phone rang and she turned to the bedside table and stared at it—a black phone sitting on a piece of ivory-colored lace beneath a brass lamp. She didn't want to answer it until she knew where she was. On the second ring it suddenly came to her that she was in Uncle Harold's house, and the tightness in her chest vanished, leaving her instead with a vaguely disoriented feeling. As she picked up the phone, she realized she rather enjoyed the disorientation, the sense of newness, of the unexpected.

It was Calvin Mason, sounding very cheery and normal.

"I got that name and address on the Toyota you wanted," he said.

"Terrific," she said, reaching for a pen.

He gave her the name and address. It was in Issaquah, a suburb farther east from Bellevue, but still close to the

Donnellys' house. The car was registered to a Susan and Brian Gilman. The brown-haired woman with the baby. Linda's half sister, Jane was sure.

"Call me back this afternoon," he said, "and I might have something on your friends at the Fellowship of the Flame. My source," he added dramatically, "didn't want to talk, at first. But I'm meeting him later. It may cost you."

"Tell him to stop the meter at a hundred dollars," she said, throwing back the covers. If Calvin Mason was chiseling her, she meant to keep it within limits.

• • •

Susan Gilman's house on a cul-de-sac in Issaquah was painted powder blue and constructed in a New England style, with wood siding and a peaked roof. Its recent vintage was revealed by its tiny aluminum-framed windows.

The yard was a bright green oval of new lawn, surrounded by huge garden beds full of orange bark mulch and dotted sparsely with small evergreen shrubs. The developer had left in a few native Douglas firs—tall, dark, and rather sinister looking in the tidy setting.

It was quite a bit different from the Donnellys' house in Bellevue. This suburb was farther away from Seattle, and, in this less affluent era, the house was more cheaply built. The architecture had a cautious eye on the past, unlike the defiant fifties rambler sprawling happily into the future.

But in another sense, this house was the generational equivalent of the house in Bellevue where Linda and Susan had grown up. It was safe, neat, quiet. There were no sidewalks, for none were needed.

Susan Gilman came to the door holding her baby on her hip.

"Oh!" she said, with a look of recognition.

"My name is Jane da Silva. I talked to your mother this week."

"Yes, I know. I saw you in the driveway, and then she told me who you were. You asked about Linda. Come in."

Jane sat in a sparsely decorated living room, while Susan Gilman arranged her baby in a yellow plastic playpen, setting some small toys in front of her.

The baby looked at Jane through the white mesh, her faint eyebrows raised in curiosity.

"She's lovely," said Jane.

Susan stepped back and gazed at her child. "I know." She turned to Jane and smiled nervously. "It's since Camille was born that I began to think more and more about Linda."

"I suppose that's natural," said Jane. "Family."

"Our family has just kind of blotted Linda out. Like she never existed." Susan sat down, smoothed out her jeans, picked at the fabric on the arm of the sofa. "I can't imagine doing that to Camille. No matter what happened."

"Do you know why I'm asking about Linda?" said Jane.

"You're trying to help Lullaby. But I'm not sure how."

"Linda's money. The money she should have passed on to her daughter. Lullaby calls herself Leonora now, by the way."

"Money? Linda had some money?"

"From her real father's family. You didn't know about that?"

"My parents are very private people. It wasn't the kind of family where we talked about anything negative, you know?"

"I know." Jane paused. "Apparently, there was an inheritance from her father's family. She came into the money when she was twenty-one, and had it very briefly. Then she turned it over to a cult called the Fellowship of the Flame. Then she died."

"The Fellowship of the Flame. That sounds familiar. I'm sure I remember my parents talking about it. Linda was into all kinds of occult stuff. And you're trying to get that money back for Lullaby?"

"I was hoping you could help me."

"Well, I don't know. I mean, it's always been so painful for my parents. I don't know whether I want to stir things up. It was all a long time ago."

"Your niece is a very talented classical pianist. She needs that money to study music." Jane leaned forward, and looked Susan right in the eye. "I've heard her play. She's a very good musician, and no one seems interested in helping her. Her mother's dead, her grandparents don't care, and her father is incapable of helping her, as far as I can judge. She's young and gifted and I think she deserves a break."

"Really?" Susan looked a little defensive. "I haven't seen her since she was a baby. About Camille's age. I don't know how I can help."

"I'm not sure either. Just tell me about Linda and the time she died."

"I was fourteen. We weren't very close. She was a lot older. She was a hippie, and she lived with that guy Ken." Susan frowned in concentration, as if she were trying hard to remember. "I'm afraid I didn't like Linda."

"Why not?"

"Oh, I don't know. My parents did a remodel that seemed to last forever, and we shared a room for a while. She had all this junk around when I was ten or so and she was in high school. Black light posters and stuff. I wanted a frilly little girl's room with a canopy bed, you know?"

She paused. "I remember our fights. I'd just scream. I used to tell her she wasn't really in our family. Just half-in, and if it weren't for her, I'd have my own room. Pretty awful, huh?"

The baby gurgled.

"Sometimes she'd lock me out of the room. I'd sit in the hall and do my homework. She'd be in there sulking. Maybe she was smoking dope with a towel under the door. Who knows. I suppose I irritated her. I'd jump up and down on the bed and stuff and have my Barbie doll clothes all over everything. It was a real disaster."

"What did your mother do?"

"Nothing. Whenever anything unpleasant happens, my mother does nothing."

"She smiles," said Jane. "I noticed that. Whenever anything unpleasant comes up, she smiles."

"That's right, that's right." Susan became a little agitated, as if pleased that someone else had noticed this about her mother. "Well, she smiled a lot around Linda. Linda would want to fight with her the way teenage girls fight with their mothers, and Mom would just smile."

"When you think back, do you think Linda really meant for that cult to get all her money?"

"I don't know. I just don't know. If Linda gave it to them, it was because they gave her a lot of attention. That's all she ever wanted, and she could never get enough. I resented her so much when I was younger because she was always causing trouble and getting that attention.

"I remember the time I had a violin solo in assembly and I wanted my parents to be there, but Linda had got into some trouble or other, and my parents had to go down to the high school and have a conference about her. She was cutting classes, I think."

Camille, who had been sucking on a plastic duck, flung it away and began to whimper. Susan went over, picked her up, sighed, and sat down with the baby in her lap. Camille put her head against her mother, looked curiously over at Jane, and began sucking her thumb in a business-like way.

"She used to stomp around the house and say 'Nobody loves me.' I just hated her for it, because she had made herself so unlovable. She was always difficult."

Susan stroked her baby's soft brown hair. "But maybe she was right. Well, Mom loved her, I guess. But Mom was always trying to be a cushion between Linda and Dad. He got aggravated so easily, and Mom always tries to protect him."

"How did they feel when Lullaby was born?" said Jane.

"Well, first of all, Linda had the baby at home. With some hippie midwife. Mom was horrified. Dad wanted to call the police and put a stop to it. Mom was sure the baby would die or Linda would die or they both would die.

"But they didn't. And my parents were so embarrassed because they didn't believe Linda and Ken were really married. That was a big deal back then." Susan sighed. "She brought the baby over one time, and I held her. I loved holding her. I hadn't really held any babies. It was when I first held Lullaby—Leonora—that I realized I wanted babies, too."

"Did anyone think there was anything strange about Linda's death?" asked Jane.

"It was a shock, of course. But in a way, we weren't surprised. Linda seemed so reckless. Not physically reckless, but it was always as if she didn't care what happened to her in a way. I mean, Linda was always very self-centered, always more concerned with herself than with anyone else. But she was wild, too, and careless about herself. So when we heard she drowned—well—Dad said she was probably on drugs."

"Do you think she could have killed herself?"

"Linda? No, I don't. Suicides are depressed, aren't they? Linda wasn't depressed, she was angry. Always angry. Fighting." Susan began to rock the baby, who seemed to be falling asleep now, her eyelids at half-mast, her brow smooth, her wet pink mouth slightly open. "That's why she was such a pain. She was always fighting."

"Fighting your parents?"

"Yes. And somehow fighting to be happy."

"What about her real father?"

"Long gone. My mother never talked about him. I

guess he was a real loser. Linda tried to find him once when she was about fifteen. His parents lived in California, I know that. They used to send her ten dollars every Christmas. We all were somehow embarrassed by that. Embarrassed that she had relatives we didn't, and that Mom had been married before to this bum. I did get the impression he was a flake.

"Linda always seemed extra, somehow. In all our family pictures she was standing off to one side. And she was darker than me and my brother. It was like she was a guest in the family, someone you had to invite.

"I'll be right back," said Susan, looking down at her baby. Camille was asleep now, and breathing snuffily. "I'll put her down for her nap." She carried the little girl from the room and returned a few minutes later. The sound of a music box chimed from some back room. "She usually falls asleep about now," she said. "She's such a good baby."

Susan sat down heavily. "Like I say, I've been thinking more about Linda now. I'm sad she never saw Camille.

"I realize I've pushed a lot of it to the back of my mind. When she died, I felt so guilty. I wished I'd been nicer to her. When I was really little she used to walk me home from kindergarten. I'd hold her hand while we crossed the street, and I'd feel proud to have a big sister. It was only later I thought of her as my half sister."

"I wish I knew more about her state of mind before she died," said Jane. "What I'm trying to do for Leonora is to see if we can somehow prove that the money your sister gave away to the Fellowship of the Flame was fraudulently obtained."

"There was her best friend in high school. She's still around. I ran into her in the Safeway the other night. Judy came to Linda's funeral. I remember that."

"Judy?"

"Judy Van Horne. She might be in the phone book."

"What about your brother? Does he remember much about Linda?"

"Gregg? He joined the service right out of college. He's based in Germany now. I don't think he and I talked about Linda more than five or six times in all the years since she died."

"I really appreciate your talking to me," said Jane. She wondered if Susan Gilman wanted to see her niece. Mrs. Donnelly hadn't asked about Leonora, which Jane thought was strange. Susan didn't ask either. She showed Jane to the door and said, "I hope you can help Linda's girl. She must be pretty big by now."

"She's seventeen. A very nice young lady."

"How do you know her?" said Susan. "Why exactly are you trying to help her?"

Jane had been waiting for this, and in fact, she wondered why it had taken Susan so long to ask.

There was absolutely no way to explain that Uncle Harold had decided Jane was going to be a nonprofit detective; that there wasn't really much else for her to do with her life right now; and that she was trying to make a big case out of an old injustice, probably in vain, so she could get her hands on some money of her own and lead a comfortable, respectable life, something that had eluded her up to now. Instead she said, "I'm a music lover, and Leonora needs some help getting herself a good education. She's a very talented pianist."

"I see," said Susan. "That's really nice of you."

As she walked back to the car, Jane thought to herself, No, it isn't. I'm not being nice at all. I'm just a hopeless case myself, getting too tired to keep living by my wits and what charm I manage to scrape together when I need it.

Chapter 9

She glanced around the cul-de-sac at all the neat homes, the tidy yards, felt the heavy stillness. She'd always felt an antipathy toward neighborhoods like this.

But the people who lived in them had figured out something she never had. They lived quiet, respectable lives and they had accepted that to do so they had to take boring jobs working for other people and doing the same thing every day.

Jane had thought she could be freer than that. Mostly, she'd wanted freedom to keep moving toward new people and new places. But she wasn't free at all, really. For years, ever since Bernardo's money had all disappeared, she'd been scrounging. And for years, while these people were building for the future, she'd been living for the future, hoping things would change for the better, that she'd somehow hit on a magic formula, a perfect job, maybe a perfect husband. Instead, she found herself at the mercy of dead Uncle Harold's whims dragging around all these oppressive suburbs like some kind of Avon lady in her Chanel suit.

Jane decided to head right back to the city and get immediately into her self-pity mode. Her theory was that feeling sorry for yourself was best tackled head-on, with calculated self-indulgence. She felt miserable, and she'd systematically cheer herself up.

She drove back across the lake and headed downtown to the Pike Place Market. Parking was tough, but she found a public lot, and pulled the car into a slot. She sat for a minute in the car, looking out over a railing and marveling that, here in Seattle, a parking garage could have a fabulous view. She was looking out over Elliott Bay, and across to dark green, forested islands, and beyond that to blue, snow-topped mountains. In the foreground, on the water, sailboats tacked around the wake of a big Japanese container ship.

She walked back to the market past a small park with a sweeping view of the sound. There, on green lawn sculpted into a hill and decorated with cedar totem poles, she watched two police officers. Giant night sticks and big guns on their belts, they patted down two Indians, a young man and a woman with glasses. One of the policemen took a couple of cans of beer away from them and poured it out on the grass, then fastidiously put the beer cans in a trash container.

Nearby, a couple of tourists, apparently oblivious to any irony, pretended not to notice, while they admired the ancestral art of the Indians.

She walked a little farther past a line of antique streetlamps with big glass globes, remembering how grim the market had been years ago when she had left. There had been rainy days when she'd come down to buy fresh produce from elderly Japanese truck farmers. Back then, there'd been empty stands, derelicts jaywalking across the cobblestones, and a few eager citizens with petitions to save the market.

It had been saved with a vengeance. In fact, it looked almost like a movie set. There was a lively crowd pushing past stands selling crafts or shiny fruits and vegetables. She admired stands selling little bunches of fresh herbs, and beautiful bouquets of flowers sitting in coffee cans. They were bouquets of the kind of old-fashioned flowers that needed more space than could be had in city gardens— lupines and hollyhocks and columbine and delphiniums. Jane bought a bunch from a Cambodian lady who wrapped everything deftly in tissue paper with small, beautiful hands.

Energetic, flirty young men in aprons shouted out the merits of their vegetables. Jane bought some fresh peas and looked forward with anticipation to shelling them—an occupation she associated with back porches and a big chipped enamel bowl, some childhood memory, she supposed. She also bought a handful of small red-skinned potatoes. Already, she was beginning to feel better.

She felt the kind of poignant intensity she had felt before, when traveling alone. It came from all the faces of strangers and from the vivid surroundings, flowers and food and vendors hustling their wares with practiced theatricality; and, from across the street, the saxophone of a street musician, running a line of slow notes in a minor key through all the festive energy. Small brown birds hopped along the ground, grazing deftly between pedestrians' feet. Restored turn-of-the-century ironwork lamps and baskets of summer flowers gave a finished look to the proceedings.

At a fishmonger's stall, she gazed happily at Dungeness crab set in neat rows and beautiful clear-eyed whole fish on mounds of ice. She bought a couple of bright red sockeye salmon steaks, and added the white butcher paper package to her collection.

A juggler was holding forth farther along, where the narrow corridor of stands opened into a kind of plaza. Children in strollers watched him solemnly. Jane crossed the brick-paved street and discovered that the area around the market had blossomed forth into dozens of restored storefronts. Overhead, on a narrow balcony looking down on the narrow street, was a restaurant achingly festive with a wrought iron railing and umbrellas over white tables. Jane bought a bottle of good wine in a shop that had grapevines growing out of window boxes in the front; three chocolate éclairs in a bakery; and a pound of coffee in an antiseptically white store with more kinds of coffee beans than anyone really needed. And then she found an international newsstand where she bought heavy, slick magazines—a French *Elle*, an Italian *Vogue*, and a *Tatler*—for an exorbitant amount of money.

Back at her car, she felt, as she set her purchases in the backseat, the usual satisfaction she felt after shopping. Here she had the makings of a lovely meal. But the intensity of all she had seen, while it seemed to have blotted out her depression, had left her with another feeling, troublesome in a different way.

Her own solitude and all that stimulation had collided in a rather unsettling way. Sometimes that feeling could be embraced and be exhilarating. Now, with the prospect of going back alone to Uncle Harold's gloomy house, she saw it might upset her. Like a drug addict who tries to control his mood with a complicated regime of uppers and downers, Jane decided she needed to make one more stop, for something to distract her more profoundly than those luscious thick magazines.

She had spotted a video rental place near Uncle Harold's house. Tired, but willing herself on, she went there, and after a slight contretemps with the owner, who didn't like it that she didn't have a Washington State driver's license and then ran her Visa card through some computer and found it wanting, she discovered he was an Algerian. In French she convinced him to let her rent some tapes and a VCR. Heading straight for "Classics," she grabbed two Fred Astaires, one early Jean-Paul Belmondo gangster film, and Gary Cooper and Madeleine Carroll in *The General Died at Dawn*. She wouldn't have time for all of them, but the whole idea of an antidepression orgy was to wallow in luxury and the extravagance of abundance and choice.

Struggling into the house with everything, Jane felt quite lovely and perfectly justified. After all, she'd been working hard. And if, after all her efforts, Uncle Harold's cronies deprived her of her inheritance, she at least deserved one decent meal and a movie, magazine, and éclair marathon on his nickel.

Chapter 10

Linda's friend Judy Van Horne was easy to find. Jane found her parents listed in the Bellevue phone book, and they gave her an address in Carnation, a small town to the northeast.

She drove through pastureland where black-and-white dairy cows grazed, startled to see such a rural landscape so close to Seattle. She was still in King County, but she could have been hundreds of miles away, or decades in the past.

The house was a low, scruffy bungalow surrounded by trees and a yard that looked as if it had never been cared for, unless the one dusty lilac by the front porch was the last remnant of someone's garden. When she pulled into the driveway, a fierce yapping of dogs began.

A couple of black Labs and a yellow mongrel rushed up to the car. Jane wondered whether it was safe to get out. Then, a tall, angular woman in jeans and a man's shirt strode out and spoke sharply to the dogs. She had a weathered face and short, rather wild hair. The dogs scuttled back toward her, but kept up their movement, obviously excited.

"Quiet, you guys," she yelled, as Jane got out.

"Hi," said Jane. "I'm looking for Judy Van Horne. My name's Jane da Silva."

"I'm Judy." She looked wary. Jane was startled to see how old she was. Because Linda had died young, it was hard to remember her contemporaries were entering middle age.

"Susan Gilman gave me your name. Linda Donnelly's little sister."

"Yes?"

"I wonder if I could ask you a few questions about Linda."

"But she's been dead for years." She had the Labs by their collars. They were panting and fractious.

"I know. I've been trying to help her daughter find out about her."

"Oh. Well, you can come in, but I doubt if I can help you."

Jane followed her up onto a creaking porch and into a living room obviously ravaged by the dogs. Upholstery and carpeting were scratched and chewed, and the place smelled of animals. A long-haired cat was sleeping on the sofa. A poster on the wall showed a monkey in a cage and read STOP VIVISECTION AND SPECIES CHAUVINISM. Another poster showed a harbor seal.

Judy sat down. "I was her friend in high school. That was a long time ago."

Jane felt awkward, but she plunged ahead. "Well, her daughter is almost grown now, and she never knew much about Linda."

"Linda and I were very close for a while. We were both unhappy at home, and that brought us together. But then she started going out with Ken in her junior year and she lost interest in me."

"I imagine that was painful," said Jane. "Young girls can be cruel."

"Humans are cruel." The yellow dog came and rested its head in her lap. She stroked its fur. "Not like these guys." The dog made a whiny sound and drooled. Jane decided she'd better show some interest in the menagerie and looked around for something else to pet. She was reasonably fond of animals, especially well-behaved dogs. They made nice companions on walks. She generally admired cats for their elegance, but found something unpleasantly cavalier about the way they treated the humans who loved them.

None of the present assembly of animals appealed to her particularly, but to be polite, she ran her hand down the back of a nearby cat, which nipped her thumb and gave her a feline sneer.

"Oh, Colonel Mustard's always crabby," Judy said casually. "He bites everybody."

Managing a wan smile at Judy, Jane shot the cat a cold look, but it just closed one eye and looked bored.

"Anyway," continued Judy, "she did invite me to her wedding."

"Oh, yes. On a mountaintop, wasn't it?"

"That's right. I don't remember much about it. I guess she was really happy. I don't think I saw her after that. I went away to college and lost track of her."

"But you heard she died?"

"Yes. I went to the funeral. Her stupid stepfather was there. I remember wondering if he was glad she was dead. She hated him."

"So Linda was pretty unhappy?"

"I think so. She was always complaining about her family."

"Why didn't she get along with her stepfather?"

"He was always nagging her. She said he treated her like a servant. It was like Cinderella. She was always supposed to baby-sit his kids. Who knows? People just seem to hate their stepparents. I certainly hated mine."

Judy leaned back on the sofa, as if her memories were collecting themselves, and her voice became more thoughtful. "Looking back on it, it seemed he'd spoiled her rotten when she was a little kid, but when she hit adolescence it kind of threw him. He used to tell her she dressed like a slut. I remember one time we were watching TV and she was lying on the couch and he came and yelled at her that her skirts were too short.

"It was different at my house. My mom was always giving me charge cards and trying to get me to wear more fashionable clothes." A look of contemptuous irritation flitted across her features.

Jane wished someone had given her charge cards in high school and set her loose. In fact, she wished someone would do it right now. But, "I see," was all she said.

"Basically, Linda was pretty out of it, and so was I, and she needed someone to sit with in the cafeteria and go shopping with. You know what I mean?"

"Adolescence is rough," said Jane, trying to look sympathetic but not pitying—as if she knew this from personal experience. Which, of course, like anyone else, she did. "Later she was involved with a cult. Do you remember anything about the Fellowship of the Flame?"

"It sounds familiar. Weren't they pretty big around here in the late sixties and early seventies?"

"That's right. Linda gave them all her money. She had an inheritance and she turned it over to them."

"That figures. She always wanted to belong. But she didn't care that I needed that too." Judy shifted in her chair.

"Ken, her boyfriend, was kind of a loser too. I mean, no one ever paid any attention to him until he turned himself into a hippie. Suddenly he grew his hair and wore these flowing blouses and stuff and did a lot of dope. They got together and she was thrilled. But she just dumped me."

"That must have been hard."

"Well, it wouldn't have been any big deal if I hadn't

already felt rejected and vulnerable. I've worked a lot of that out in therapy since."

"Linda was seeing a therapist in high school, wasn't she?"

"That's right. Dr. Hawthorne. She was crazy about him. Her parents sent her there and she really took to it."

Judy cleared her throat and wrenched the conversation firmly back to herself. "My own therapy really helped with rejection. I realized in group that Linda had truly hurt me in high school. We spent half a session on it, I think." Judy frowned. "And what was really strange was that there was this guy there who'd known Linda later—around the time she died.

"Afterward, he came up to me and asked about her. He seemed really agitated. He wanted to know about her family and what kind of a person she'd been."

"Really? Who was he?"

"We only knew each other's first names. I think his name was Rick. He was an okay guy, I guess." Judy sounded reluctant to concede that anyone was worth liking. "He kept saying he had a lot of guilt to work out, but I can't remember much more about him. A lot of these people have pretty boring problems, actually."

Jane imagined a circle of people on folding chairs, all waiting impatiently to discuss their own fascinating cases. "Thank you very much," she said. "I hope this wasn't too painful." Jane hated thinking about her own past, even though she often felt a longing for other eras, even eras she hadn't personally experienced. But to reminisce about people and places she'd lived through herself she usually found vaguely depressing, even when the memories were pleasant ones.

"Like I say," said Judy, standing up and jamming her hands into the pockets of her jeans, "I've worked a lot of the rejection thing out. I've learned not to count on other people. Just my babies." She smiled down at a drooling Lab and scratched its head.

As she walked Jane back to her car, she said suddenly, "That guy from group I was telling you about? Rick? I remember now. He was a special effects guy. You know. For commercials and stuff."

"In Seattle?"

"That's right. He was really interested in Linda. But after that session where we talked about her, he never came back. I remember wondering what had happened to him. I thought it might have been helpful for me to have him there while I talked about Linda's rejection of me."

Losers! thought Jane as she pulled away from the yapping dogs. Uncle Harold gets twins separated at birth and Russian spy impersonators, and I get the dysfunctional Donnellys and whiny Judy and Colonel Mustard, the crabby cat.

If Judy's shrink had any sense at all, she thought, he'd tell her to start thinking about others—preferably others of her own species—for a while, and get the focus off herself. And, for short-term depression and self-loathing, the éclairs, magazine, and video cure could be very effective. As she got closer to Bellevue, she pulled over to a 7-Eleven store, bought herself a giant Coke, and flipped through an Eastside phone book. A Dr. Hawthorne was still in practice, and he was in downtown Bellevue. Jane figured it wouldn't hurt to show up in person and try to get an appointment.

Chapter 11

After Calvin Mason had provided Jane da Silva with the name to fit the license plate she'd asked about, he was puzzled by a vague feeling of anticlimax. Oh well, he thought, she'll call back to find out about the Fellowship of the Flame. It was this thought, somehow cheering, that made him aware of the reason for his let-down feeling. He wanted more contact with Jane da Silva. He found her intriguing, and he wanted to find out more about her.

But why wait to glean polite snippets about her from casual conversation? Shamelessly, Calvin Mason decided to devote a couple of hours to finding out what he could about her.

There wasn't much. A couple of phone calls later he determined her dead uncle, in whose name the phone was still listed, had been one Harold Mortensen. A trip down to the King County Courthouse, and a glance at the probated will, didn't tell him much more that he didn't know, other than that Jane's last address was care of American Express, Amsterdam.

Calvin liked that. He thought it spoke of a certain casual, transitory, expatriate life, rather at odds with the somewhat formal, cool woman he'd met. She acted self-possessed, like someone who had a good, solid address. Or maybe two.

He knew a lot of skittish women who kicked around and never settled in, whose lives were always in flux. Nice, often artsy women who bounced around from bad relationship to bad relationship, dragging a few kids with them sometimes, never having enough money and always involved in some low-level hassle. A lot of his clients were like that.

Calvin sometimes thought he had a sign on his forehead reading NICE GUY that only these women could read. They were pleasant, but clingy, with soft voices and vulnerable faces. Women who would never come out and ask you to take care of them and all their problems, but who nevertheless made you feel somehow guilty if you didn't help them; and you never could help them enough.

Jane da Silva was polite, but on the other hand she had a kind of kick-ass aura about her that he liked. That, and her having been a singer, reminded him of some smoky old film noir, in which the heroine's been around and can handle herself anywhere.

He left the King County Courthouse and wandered up Third Avenue, turning into a little brick courtyard between high rises. Like any odd little corner of Seattle, it had lots of flowers and an espresso stand and white plastic chairs and tables.

Calvin bought himself a double *latte* from a cheery redhead with a jewel in her nose and a row of tiny silver rings working their way up the cartilage of her ear. He sat down at one of the tables under a scrawny sycamore, and observed the full ashtray. Smokers loved these little spots around town. It was the last place left they could sit down and have a quiet cigarette. The tree above him shivered, and a breeze smacked him in the face. These damned high rises, thought Calvin irritably, had filled the city with pockets of updrafts.

He sipped the coffee, felt the caffeine jolt, and resumed thinking about Jane da Silva. It had long been one of his fantasies—Calvin Mason never shared his fantasies, but he wasn't ashamed to spend a lot of his own time wallowing in them—to have some smoky female sashay into his office like Veronica Lake or Lizabeth Scott, some sultry type with a low voice who didn't smile too much. He'd solve her problem and they'd end up in the sack. And it would be great. Naturally, this class broad would never presume to cling or need him too much. But she'd always be available and thrilled to see him.

Instead, he got all those nice, sweet, clingy overeducated welfare mothers. Instead of women with a cool, level, smoldering gaze, he got women who bent their heads helplessly forward and looked up at him shyly. All very appealing in its own way, but Calvin had to admit that his own life was clinging to the margins as it was, and he couldn't afford to get tangled up with someone else in the same boat but even less competent.

Unlike his fantasy, Jane da Silva hadn't come into the office wearing a black veil, suede gloves, stockings with seams, and tarty shoes with ankle straps. She'd been wearing jeans and a sweater. But then, if anyone wearing all that gear had shown up in his office in this day and age, Calvin would have checked the feet and shoulders and Adam's apple to see if he was dealing with a drag queen. No one else would wear a hat and gloves nowadays.

Anyway, Calvin sighed, he supposed he'd better stop thinking about Mrs. da Silva. It would just get him all bent out of shape. In recent years, Calvin had postulated a model of sexual attractiveness and availability. He'd even thought a software program could be developed around his theories, which were based loosely on the behavior of lesser primates.

First of all, men and women were looking for different things. Sure everyone wanted love and companionship and all that, but men cared more about youth and beauty and women cared more about babies and security. And these were the bargaining chips with which the deals were made, especially as the participants got older. (Young kids and people out of town on business were the only ones who just went after each other out of sheer, happy lust.)

The idea would be to establish a curve and find out just where the trade-offs intersected. The older and homelier the guy, the more money and power he had to have. Which, thought Calvin Mason, probably meant that he and the da Silva woman weren't in the cards. She had sex appeal and pretty good looks and class—and the confidence to carry it all off. If she was completely broke, she could still do better than Calvin, who figured that the points he got for being reasonably attractive and an enthusiastic lover and a nice guy and having all his hair and a flat stomach weren't enough to squeak him into contention, what with his lousy practice and his beat-up car.

The best thing to do was to get her off that stupid pedestal in his mind. And he knew just how to do it, too. After all, he told himself as he headed up to the library, no one is really like those torrid movie ladies, anyway. Everyone started out insecure, and part of them stayed that way.

He found what he was looking for. There was her twenty-year-old class picture in the Roosevelt High School yearbook. She looked pretty cute in her picture. Same eyes and nose and mouth, but softer, with fewer planes in her face. Not anybody you'd peg for a steamy film noir heroine. She said her ambitions were to travel and meet interesting people (implied in this goal was a certain contempt for the people she already knew). She'd been on the tennis team and in French club and in the choir. He flipped around some more and found her in the French club group shot, wearing a cardigan sweater and a pleated skirt. A good girl. Definitely. In the tennis team shot she was in the back row, squinting a little into the camera. Apparently she'd been absent the day the choir shot was taken.

She was just a reasonably intelligent, attractive woman on whom he'd projected yet another of his fantasies, Calvin told himself. And what was he getting all fired up about, anyway? After all, there was always good old Marcia, who was a lot of fun and liked to cook and bounced around a lot in bed. Marcia also had the good taste never to use the dreaded C words: *commitment* and *call*, as in, "You said you'd call. Why didn't you call?" In fact, Calvin had the feeling she'd dump him in a minute if someone more solid came along.

Chapter 12

D r. Hawthorne's office was in a small, square building stained a milky pale gray and softened by vaguely Japanese-looking landscaping—low shrubs leading the eye serenely from the gravel parking lot to the heavy front door.

Jane had parked and was crunching through the gravel as a plump middle-aged woman in a plaid skirt and a polo shirt came out of the building. She was wiping tears from her face, working hard to keep the mascara on the bottom lashes from smearing. Jane sighed. Another unhappy customer. She shouldn't be crying as she came *out* of the building.

Inside, the waiting area was gloomily tasteful. Artfully lit pre-Columbian artifacts sat in glass niches in the walls, their faces with startled eyes and round mouths looking suitably neurotic, or at least anxious. Vaguely sinister plants loomed in the corners. There were two long black leather sofas facing each other over a glass-topped table with *Sunset* magazines laid out in a neat, overlapping row. Track lighting sent bursts of illumination onto the sofas and the reception area.

Behind the desk sat an extremely serious-looking middle-aged woman with steel-gray hair and glasses. Jane thought she'd look serious, too, working in a space that resembled the set from the last act of a depressing play, or a sort of

85

temple of malaise. Usually, Jane managed to avoid bleakness. Lately, she seemed surrounded by it. She hoped it wasn't catching.

She gave the woman a kind, gentle smile, and asked in a genteel voice if it were at all possible to see the doctor, not on a professional basis but on another matter entirely. As she said this, it occurred to her the woman probably thought she was in deep denial about her psychological problems and was desperate for therapy.

"What is it concerning?" she asked flatly.

"I have some questions about a patient he had once. It's a family matter. Linda Donnelly."

The woman raised an eyebrow skeptically and checked a schedule book. "I'll see," she said.

She withdrew into an inner office and returned, apparently surprised. "Dr. Hawthorne says to come right in," she said.

After the grim waiting area, Jane was surprised to see that Dr. Hawthorne's inner office was an oasis of calm and diffused light. Across from his desk was a pleasant view, through French doors, of lacy green foliage against a cedar fence. (Of course, the patients faced him, so he had the view.) The walls were a glowing peach, and there were abstract pastel watercolors on the walls.

Dr. Hawthorne himself stood in the center of the room in a dark gray suit of fine wool. His abundant hair was silver, and he had a beaky nose, a light tan, perfect white teeth, and remarkable eyes. They were pale and piercing, but with a light in them that gave them a look of intellect and spirituality.

"I appreciate your seeing me without an appointment," Jane said, shaking his hand. He indicated a chair facing his desk and sat down himself.

"You wanted to talk about Linda Donnelly," he said.

"Yes. I'm a friend of her daughter, and I'm collecting some facts about her," said Jane.

"And why are you doing that?" He tilted his head a little and looked at her curiously with his shiny eyes.

"Well, to be quite honest, I'd like to recover some money her mother had."

"Yes," mused Dr. Hawthorne. "There was an inheritance of some kind, as I recall." He sighed. "I remember her talking about turning the money over to some odd group. She was under some pressure from her husband not to do it. Ambiguous family dynamics created unresolved conflicts for her."

"Did you try to stop her from giving away all her money?"

The doctor smiled at her piteously. "I can see you've never been analyzed," he said. "Of course I didn't. The analyst doesn't dissuade, persuade, suggest, cajole, wheedle ..." He trailed off.

"No, of course not," said Jane. "I also hoped you'd be able to tell me about her state of mind, around the time she died." She paused. "If it wouldn't be a violation of confidentiality."

"We are allowed to speak ill of the dead," he said with a little smile. "Or well of them. We are allowed to speak of them in general. But of course, we don't have to, either." He looked pensive, as if trying to decide whether to talk about Linda or not.

"Her daughter, would, I think, like to know more about her," said Jane, trying a different tack.

"Her child." Dr. Hawthorne gazed over Jane's shoulder out into the garden, giving the impression he was thinking deep thoughts. Jane wondered if it really meant he was simply looking out the window. But with those eyes, it was hard to believe Dr. Hawthorne ever simply looked out the window. "It would be interesting," he said, "to learn how the dynamics of Linda's personality would affect the character development of a vulnerable offspring."

"Leonora was raised by her father," said Jane.

"Yes. I remember him. Passive. A classic oral-dependent type." Jane detected a hint of a sneer. "Well, Linda was making progress, but she was at risk for suicide. She'd had an early loss, social isolation, critical parent introject. She was impulsive and rigid and emotionally labile. She used acting out as a primary defense."

"So you think she killed herself?"

He shrugged. "She made many self-destructive gestures."

"It's funny, I had a different impression of her," said Jane. "She was always searching for herself, and she seemed rather enthusiastic about the task at hand."

"Yes, she had some defenses," said Dr. Hawthorne. "But, although Linda was morbidly introspective, she never remembered her dreams, I'm afraid." He gave a little frown of disapproval. "There was resistance on a subconscious level."

"The cult she was involved with was called the Fellowship of the Flame," said Jane. "Do you remember that?"

"Yes. Seething with hostility. They're very angry people. Or were. I haven't heard much about them lately."

"And Linda was angry?"

"Oh yes. It was repressed anger. She had difficulties with her parents. Repetition compulsion made her a slave to her unresolved oedipal conflicts—or in this case, an Electra complex. The Electra complex is much less interesting than the oedipal conflict, I'm afraid."

"I understand she didn't get along with her stepfather."

He nodded. "When the child makes tentative seductive moves that lead to rejection by the parent, the child needs to establish identification with the same-sexed parent. It makes it much harder if the same-sexed parent is particularly weak."

Jane nodded. Linda's friend had told her that Linda's stepfather had yelled at her that her skirts were too short. She had a depressing picture of a sullen teenager with one of those adolescent bodies bursting out of her clothes,

miniskirt hiked up above her newly mature thighs, lounging sulkily on the sofa while her stepfather shouted at
her, not knowing why, and her mother smiled grimly
from the sidelines.

"It seems odd to me," said Jane, "that she would
continue to see you while simultaneously buying into the
Fellowship of the Flame."

"It happens all the time." He smiled and spread out his
hands. "There were many splits in her ego, allowing her
to function appropriately in situations that are apparently
contradictory, while experiencing no emotional conflict.
Classic dissociation. And, because of Linda's hysteria, the
opportunities for self-dramatization the group would pro-
vide her would be extremely seductive."

"It seems a shame they got all her money, though,
doesn't it? And apparently, they did."

"Oh yes. She gave it to them all in cash. She told me
how happy it made her to turn it all over. There was a
whole suitcase full of it, as I recall." He smiled indulgently.

"But do you think she was mentally capable of making
the decision?" Jane felt impatient. "What exactly was your
diagnosis?"

The doctor looked thoughtful, as if he was trying to
remember. "Histrionic personality disorder with borderline trends suggestive of severe emotional instability."

Jane had once spent six disastrous weeks imagining
herself in love with a rich, handsome neurotic. Anthony
had been a professional analysand, visiting his therapist
Monday through Friday, and discussing his own therapy
and psychoanalytic theory in general at great length on
the weekends. Jane remembered some of the jargon.

Consciously combining this knowledge with careful dic-
tion and a ladylike demeanor, Jane did her best to assure
the doctor he was dealing with an intelligent woman,
equal to him in class and intellect and therefore worthy of
his time, attention, and confidences.

"So in other words, to Linda, life was a stage. While she may have appeared and acted passionately, she was in reality rather shallow of feeling, and, as she would be unable to tap her own resources, she might be very receptive to a powerful person or an organization that promised to save her, bring her happiness."

"That's right," he said.

"And so it would be very easy to separate her from her money with some promise of personal salvation. Isn't that undue influence?"

He gave her an attractive but slightly patronizing smile, and allowed his blue eyes to glow at her softly.

"She was sane enough to give away her money. The money seems to concern you a great deal. What happened to the money is of no concern to me. My accountant will tell you I don't concern myself with money at all. He finds this somehow threatening. But I'm a psychiatrist. It is the wellness of the mind, or soul if you will, that is my responsibility."

"Yes, of course. I suppose psychiatrists are the priests of our secular age," she said, tempted to add they were spared a vow of poverty. If, through carelessness in financial matters, the doctor needed some quick cash, he could always sell those Incan relics in his waiting room, or the Jaguar sedan she'd seen in the parking lot.

"I've heard that analogy many times," said Dr. Hawthorne. He said it pleasantly but she had the impression he was determined not to let her think she'd had an original thought.

"I suppose I had seen Linda somewhat as a victim of the sixties," said Jane. "But you have put it all in very clinical terms, as if she would have developed the same way whenever she had lived."

"Well, we can't discount societal influences entirely," said Dr. Hawthorne, sounding as if he wished he could. "The sixties were a difficult time. But I still believe

Linda's case would have had the same tragic conclusion, whatever happened to her."

"You think she killed herself, don't you?"

"I think it is likely. That's what I told the police at the time."

"I really appreciate your talking to me," said Jane. "And I'm impressed that you remember it all so well. Did you consult your notes?"

"They were destroyed," said Hawthorne. "We don't keep them after a patient dies."

She'd hoped they'd be around. "You have a remarkable memory," said Jane. "It's been so many years."

"Yes. It's strange, how vivid it all is. I think it's because it was an intense time in my own life. I was divorced around that time."

"Oh. I'm sorry," said Jane, rather astonished that he was telling her anything about himself. Maybe he got tired of listening silently to patients hour after hour. "That is always difficult."

"Well, it was the wisest course of action," said Hawthorne. "Caroline's character development was hampered by her dependent relationship with me. Even though she had been an independent woman, putting me through medical school, for instance, her relationship with me was based on her transferential perceptions about me. It was even interfering with proper working transference with her own analyst.

"As long as she loved me the way she did, her personality conflicts remained unresolved." He sighed. "I did it for her."

Jane nodded solemnly. This was the weirdest reason for a divorce she'd ever heard. "Did you remarry?" she said.

Hawthorne's face lit up. "Yes. I was fortunate in finding a woman, much younger than Caroline chronologically, but with a more fully integrated, independent personality. Tammy and I have been very happy." Jane smiled politely. It didn't take a medical degree to figure out he'd dumped his old wife and hooked up with some young tart, probably not in that order. He'd managed, however, to cast himself as the hero of the piece. Jane hoped Caroline got a great big fat settlement. After all, she'd put him through medical school.

He twinkled at her. "Time's up," he said.

She rose to go and thanked him again.

"But tell me, Mrs. da Silva," he said, taking her hand, "why you're so interested in all of this. You've said it's for the daughter's sake. Just what are you trying to accomplish?" He said it teasingly, and seemed to imply she was in it for some neurotic reason of her own.

"I'm just trying to help," she said.

"Help. I see." He nodded slowly. "I hope you'll call on me again if *you* need any help understanding Linda. Or your own motives." He shook his head a little, as if to suggest she was a mentally sick woman. "I'd be glad to see you."

Out in the parking lot, she thought about that suitcase full of absolutely untraceable cash. It was an impossible task, getting that money back for Leonora. Maybe the doctor had a point. She probably should have her head examined.

Chapter 13

Jane had meant to spend the rest of the afternoon with Linda Donnelly's notebooks, but the idea depressed her. Jane shuddered at the thought of all that woozy spiritual search, all that bad prose describing real pain.

Instead, she made herself a sandwich and grabbed the Yellow Pages. It was easy. Right there under "Motion Picture Special Effects": Richard English Productions. Optical Effects. Animation. Computer Graphics.

She called the number.

A receptionist answered. She sounded about sixteen. "Yes, he's here. One moment please."

"Rick English." It was a cheerful voice.

Jane found herself making her voice sound cheerful, too. "My name is Jane da Silva, and I'm calling you about someone you may have known years ago."

"Oh yeah? Who's that?"

"Linda Donnelly."

There was silence. Finally, Jane said, "Mr. English?"

"I'm here." He didn't sound happy anymore.

"Do you think we could get together? I'm trying to find out about her."

Jane wished she'd just dropped in on him, the way she had with Susan Gilman and Judy Van Horne.

"I'm a friend of her daughter. I'm helping her to find out a few things about her mother."

"I suppose we'd better talk," he said. There was an air of resignation about his voice now. "Who gave you my name?"

Stupid, thought Jane to herself. I wasn't prepared for that. Judy Van Horne hadn't said not to use her name, but if it wasn't considered unethical to reveal the names of the other people in one's therapy group, it should be. She extemporized hastily.

"Linda left behind some notebooks. Your name was there."

"That's impossible!" There was another pause, and then he said, "Can you come by after work?"

"Sure. Tonight?"

"No, no. I'll be shooting all night. Tomorrow night. After seven?"

"All right." She repeated the Pine Street address in the phone book.

"That's right. Maybe you'd better bring those notebooks."

"Oh, all right," she said, not intending to do any such thing. "Well, thank you, Mr. English. I really appreciate it." She tried to sound casual.

He hung up without saying good-bye, which seemed strange.

She went into the kitchen for a cup of tea, and while she waited for the kettle to boil, she stepped out onto the back porch and looked out over the garden.

It was kind of dark. Pruning, Jane decided. It all needed pruning. And a deck, a sunny deck with pots of flowers—geraniums and lobelia. And maybe in the garden she could grow some old-fashioned flowers like she'd seen at the market, tall and flouncy and delicately colored.

The water in the kettle boiled and she made herself tea, critically examining Uncle Harold's teacup in an uninspired pinkish floral pattern. She wanted her own plain white cups. She'd seen some in the coffee store at

the Pike Place Market. Very simple and restful. That's
how she wanted this house to look, lighter and simpler, so
the lines stood out. She wanted everything utilitarian to
be plain, and let the things for the soul stand out, books
and pictures and flowers, and eventually, people.

The phone rang and she went into the hall to answer it.
She wanted a kitchen extension, too. It was Calvin Mason.

"Great, you're home," he said in his usual enthusiastic
way. "I got the basic information about the Flamers. Want
to hear about it?"

"Sure."

"I just sent out for a pizza. You want to come over here?"

"All right." She realized some company would be nice.
"I'll be there in twenty minutes."

"That's what they said at the pizza place too. Don't let
the guy trample you in the lobby."

•   •   •

"I'm glad you could come," he said, when she had
arrived. "I hate to eat alone. I usually grab dinner at the
coffee shop on the corner, but I don't want to answer a lot
of stupid questions about my face. You want a beer?"

"A beer sounds great," she said. "It's been a long day."

"Well, at least no one messed up your face," he said from
the kitchen, coming back with two cans of Rainier. He sat
opposite her and handed her one. "So why don't you tell me
what you're up to? How's the hopeless case business?"

She thought about it for a moment and looked over at
him. His lip was swollen, as was one eye, but the other
one looked kindly. "Strictly confidential," she said.

"Sure."

"I found that hopeless case right here in your building,
as a matter of fact."

"So how about my finder's fee?"

"You're kidding, aren't you?"

He laughed. "Yeah. I'm kidding. A day late and a dollar short. You get used to it."

"I'm trying to get some money back from someone. For Leonora. Kenny's kid. You know, the painters."

"Getting money back, huh? I been there. Good luck."

"Maybe it is impossible." She sketched out the details of Linda Donnelly's inheritance and how the Fellowship of the Flame got it all before she died.

"So if you get this all straightened out somehow, you get that ride on the gravy train as per your uncle's screwy will, which was prepared by Bucky's own whacked-out uncle?"

"That's right."

"Do you really need to do all this?" he said.

"What do you mean?"

"I mean, you strike me as a fairly solid citizen. Why do you want to run around looking for some hard-luck case and hassle around and hope you pass muster with the trustees to get paid?"

"To be perfectly honest, I don't know what else to do," she said. "I think I'm having some kind of midlife crisis." She collapsed into the sofa cushions.

"So you want to throw it all over and live on the edge?"

She laughed. "No, I want to settle down and be respectable. A midlife crisis means you mourn the loss of whatever you didn't bother to do. For most people, it means they want to live recklessly, run off to Tahiti. For me, it means I want to settle down in Seattle and do an honest job and get paid a lot. I guess."

"You should have gone to graduate school. Got yourself a teacher's credential or something," he said, shaking his head. "Or worked for the government. They have tests and stuff you can take. You hang in there long enough you get yourself a pretty safe, sweet deal." He shuddered. "Not my style, but some days I think I should have done something like that."

"But you couldn't, right?" she said.

"Right." They were silent for a moment.

"Me neither," said Jane.

"Maybe we're just a couple of losers," he said. "Kidding ourselves."

"Are we kidding anyone else?" she asked.

"I don't know." He shrugged. "You're a pretty class act. In that suit eating lunch with Bucky I thought you were rich and sassy. I don't know about me." He looked at her expectantly.

"You've got a certain sassy charm yourself," she said. "Let's not call ourselves losers yet."

The pizza arrived. Calvin pushed aside some magazines and papers on the coffee table and they started eating.

"So what have you done so far?" he asked.

"Well, I've talked to her family and her best friend in high school and I even talked to her old psychiatrist. Just to get a general background, you know?"

"Yes, I know. But you're really setting yourself up for a lot of heartbreak. This happened sixteen years ago. There's a statute of limitations on practically everything. Including fraud, if that's what you're alleging. Besides, these guys are tough nuts to crack. Want to hear what I got on them?"

"Yes," she said. "I do."

"The Fellowship of the Flame first emerged in the mid-sixties. They went legitimate and applied for non-profit status in 1967. Until then they'd been a loose sort of commune that operated out of a house in the University District. Like all these outfits they had a main guy with a direct pipeline to Universal Truth.

"They called him the Flamemaster."

Jane giggled. "Sounds like a kitchen appliance."

"Actually," said Calvin, "it's a Chevrolet engine from the fifties."

"What did these people believe, exactly?"

"Other than that the Flamemaster had a monopoly on truth, it's a little vague. Apparently the main deal was that modern living had suppressed our true nature, and that we all had to get in touch with the fire that burned in our souls. All unhappiness came from weak flames, and the idea was to get your flames going real good and your passionate nature would give you individual power and happiness." Calvin coughed. "I happen to know from personal experience that your passionate nature can get you into lots of trouble, but back then, these kids were just coming off 'Leave It to Beaver' and 'Ozzie and Harriet,' you know? They were just babes."

"Yes, I know. What did the Fellowship do?"

"Well, the Flamemaster took them through a series of exercises. I don't know, shouting, chanting, orgies, who knows? Anyway, it was plenty noisy. It went on all night, apparently."

"Sleep deprivation," said Jane.

"That's right. That's standard in these cults, I guess. Anyway, the neighbors complained and the cops were over there every night. Pretty soon, the Flamers were getting weapons."

"Flamethrowers?" said Jane.

"No, rifles and handguns. All legal, but pretty scary, nevertheless. They started talking about police harassment. There were some lawsuits."

"What happened?"

"About that time, the group came into some money. They all moved to the country. Bought an old farm out on Vashon Island."

"When was this?"

"Nineteen seventy-four."

"Just about the time Linda gave them her money. How were they financed before that?"

"Everyone turned over their assets to the group. The Flamemaster had them all out working two jobs, and spending the rest of the time working on their own internal combustion."

"So what happened? Are they still out there?"

"No. Everything kind of fizzled out after they moved to the country. There are some jobs on Vashon, but not enough for the people who want to live there. It's an island for commuters dedicated enough to country life to ride those ferries every day. I guess the commute killed them and they drifted away." Calvin shrugged. "Maybe they got their heads clear on the ferry ride every day. Maybe they just grew up."

Except Linda, thought Jane. "What happened to the Flamemaster?"

"Beats me. Probably working some other scam. Maybe he went to law school or something. Maybe he just got burnt out. Ha-ha."

"Where did you get all this information?"

Calvin looked a little edgy. "He wishes to remain anonymous."

"Why?"

"He had a bad run-in with these people back in the old days. He's the guy I represented in a custody matter. He was hot for this girl, he joined the Flamers so he could be with her, and then he got kind of sucked in himself. They got married, had a little kid, and then he snapped out of it. There was a fight over the kid."

"Did he get the child back?"

"No, but his ex-wife left the group, so he dropped his case. She got into feminism. Decided the Flamers were too patriarchal. Last I heard she was into Goddess worship."

"Why can't I talk to him?"

"He says he's afraid of them. During the custody thing they got pretty weird. A couple of thugs showed up at his house. Pushed him around a little. And the Flamemaster put out the word that he was on the enemies list. He was afraid that would be enough to get one of the more fanatical followers to take matters into his own hands."

"But he can't still be afraid of them," she said. "They've disbanded."

Calvin shrugged. "As far as I know. To tell you the truth, I think my client is just embarrassed that he had anything to do with those people."

"I'm not surprised. But all I want to find out is if he remembered Linda."

"Well I can ask him for you," said Calvin with a pleasant smile.

"Yeah, I know. For a fee."

"Got a picture of her?"

"I'll get you one. I just want some background. I'd like to know what was going on at the time Linda turned over those funds, and around the time she died. See if you can set up a meeting. Or have him call me so I can talk to him over the phone, will you?"

"Okay. I'm telling you, though, you won't get anywhere with this. That girl's money is gone."

"Sounds like they bought that place over on Vashon with it," she said. Then she added impatiently, "Come on, can you call the guy now? See if he'll talk to me?"

"All right." Calvin went over to his desk and flipped through his dog-eared Rolodex, then punched up the number. Jane listened carefully to his half of the conversation.

"Hi. It's Calvin. Yeah. Remember the woman I told you about? The one who wants to find out about the Fellowship?" He paused. "Just relax, will you? She's here now. Would you mind speaking to her?" He paused again. "Come on now, aren't you being just a little paranoid?"

He held his hand over the receiver for a moment. "Wonders if you aren't one of *them*."

"Oh, for heaven's sake, let me speak to him," said Jane, walking over to the desk and taking the receiver.

"This is Jane da Silva," she said in businesslike tones. "I understand your need for, er, privacy, but I just want to ask you a few questions."

"Okay. But I might not answer them," said a frightened voice.

"That's fair enough," said Jane. "I just wondered if you knew a Linda Donnelly. She drowned sixteen years ago. She was part of the Fellowship." She couldn't bear to add "of the Flame." It sounded so corny.

"There was a girl who drowned. I vaguely remember that," said the voice. "But I don't remember her name."

"Do you remember what she looked like?"

"I think she had dark hair. That's all I remember. Why do you want to know about this?"

"I'm looking into her past for a member of her family," said Jane. "She gave a lot of money to the group at one time, I believe."

The man gave an audible sniff. "I can believe that," he said. "We all did. They told us if we didn't turn over everything our flames would go out. We'd die a cold, quick death."

"Who said that?" said Jane, excited. Threat of death. It sounded like fraud, or maybe even extortion.

"The Flamemaster, of course." The voice was less fearful. Now it was a little snippy.

"Yes, naturally."

"As a matter of fact, that's why I remember the girl who drowned. He said she wasn't generous enough. She was holding back. He said that's why she'd died."

"Do you suspect—" she began. But he interrupted her.

"I don't want to talk about it. These are dangerous people." She was afraid he was going to hang up.

"Wait," she said. "You talk as if they're still around."

"Oh, they're around all right," he said, rather bitterly.

"You mean you think that the group still exists."

"In a different form, perhaps. But they're around. Doing the same old mind trips on people."

"Who was the Flamemaster?" she said.

"Uh-uh. I'm not going to answer that one," he said.

"Listen, I don't know who you are. Calvin says you're okay. So take some advice. Don't mess with these people. If you do, protect yourself somehow. That's all."

He hung up.

Jane replaced the receiver and stared at Calvin Mason.

"He's really frightened," she said. "He acts like these people are still around."

"Yeah, well, he is kind of a rabbity little guy."

"He practically accused them of murdering Linda."

"That's good news," said Calvin. "There's no statute on murder. Not that that means you could get Leonora's money back."

"I wonder if Uncle Harold really wanted me to tangle with thugs?" Suddenly she felt indignant. The way this guy talked, she could get killed. And it would be Uncle Harold's fault. She felt as if Uncle Harold had planned to manipulate her from beyond the grave, but had somehow screwed up and got her into a dangerous mess. Why couldn't he have either left her his money, or cut her off entirely? Instead she was operating in a scary, gray area.

"Look, Jane, take my advice. If you track these people down, be prepared to back yourself up with some muscle."

"You mean like a bodyguard?"

"Well, they did have guns, they did push my guy around, and now you're saying they might have killed someone."

"Maybe you're right," she said.

"I'd be glad to help," he said. "Same rates as investigative work." He pointed to his swollen face. "See? I'm fearless."

Jane smiled back. "No offense, Calvin, but if your knuckles looked like your face," she said, "I'd take you up on it."

Chapter 14

The Fellowship of the Flame! You're kidding." Bucky's voice sounded pleased and amused. "I've had some dealings with them myself."

Bucky had called her to ask—in a rather patronizing but eager way, Jane thought—how she was doing.

She figured she'd better tell him something that indicated she was being industrious, so she told him very briefly that she was checking into an old injustice perpetrated by the group.

"The Fellowship of the Flame," he repeated with a knowing snicker.

"Don't tell me you were the Flamemaster," she said. She imagined Bucky for a minute in an asbestos jumpsuit—the shiny silvery material of ironing board covers.

"Wasn't a bad gig," said Bucky. "That guy raked in plenty."

"Tell me all you know about them," said Jane.

"Hmm. I really shouldn't. It has to do with a privileged matter."

Jane knew she had him. If he'd been a correct, discreet sort of lawyer, he wouldn't have volunteered that he knew about the Fellowship at all, and he certainly wouldn't have bandied about that it was a privileged matter. He was clearly dangling the bait in front of her. She thought she'd better bite.

"Just a little general background would be immensely helpful," she said. After a pause she added, with just a hint of a tremble to her voice, "I'd be so grateful. This isn't easy, you know, and I'm all by myself." She stopped herself before she added, "I have always depended on the kindness of strangers," in a Blanche DuBois accent.

"Well," said Bucky, now obviously very pleased, "maybe we can do a little something for you. Let me make a phone call and get back to you. Or better yet, maybe we can talk about it over dinner."

"Dinner would be lovely," said Jane, trying to sound sincere but not too enthusiastic. "But I wish you'd call me with the information right away. If you get any, that is. Time is really of the essence here."

"All right," said Bucky. "That way dinner can be strictly social."

"Umm, yes," she said. Bucky was a transparent jerk, but he was reasonably amusing, and she had been feeling socially deprived. In a new town, you had to start somewhere. Besides, he had a pipeline to the trustees—those querulous old men who were standing between her and her money. The specter of his hand on her knee in a dark restaurant, followed by a tussle at her doorstep, flitted briefly into her consciousness, but if anything like that came up, she imagined Bucky wouldn't be too hard to handle.

She checked her watch. "I've got to go," she said. "I've got an appointment."

"Mrs. da Silva, on the case," said Bucky. "Righter of wrongs and bringer of hope."

He really was irritating. It was easy for him to laugh. He didn't have a lot of cantankerous old men to answer to.

"Or are you going off on some more mundane errand?

Maybe aerobics or just to buy Drano or something. What *is* your life like?"

"I really have to go," she said. "I'm checking out someone on Capitol Hill who runs a special effects business." Why was she bothering to tell Bucky? She supposed she wanted him to know how hard she was working so he'd tell his ridiculous uncle. There was something so undignified about the whole procedure. It was rather like a perpetual job interview.

• • •

Richard English's studio was at the base of First Hill, an older neighborhood that had so far defied complete gentrification and persisted in remaining a jumble of businesses, small groceries and restaurants, tough-looking taverns, chic apartment buildings from the twenties, and a few tumbling-down old houses covered with asphalt siding and morning glory vines.

She pulled up in front of an old brick building on Pine Street that looked as if it might once have been a livery stable. There were no windows, except for a row of small painted-over panes up high, about ten feet from the ground. The small door was painted blue with white numbers and letters. RICHARD ENGLISH PRODUCTIONS. PARK OFF OF ALLEY IN BACK.

But she didn't have to. There was a meter right in front. She didn't even have to feed it, as it was after six. It began to rain a little, and she smiled, recognizing the Seattle smell of wet summertime pavement from her childhood, a smell of dust turned into something sharper by raindrops.

Inside, there was a small reception area. There was no one there. She called out "hello" and walked back through a door that led farther into the building. A short passageway led to a vast room, dimly lit from above. She looked up to see a grid of metal bristling with lights. Ahead of her, one long wall was painted bright blue. Another wall was stacked with giant paintings; they seemed to be realistic but rather lurid landscapes.

There was an eerie stillness here, but a palpable presence, too. Nervously she glanced into a corner where a clutch of five-foot-tall masks stared back at her. She gave a little start, then forced herself to look at the garish faces, wide eyes with Disneyesque lashes, grinning red lips.

Straight ahead, there was a table that seemed to be dominated by a crumpled mass of cloth. She stepped toward it and got the impression of a bundle of old clothes.

Just then, the lights went out. Instinctively, she stepped aside quietly, hoping her eyes would adjust to the dark. They didn't. The place was apparently sealed against any outside light. She remembered the small row of window-panes she'd seen from the street. They had been painted over.

She moved three steps over and two back. Then she heard someone else's steps coming toward her. Small, neat, careful steps. She moved back once more, as quietly as she could, on the balls of her feet.

She started to speak. "Mr. English?" she was going to say. But she stopped. Why the silence? It was unnatural. Something told her she shouldn't let whoever it was know exactly where she was. She stepped a few steps to the side. The pattern of those other feet made the same number of steps. It was as if they were moving blindly around a chess board.

If only she could get around and back to the entrance. She was being stalked, she knew that now. Knew it from the silence and from the way those steps moved toward her, a few at a time. She fell to her knees and crawled backward to where she thought that long table was. If she could get around in back of it and then skirt along the side of the room, she could negotiate her way to the door and back to the reception area. Then what?

She'd have to decide that when she got there. She had no choice now but to find a way out, and the way in was the only way out she knew.

Her heart was pounding. She was sure the other person could hear it. She wanted to gasp, to cry out, but she tried to keep her breathing shallow and silent. She thought about leaving her purse on the floor, then remembered she'd need her car keys. She wrapped the strap over her shoulder, crossing her chest, and began once again to crawl on her hands and knees. It was a much quieter way to get around.

She hoped she was heading toward the table. The other person had stopped. She hadn't heard footsteps for a few seconds, although who knew how long she'd been there. The complete absence of light made it seem as if she were in another dimension entirely. She felt with one arm for the table leg. Nothing. And then she heard the steps again, nearer this time. She felt the air above her move as if an arm had passed over her back. If she'd been standing, that arm would have found her.

She stayed as still as she could, squeezing her eyes shut like a child does when it's afraid of the dark, as if it can shut out the monsters. She heard breathing now, a nervous breathing, like hers, and she sidled away from the source of the sound.

She made circles in front of her with her palms, looking for obstacles, hoping to find the legs of the table. When she finally touched metal, she groped it gingerly. She heard a crash from about three feet away, but no human sound. She guessed that one of the lights she'd seen on tripods had crashed over. She tried to pinpoint the direction of the sound and stay away from there.

Her hand crept up the metal she'd discovered. It felt

like a tubular steel table leg. She hunched closer to it. Slowly, she raised one hand above her head, palm up. It touched cool wood. She was under the table.

Still trying not to breathe, she sat, encircling her knees with her arms and pulling them toward her chest, as if to stifle the pounding of her heart.

She willed herself to think despite the fear. She had managed to get a basic orientation before the lights went out. This table was parallel to the blue wall; the door was opposite and on her right. But she wasn't sure which direction she was facing.

She heard the breathing again and pulled herself further back. Then she felt the table above her bump and heard a grunt. Someone had walked into the table. She crept back and thought for a minute about getting up on the table itself. They'd never think to look there. If they bumped into the table again, they'd veer off.

She crept back and to one side until she brushed the table leg again. Then she slid out, and, still on her knees, felt above her for the rim of the table. She wrapped both hands around it and pulled herself up so she was on her feet again. Then she felt with her knee for the top of the table. She pushed herself up and climbed so both knees were on the table, and, that done, she fell forward on her hands.

Then she felt it. The crumpled mass of cloth. It wasn't a bundle of clothes at all. It was a body. It was still warm, but she knew, even in the blackness, that it was a dead body. It was completely inert.

She screamed and tried to roll back off. A second later, she felt a man's arm around her waist, felt his breath in her face, and, still screaming, felt herself being shaken from side to side.

"Stop it!" she shouted, but he didn't answer. He just kept shaking her until her neck snapped and her eyes rolled around. "Who are you?" she screamed, and he was still silent and still shaking her. She was frightened at the sound of her own screaming. She heard herself shout hysterically, "It's dark," and then she couldn't scream anymore.

He had his thumbs together on her windpipe and then he slammed her head down on the concrete floor. She heard a sound in her head that had to be her skull cracking, and she couldn't breathe. Her head felt as if it would burst from within and without. "Please, God," she said inside her head, and then she could breathe a little. He'd loosened his grip on her throat.

Then, she felt a blow across her face. It was surprising and horrifying, because she couldn't see it coming, so the blow just exploded across her face. She went limp, and instead of struggling, pretended to lose consciousness. It wasn't hard to pretend. She felt herself slipping away.

Her arms were splayed out on either side of her, and she felt a gloved hand run along the length of her right arm, as if it were looking for something. The hand stopped when it reached her wrist. He was feeling for her pulse. Yes, there's a pulse there, she thought. I'm still alive. It was her last thought before the blackness.

Chapter 15

Her eyes were open now. She didn't remember whether or not they had ever actually closed, and she didn't remember opening them, but here she lay, staring up at a ceiling full of gridwork with lights clamped onto it at intervals. None of those lights was on, but she could see now.

Her head pulsed and her throat was sore where those thumbs had pushed into it. Her body felt the cold damp of concrete through her clothes. She tried, with difficulty, to sit up, finally settling for being able to turn her head to one side to get her bearings.

The door from the studio to the office was open. He must have left that way. There was a strip of light between the door and the frame, enough to vaguely illuminate the room. She saw the shapes of the horrible masks, the outline of the klieg light that had crashed to the floor. Slowly, she remembered the details of how she had come to be here.

She seemed to be alone now. Her face contorted with pain, she managed to lift her head off the floor and pull her body up into a sitting position. She propped herself up on one elbow and felt her face with the tips of her fingers. She felt blood. Cool and tacky. She'd been here a while.

She twisted her torso and looked over in the direction of the table. That shape she'd seen as a mound of clothing and later felt as a dead body was still there. She managed to roll over onto her hands and knees. She stayed like that, wobbling, for a second, then struggled to push herself up.

With the feeling coming back a little more at every step, she made her way over to the table. The body was covered with a large piece of black velvet. She lifted one corner of it and looked into a dead man's face.

It was pale and bloodless, and his lips were pulled back so his teeth and gums showed. His eyes, blue-green, looked like milky glass. He wore a brown suede bomber jacket over a striped Oxford cloth shirt and jeans. There was a huge, dark stain on the shoulder of the jacket.

Without touching him, and still holding the corner of the black velvet in the tips of her fingers, she circled around and looked at his head from the end of the table. There was a lot of blood in his sandy hair; in fact, his head seemed to be lying in a thick patch of it. He must have been struck from behind, and the blood had run down over his shoulders.

Jane thought it was certain that whoever had hit him had also hit her.

She dropped the corner of the cloth, watching with relief as it covered him again. Then she stepped back and felt something squishy underfoot. She backtracked a little more and bent down to look at it. It was a cartoonish dinosaur, and it was holding a miniature pizza with a perfect little circle of blood on it. The dinosaur was smiling.

She realized she had better call the police.

When she got out of the studio area, into the front office, she heard birds singing. It was dawn. Through the window, she saw a rosy gray patch of sky, illuminating a pale, deserted street. The phone had an alarming array of buttons, and for a moment, after all she had been through, it seemed too much to have to figure out how to get an outside line. She began to cry. Snuffling a little, she pushed down the top button, then dialed 911. It worked.

Later, she could barely remember the interval of time between the wonderful sound of a police siren coming over the hill down Pine Street, and the sensation of cool hospital sheets.

There had been the police. First two, then a lot of them. Their radios had crackled in the morning air and they'd bent over where she sat in the receptionist's chair and she'd told them to go back and find the body.

Then a fire department aid car arrived, and a man and a woman in dark blue uniforms looked her over and told her they'd take her to the hospital. She kept telling them she was fine and didn't want to go to the hospital.

Next, two detectives arrived. A tall, dark one sat opposite her and asked her questions.

"I had an appointment with Richard English," she heard herself say in a deceptively calm voice. "I was here on time—at seven—and I walked in and went back there." She pointed to the studio door. "It was dark, but there was some light. Then, all of a sudden, all the lights went out, and he attacked me. First, he stalked me in the dark. Then, when I fell over the body, I screamed, so he found me."

"Do you know who attacked you?"

"No. I never saw him."

"Not at all?"

"It was pitch black. That studio is sealed against any light."

"But you knew it was a man?"

"Yes. He walked into a table in the dark and then he groaned a little, and I thought I could tell it was a man.

Later, when he was choking me, I knew for sure it was a man. I could feel it. All I know is that he was taller than I am."

"And how tall are you?"

"Five-six."

"What were you seeing Mr. English about?"

"The dead man—he's Richard English?"

"Looks like it. His wallet was in his pocket, with his driver's license. You never met him before?"

"No." And then, in her woozy state, she heard herself say, "There was a dinosaur with a pizza."

"What?"

"On the floor."

"That's right. It looks like he was working on a pizza commercial. Clay animation. We found a what-do-you-call-it—like a comic book of the script." He had a nice voice. Why was he talking about pizza commercials? He must be humoring her.

"A story board," she said. She put her hand up to the back of her head.

"The medics here say you should go to the hospital," he said now.

"I already told them I don't want to."

"You're not thinking clearly," he said. "Sometimes when people get hurt they think that by pretending nothing's wrong, everything will be all right. But you could be seriously injured. You might have a concussion, or even a fractured skull. You've got to go to the hospital."

"Can you make me?"

She looked at him carefully for the first time. He had an amiable face with crinkles around his brown eyes. He was smiling at her, and he said, "Well, I suppose I could arrest you as a material witness."

"Don't be patronizing," she said. "Just because I've

been beaten up doesn't mean you can treat me like a child."

Now he took on a brisker tone, and looked away from her face. "Tell me what you were doing here."

"I wanted to talk to Richard English."

"What about?"

Jane didn't know what to tell him. She had to have time to think. "All right," she said. "I'll go to the hospital."

"Fine," the detective said after a little pause. "I'll see you there later. We can talk then." He gestured to the two medics.

Jane shook her head. "I can drive myself," she said.

"No, you can't. We're going over the car. The rental car at the curb. He searched it."

"He did?"

"That's right. And your purse too. I'll bring it to you after we've finished with it. The contents are scattered all over the floor. They're photographing and fingerprinting now."

"They won't find any fingerprints," she said. "He wore gloves. Thin rubber gloves."

"He did? You felt them?"

"That's right. When he had his hands around my throat. They felt clammy." She thought for a moment about her purse and what had been in it. She had an international driver's license and her credit cards had an address in Paris. Her printed checks hadn't arrived. And the car rental papers had been filled out with the name of Mr. Montcrieff's firm. She had thought it looked more respectable and was afraid of what a check on her Visa status would reveal.

"There wasn't anything there with my address on it," she said. "I'm pretty sure of that."

"I noticed that," he said. "Just what is your address?"

She gave him the address on Federal Avenue.

"Until we find out more about this," he said, "I'm holding your name and address. I don't want the press to get at you. And I don't want your assailant to find you. He may have thought he killed you. Any idea what he was looking for?"

"I'm not sure," she said. But she did have an idea. She'd told Richard English she'd be bringing Linda's notebooks to their meeting.

Chapter 16

Jane had spent the morning in a hospital gown being examined by doctors. They looked in her eyes, lifted up her hair and peered at her scalp, and ran her through a CAT-scan. She was also, she discovered, a piece of evidence in a homicide investigation. Her bruises were photographed, scrapings were taken from under her fingernails, her clothing was taken away in a search of hairs and fibers.

Then she was put to bed and fed. She polished off the whole tray—mixed vegetables, some sort of a meat patty, roll, butter, and lime Jell-O with fake whipped cream. After lunch, she lay in bed and closed her eyes, and listened to the hospital sounds: nurses chatting at their station and metal carts being wheeled down the hall, and the steady hum of television sets. She had to decide what she'd tell the police. She had to tell the truth, of course, but she didn't want them to constrain her in any way from pursuing her own hopeless case.

A woman wearing a blue dress and carrying a clipboard came into her room and asked her about health insurance.

"Health insurance?" Jane repeated blankly. "I forgot all about it. I've lived in Europe so long, I just assumed—"

The woman frowned. Jane imagined the woman wanted to stuff her into a cab and ship her off to some Dickensian public ward. She supposed she should feel pathetic. An indigent, whom no one would want to care for. If she let herself, she could fall apart now. But she wouldn't let herself.

"All my bills will be taken care of by my lawyer's office. That's Carlson, Throckmorton, Osgood, Stubbins, and Montcrieff," she said grandly. She'd faked her way through worse situations than this.

The woman wrote down each partner's name suspiciously. "I'll still need you to fill out the rest of this form," she said, shoving the clipboard at Jane.

Jane didn't reach for it. "Carlson, Throckmorton, Osgood, Stubbins, and Montcrieff handle all my paperwork," she said. "They know my social security number and all that kind of thing." The woman glared at her and Jane smiled a condescending smile.

Damn, damn, damn, Jane thought. This is all Uncle Harold's fault. Why should she have to put up with all this? She'd been given a vague task, been beaten by an unknown assailant, and now she was being hounded by this woman in blue who presumably had health insurance of her own and remembered to clean out her gutters when they filled with leaves and returned her library books on time and led a thoroughly respectable and dull life. Why couldn't Uncle Harold have left Jane his money? Period.

"We need some basic information, or we can't treat you," said the woman.

"I've just had a blow to my head," said Jane. "I'm not filling in anything right now. I'm sorry."

"Is there someone who can help us? A husband or someone?"

"There isn't anyone like that," said Jane, feeling rather ashamed that there wasn't. Most people had people who cared about them near at hand. "Call my lawyers. They'll straighten it out."

The woman sighed and left.

` Through the pain, and blotting out the self-pity, Jane felt a surge of energy and an eagerness to press on. She was too damned angry at whoever it was who had beat her to stop now. There was a lot to do. A lot to find out.

Jane picked up the telephone at the side of her bed and called Calvin Mason. A recording came on. "We've stepped out of the office for a moment," it said. Who "we" were, Jane couldn't imagine, unless you counted the orange cat. "Just leave a message and we'll get back to you."

"This is Jane da Silva. I'm in the hospital. I was attacked. I need you to—"

Just then Calvin's real voice came on. "My God," he said. "What happened to you?"

Jane told him about her appointment with Richard English and its aftermath.

"My God," he repeated softly. "If I'd known it was going to be like this I would have tried to stop you. How are you feeling now? Is anything broken?"

"No bones. I just feel the way you looked the other day. I should have been more sympathetic."

"Yeah, well I wasn't stumbling over corpses. This is pretty major shit you're talking about."

"Anyway," she said, "I was hoping you could go to my house and get three notebooks from the drawer in the bedside table in the main bedroom upstairs. And then hang on to them."

Calvin, bless his heart, didn't ask any more questions. "All right," he said. "Is there a key?"

"No."

"Is there an alarm?"

"No."

"Okay. No problem. Just give me the address."

"Be careful," she said. "Whoever attacked me might try to search my house."

"Don't worry about me," said Calvin heartily. "Just get some rest. I'll come by and see you later."

"Don't bother," she said. "I'm checking out."

She hung up, and a volunteer with a cart of magazines came into the room. "The police won't let me have my purse," Jane said. "Do you think you could get me a brush and a mirror?"

The volunteer, a pleasant-looking woman with a round face, seemed glad to be able to help and left on the errand. When she'd gone, Jane decided she'd better call Kenny and Leonora and warn them.

Kenny answered.

"This is Jane da Silva. I'm in the hospital."

"What happened?" Kenny sounded shocked.

"I had an appointment with Richard English. Someone who apparently knew Linda years ago. Around the time she died. I was attacked in the dark."

"My God!"

"Well, it was worse for Mr. English. He was murdered."

Kenny was silent for a moment. "It's the Fellowship of the Flame. You must have let them know, somehow, that you were after them. Jesus, we never should have opened up this can of worms."

Jane didn't point out that Kenny hadn't opened up anything.

"I guess you'd better drop the whole thing, huh." He sounded frightened. "I'm sorry I ever let you get involved. It was crazy."

The volunteer came back and handed her a small pocket mirror, a plastic comb, a toothbrush, and a bottle of hand lotion in a plastic packet. Jane, still on the phone, mouthed a thank-you.

"Well, my main concern," said Jane, "is that Leonora might be in danger." She looked at her face in the mirror and gasped. Half of her lower lip was swollen. There was a purplish mark along one side of her face, and a red, scratchy patch on the other. On her throat were two dark blue marks, where a pair of thumbs had pushed their way into her windpipe.

"Bastard!" she said to herself.

"What?" said Kenny.

"I'm sorry," she said. "I was just inspecting the damage. I was hurt badly. I think he might have been after Linda's diaries, and I'm worried about Leonora. Is there somewhere else she can stay?"

"I guess so." Kenny sounded overwhelmed. "I guess it'll be okay. I mean, we'll just drop it."

"Drop it? Hell, no," said Jane, turning her face in three-quarter profile to the mirror. "They killed a man. And you should see what they've done to my face. Kenny, I want you to tell me about Linda's last days. Where was she going the last time you saw her? Were there any special friends she had in the group?"

"It was so long ago," said Kenny. "She was all wrapped up in this Flame stuff, and she wanted to move in with them. She was there all the time and I was home with the baby.

"Anyway, the last time I saw her, she left with some woman. Her name was Robin; she was one of these Flamers and they were going off to a special meeting—for the chosen few or something. The whole thing was so dumb.

"We had a fight about it, I remember. Anyway, she kissed the baby good-bye, and then she and Robin drove off. Some guy picked them up."

"Who was Robin?"

"Just some chick. That's what we called women then. Anyway, like I said, Robin was one of the Flamers. They sometimes went around in pairs, like nuns. You were supposed to have a buddy, like when you go swimming at camp. Another member of the group to keep you brainwashed, basically.

"Robin was your typical airhead, but she had great legs. I remember that day when Linda left and didn't come back, Robin was wearing a purple suede miniskirt, and I was looking at her legs. She had a cute little black mole on one thigh, like a beauty spot. I remember Linda and I were squabbling and I was holding the baby, who was squirming, and I looked at that thigh and that beauty spot and thought what the hell am I doing here? How did I get trapped like this?"

"Do you remember anything else about her? What she did for a living or anything?"

"No. I never saw her again. You see, I didn't report Linda's being missing for about a week. I figured she'd gone away on one of those Fellowship retreats or something. Boy, I was really pissed off at her, too.

"Finally, I got scared and I went to the police. They had me come down to the morgue, and there she was." He stopped for a moment. "She looked terrible."

After some time in the water and nearly a week in the morgue, Jane was sure that was true. "It must have been horrible," she said simply. "But what happened to Robin? Did she tell you what happened?"

"No. I never saw her again. I didn't know her last name. I told the police about her, but I doubt they looked for her. They did talk to the Fellowship of the Flame, and those liars said they hadn't seen Linda for some time, and they never heard of Robin. The death was listed as an accidental death, but everyone thought it was suicide."

"Except you."

"It was such a confusing time. Maybe she did kill herself, but she never seemed like she would. She had a lot of crazy energy, you know? It's true, she wasn't happy, but Linda never was. She kind of got off on being miserable.

"Anyway, I've always blamed the Fellowship of the Flame, and thought they were responsible, whether or not they'd actually done it. In a way, they'd already taken her away from us. From me and Leonora."

"Is Leonora there?"

"No, she's not. She's at her piano lesson."

"Well, tell her I'll call her later. I hope neither of you are in any danger. Be careful, will you?"

A nurse came in carrying Jane's clothes—presumably neatly vacuumed by the police—and her purse, and put them on the chair next to the bed. "The police say they'll be back to interview you this afternoon," she said, fluffing up Jane's pillow.

After she left, Jane got out of bed and started dressing. When she was almost finished, she rang the buzzer. She was sitting on the bed, looking through her purse, when the nurse reappeared.

"I'm leaving," Jane said.

"Oh, but you can't. The doctor—"

"If you get the doctor here, I'll be glad to listen to any reasons I should stay here, but otherwise I'm leaving. I feel fine." This wasn't strictly true. Her head ached.

The nurse scurried out of the room and returned just as Jane was tucking her blouse into her skirt and slipping her feet into her shoes. The nurse had a young, curly-haired male intern with her.

"We'd like you to stay just for the night," he said pleasantly. "Just to be sure."

"I'm sorry," she said. "I'm leaving. But I would like you to tell me what you found out from those tests."

"You've got a pretty hard skull. You don't have a concussion or any fracture. Still, we'd like to observe—"

"I don't have time," said Jane.

The nurse and the doctor exchanged glances.

"And I had a watch," she said. "Where is it?"

"But if there's anything wrong with you—" the doctor began.

"I know, I know," she said impatiently. "If there's anything wrong with me, you're afraid I'll sue you." From what she'd heard, Americans had spent the years she was away in a litigious frenzy. "If you want, I'll sign some form that says I'm leaving against medical advice. Would that make you feel better?

"You'd better hurry, though," she added, looking back in her pocket mirror and fluffing up her hair. "Because I'm on my way out."

The nurse rushed away and came back with the woman in blue and her clipboard. Jane hurriedly signed something they thrust in front of her. "If my brain is scrambled," she thought to herself, "my signature won't mean anything anyway." The nurse handed Jane her watch, a simple gold circle on a brown leather strap. She noted with chagrin that the crystal was broken.

The first place she went, after emerging onto the street, was a drugstore. She bought a bottle of face make-up, and a lipstick that covered the bruise on her lip. She put it on at the mirror on the cosmetics counter, while the clerk, a young girl, stared at her, fascinated. Her lip hurt as she applied the lipstick, purplish to match her bruise.

Jane toyed with the idea of coming up with some explanation for her battered face, and then decided to forget it. Women mostly got beaten up by men they loved and then lied about it. The girl wouldn't believe her anyway. Jane smiled at her, and she looked away, embarrassed.

Then Jane went to a pay phone and looked up two numbers in the directory. The first was for a car rental place. The detective had told her the police would be going over the other car, looking for evidence. They'd probably towed it away. And if they hadn't, if they were checking it out where it was, they might be there and they'd want to ask her more questions.

She figured it was about a ten- or fifteen-block walk

from the hospital on First Hill to the downtown office, so she set out on foot.

Once she got there, she rented another car and headed toward the freeway, going south. It had all taken so long, and it was getting dark. About forty minutes later, after having been lost twice, she found what she was looking for.

It looked like the right place. It sat back from the road in a neon-lit strip mall—a squat, concrete block building, painted bright white with a red-and-black sign. MUSCLE HOUSE, it read. Beneath that, in quotes, was the slogan she'd read in the Yellow Pages—"HUSTLE IN AND MUSCLE UP." She'd eliminated any gym that had the word *fitness* in its ad, and counted on the neighborhood, Burien, a southern suburb with a reputation for toughness.

Inside, she was assaulted by a barrage of heavy metal music, with unintelligible, angry vocals, resentful music of the socially powerless male. There was also an overpowering smell—rancid sweat. At the door, like lions couchant, two giants—one black, one white—sat on stationary bikes. Their faces were impassive. Their huge forearms rested on the handlebars. Their massive thighs circled.

The floor was covered with orange indoor-outdoor carpeting, dotted with black rubber pads. The large, square room bristled with body-building equipment made of dark steel in frameworks coated in orange chipped paint. It all clanked rhythmically as male bodies of various sizes, shapes, and colors pressed, squeezed, lifted, heaved, pushed, and groaned.

Off to the left was a small office. The door was open, and she went in. The smell hung heavily in the air here, too. There was a desk, littered with papers, and behind it another giant. This one had a brick-red face and a shock of bleached hair. The gray fabric of his sweatshirt strained to cover a massive chest. Jane figured he had a forty-inch neck.

Brick Face gazed up at her with a pair of china-blue eyes and smiled with a row of perfect teeth. If he noticed the scrapes on her face, he didn't let on. She appreciated that.

"I'm looking for a bodyguard," she said.

He was silent for a moment, looking up at her. "Yeah?"

A small woman in red sweatpants and a tank top came over to his side. "Here's the bad checks for this month," she said. "Eight of 'em."

"Shit, Tracy," said Brick Face. Jane watched the woman's arm as she handed over the stack of checks. It was like a man's—fully developed with a network of raised veins, ending incongruously in a scarlet vinyl nail job. Jane glanced at the woman's body: massive shoulders, small breasts above a huge rib cage, narrow hips. Above her powerful neck, she had a sweet, small face that could have belonged to a kindergarten teacher.

The man made a clicking noise with his tongue and pushed aside the bad checks. "I guess we gotta lean on these guys," he said, bringing up a horrible picture of huge, crushing men pummeling each other to death. Although Tracy could probably scare the hell out of a deadbeat or two all by herself.

Brick Face turned his attention back to Jane. He winced a little as he examined her face. "You're sure that's all you're looking for?" he said. "Maybe you want someone to beat up your boyfriend, or whoever did that to your face."

"I just need someone to make me feel safer," she said.

He looked down at the checks in front of him. "Try Bob. Bob Manalatu. Big Samoan over by the wall. He's three months behind on his gym bill, and he just wrote us a bad check. He could use some spare change. He's three hundred pounds or so, and too dumb to be scared. Take a look at his gut, and you'll see what I mean."

Bob wasn't hard to pick out. He was on his back,

pushing several hundred pounds of steel up over his neck. He had a flat face, and his body, though muscular, had a balloonish quality. He wore orange Day-Glo shorts and a white T-shirt that didn't quite cover his solar plexus. There was a twisted white scar there that could only have come from a knife.

She cleared her throat. "Bob?"

After three more reps, he fell back for a second, then scrambled to his feet. Standing, the sheer mass of him was awesome.

"Yes?" he said politely, pulling down his T-shirt.

"I may be doing business with some scary people. If I go see them, I'd like to take someone along for protection."

"Sure," he said, apparently uninterested in the nature of her errand.

"Great. How can I get in touch with you?"

He went over to a gym bag. There were a lot of similar bags lining the walls. There didn't seem to be a locker room here. It certainly smelled like there were no showers.

She watched his arms and legs as he bent over. They were like huge satin pillows.

"Here," he said, handing her a card. AMERICAN-SAMOAN COLLECTION AGENCY, it read. There was a small graphic of crossed American flags, his name, and a phone number.

"Fifty bucks an hour," he said. "More if I have to hit somebody."

"What if they hit you?" she said.

He smiled. His teeth were beautiful. "It won't happen," he said, demurely lowering his lids over velvety brown eyes.

She shook his hand in its black glove, rather like shaking a leg of lamb. "Thanks, Bob," she said. "I'll be in touch. My name's Jane."

Out in the parking lot, away from that sour, cloying smell, she realized it wasn't just sweat she'd been breathing in there. The place must have been heavy with male hormones or pheromones, or whatever they were called. It smelled like men.

Out in the fresh air, she discovered it was a smell with pleasant associations. In the car, on the way back, she found herself thinking of some energetic phantom lover, with soft, scented skin over hard muscle. She supposed her erotic thoughts meant she was on the road to recovery. Anyway, it beat the hell out of thinking about getting choked by a mysterious assailant in the dark.

Chapter 17

When she got back to town and pulled up in front of her house, she was suddenly afraid. The house looked big and square and dark. What if he was in there? Waiting for her. She tried to tell herself it was silly to be frightened, but she came to the conclusion it wasn't silly at all. It was damned realistic. After all, she had been attacked. Her face ached, and her head still hurt.

She sat at the wheel of her car, and thought for a moment. Perhaps she wasn't acting completely rationally. If she were rational, she'd forget all about the Fellowship of the Flame, and Leonora's money. Maybe she'd leave Seattle and try her luck again in Europe.

No one had ever struck her before. She'd never felt physical fear like this before—a lightness in her limbs, a heaviness in the pit of her stomach, a prickly, itchy anticipation and dread. It was different than the helpless fear she'd felt before Bernardo's races.

But she didn't want to stop now.

Jane wanted Uncle Harold's money. She wanted charge accounts at Nordstrom and I. Magnin and vacations and books and records and fresh flowers. She wanted to meet nice people and give dinner parties. She wanted to go back to the Pike Place Market and learn every little nook and cranny there and find all the best and tastiest of everything. She was too old to be broke all the time. She wanted to be relaxed and respectable, and for that, she needed money.

But there was more. Jane was angry. Angry at whoever had beaten her and killed Richard English.

Richard English. Had she somehow caused his death? All she'd done was make an appointment with him. And he was dead when she got there. She had lied, and told him she'd learned about him from Linda's notebooks. Had she stumbled onto his murder scene coincidentally, or had someone killed him because that someone thought he had the notebooks with his name in them? In that case, he had to have talked to someone else. His killer.

Had she killed him with her lie?

She asked herself if she'd want to keep on if it weren't for Uncle Harold's money. She was pretty sure she would. But the money would be awfully nice.

She still didn't want to go into that house. She should have brought Bob the Samoan back with her and parked him on the sofa. Instead, she started the car and headed toward Calvin Mason's. She hoped he wouldn't mind, but she didn't care too much if he did. She'd sleep on that lumpy sofa of his in the office or living room or whatever it was. Besides, tired as she was, she wanted to read the diaries, and she wanted to read them right now.

Calvin drew the door open a crack and surveyed her from behind the chain. A television blared in the background.

"Oh," he said. "It's you." He unfastened the chain, and gestured at it. "You never know, at this hour it might be an irate husband or something," he said airily. Then he took a good look at her face, and sucked in his breath sharply. "You look terrible," he said.

"I know."

"Did they give you pain pills or anything?" He was scrutinizing her face and wincing in sympathy.

"In the hospital. Until they found out I didn't have insurance. Then I left."

"I hate hospitals. Sit down. I'm having beer and Cheetos. And I have some Darvon from when I got worked over. Want some?" He went over to the television and turned it off.

"Beer, thank you. Hold the Cheetos and the Darvon. But mostly I want the notebooks. Did you get them?"

"Uh-huh. Looked like no one had been to your house. I got in through the basement window. It was easy."

"Thank you. I'm glad they're safe."

"Be glad that whoever it was that beat you up probably didn't know where you lived. If you think they were after the notebooks. You want to tell me what's going on? Who hit you and why and what these notebooks have to do with it?"

"Maybe he wasn't looking for these at all," she said. Calvin was handing her three spiral-bound school notebooks in hot pink, shiny orange, and dark turquoise. Sixties colors, back in fashion again, like short skirts.

"It's hard to believe. They're pretty awful."

"You read them?"

"Of course. Some, anyway. Word salad, most of it. Whatever she was smoking I wouldn't want any part of." Calvin popped a can of Rainier beer for her and handed her half a bag of Cheetos.

Jane flipped open the hot pink book. In green ink she read:

> *Lullaby was fussy today. I stared and stared at her face. I wonder if I knew her in a previous life. It's like she came from another dimension, and my body was her gateway from one world to another. It is so incredibly weird and beautiful.*

Beneath it, in red ink, she read:

Lately, I have felt perfect glow control, reaching up from my feet through all my chakras and shining from my third eye like Flamemaster has taught us. Now it's my task to learn to move that flame up and down at will. The Fire Dance last week gave me just a taste of this bliss, and it's every bit as outrageously wonderful as I knew it would be...surging love and power. I had energy for hours and hours, and the room glowed with the fabulous flaming energy of all of us. What we are doing here is so important, and the Flamemaster is so exciting and wonderful. To be part of this at the beginning is such a privilege. I know now that all my other searching was only meant to lead me here, among the Fellowship.

Someday, if a history were to be written of the world's changing consciousness, I would be in it, as one of the first to master the secrets of the flame. But there will be no need for history books. All wisdom will live in the souls of all people, and in the common soul of all of us, a glowing, flaming thing, leaping now and then into ecstasy, glowing with happiness and health, never dimmed or cold. And I have been chosen to ignite that flame for the world.

A third paragraph was in purple ink.

Plants. Jungle plants with big leaves. Veins in the leaves are full of blood, and when the branches are cut, blood runs out of them and onto the ground. Where the blood spills, new plants grow and they have big white flowers. Who is cutting the branches? I know not. But I am there, and blood splashes on my arm. Plants grow from my arm, pushing roots into my veins and our blood mingles together. I pull the plants from my arm and blood is clotted on the roots. I throw them onto the

*ground and they take root and grow, the flowers looking
up at me.*

"Yech," said Jane. "There's some creepy stuff in here.
All about bleeding plants growing out of her arm. Dr.
Hawthorne would say this little fantasy reflected an am-
bivalence about motherhood."

"I hit a thing about flocks of laughing winged unicorns
beating their way across a tangerine sky," Calvin said.
"'The unicorns are my friends,' she'd written. What a
fruitcake."

"If I hadn't just seen the blood on that man's head,
those bloody plants wouldn't get to me," said Jane, shaking her head so she wouldn't feel woozy.

"Yes, why don't you tell me all about that," said Calvin.

Jane went over it again. Some of the terror went out of
it in the re-telling.

"What do you think?" she said.

"I think you're a lot tougher than you look."

She leaned her head against the back of the sofa. "I
kind of like the idea of turning into a tough old babe,"
said Jane. "But no bruises. I'd like to be a ladylike, polite,
well-heeled tough old babe."

"My favorite kind," said Calvin. "Once in a while, they
take off the white kid gloves, and *wham*. But only when
they're cornered."

Jane laughed. "The kind that know the rules, so that
they know when to break them and can break them with
some style."

"I also think," said Calvin, "you'd better find out who
the hell this Richard English was and what he had to do
with Linda. Could be, of course, that he was caught up in
some other deal, and you just happened to wander in."

"But why beat me up, search my purse and car?"

"Who knows? To find out who you are, maybe."

"I still think it's connected somehow. It's too much of a coincidence."

"If it's connected, then you know a little more now."

"Like what?" Her head was pounding again. She realized she had been moving ever since she left the hospital. Moving without thinking.

"Well, whoever killed English was someone he got in touch with soon after he heard from you. Someone who was afraid he'd talk, maybe."

"Okay. What else?"

"There's a lot more to this than bilking some little hippie out of her money. You don't kill over that. It's something bigger."

"I know." Jane looked down at the notebook in her lap. "Maybe they killed her."

"You'd better tell the police all about this," said Calvin.

"No," she said. "I can't. I've got to take care of it myself. That's the way Uncle Harold wanted it. I'm not letting those old bastards the trustees say I didn't take care of this myself. I'm not getting beat up just to let the police finish up and screw myself out of that money. I'm sorry, but I'm not." She picked up her beer and took a drink. American beer wasn't all that bad, she decided. "You can help me if you want. I still have plenty of money, but renting that car is costing me a fortune, and I might run out before it's all over. If that happens, you'll have to work on speculation, and hope that I collect Uncle Harold's money."

Calvin Mason sighed.

"At which point you can expect me to be very generous," she added, in a level voice. He'd help her. She knew he would. Calvin Mason always took on pathetic cases. That's what Bucky had said.

"What do you need?"

"I'm not sure. I'll let you know tomorrow. For now, though, I'd like to read these notebooks. And I'd like to read them here, if you don't mind. I don't feel safe reading them at home."

"I'll get you a pillow and a blanket," he said. "Spend the night on the sofa if you want."

"Thanks," she said. "I appreciate it." She was glad he didn't gallantly offer her his bed and move onto the sofa himself. She smiled for the first time in a long time. It hurt her lip. "And can I use your phone? I want to call Leonora."

Leonora was home. She sounded anxious. "Dad said you were hurt. Where are you? Are you still in the hospital?"

"No, I'm all right now. I'm at Calvin Mason's house, looking at some of your mother's papers."

"What happened? Dad says the Fellowship of the Flame is after you."

"Maybe they are. That's why I want you to be careful. Is there somewhere else you can stay? They might be looking for the papers you gave me."

After some discussion, Leonora said she'd spend the night at her piano teacher's house.

"I feel bad I got you into this. Maybe we should drop it. I mean, I didn't know—I didn't know it would be so important." The girl sounded frightened.

"That's exactly why we shouldn't drop it," Jane said matter-of-factly.

"It isn't just the money. It wasn't really getting back the money that made me ask you to help us," said Leonora, sounding less shaky now.

"I guess you wanted to know more about her," answered Jane, wishing the Linda of the diaries had come across as a better mother.

"That's it exactly. I guess I wasn't being honest with myself."

"Your mother died young, Leonora. You'll never know

what she would have been like now. She was searching for something. Maybe she would have found it."

"She should have had that chance," said Leonora. "And I should have had the chance to know her."

"Listen," said Jane. "When I get a little more organized, we'll get together. You can look at the diaries. I'll tell you what I've learned about Linda. I've been thinking about her a lot myself."

"All right," said Leonora. "That'll be really good. You know, I used to think the reason Dad never talked about her was that he loved her so much his heart was broken when she died. But I don't think that now."

"I guess he just doesn't know what to say," said Jane.

"I don't think he loved her. I don't think her parents did either. It means no one really loved her, doesn't it?" said Leonora.

Now Jane didn't know what to say. "Sometimes, it seems we're all alone. And other times, it doesn't."

"I know," said Leonora. "But when we feel most alone, we can't remember those other times."

"Are you going to be all right?" said Jane, changing her tone. She suddenly remembered how young Leonora was. How young and motherless.

"Yes, I'm all right. But I'm worried about you."

"Well, don't be," said Jane. "I'll be in touch. I'm not giving up, and I'm going to find out about your mother for you."

"Is the kid okay?" Calvin asked after she hung up. "That sounded like pretty heavy-duty stuff you girls were talking about."

Jane sighed. "She's so young. And she already knows what a bitch life can be." She looked down at the notebooks. She wished there was more there for Leonora.

"There aren't any dates on these things," she said, riffling the pages. "Which one do you think is the last one?"

"One of them was only half-full," said Calvin. He flipped through the pages of the hot pink one. "Here. This one."

She opened it up somewhere in the middle. In purple she read:

> *A flock of robins fly into the window and around my bed. They want me to fly with them. It isn't the flying dream, though. Instead, one of the robins grows big and speaks to me in a voice of chimes. Follow me, she says. I have what you're looking for.*

So purple must mean dreams. Green seemed to be mundane daily matters and red was a sort of journey of the soul in the waking state. Jane read a few more passages to check this theory.

In green:

> *Kenny's taking the post office test. I hope he doesn't get it. Who'll take care of Lullaby? I want to be able to come and go when I need to. He says they have good medical benefits. It's so pathetic, he doesn't realize we are protected by our own—my own—spiritual strength.*

Jane flipped forward a few pages. If only Kenny had got that post office job, he and Leonora would be in fat city. He'd almost have enough years for a decent pension.

In red:

> *I feel closer and closer to the center. I know that I am being called to a great spiritual life.*

Jane flipped to the last pages of the pink notebook that Linda had written.

In green:

Went over to Mom's. She and Dad are impossible. They nagged me again about the money. I don't care about money. What happiness has it ever brought them? They are such tiny people with such tiny minds. Won't they be surprised when the End Time comes and they aren't part of the New Time. It is the bad energy of people like them that's dragged the world down into the totally screwed-up place it's at now. I borrowed Mom's sewing machine to make new curtains for the living room. I found some cool material at Home Yardage. Big red flowers on dark blue with red leaves. It was $1.19 a yard, and there were three big remnants, so I'll have enough. Maybe I can make some pillows to match. Totally bummed out by Mom and Dad and their attitude. They are so closed to spiritual development. But they're probably too old to learn, anyway. Came back and did a couple of numbers with Kenny, and calmed down. He really is sweet. Even though he's not as spiritually developed an entity as I am, he really helps me get mellow when I need it. I'm glad he's here to take care of Lullaby. If I had to think about her all the time, I couldn't do what I'm meant to do. This is such an important time for me now—and for the world. In his own sweet way, Kenny's place in the whole Plan is important, too.

In red ink she had continued:

It's weird how calm I am. I keep on living my regular daily life on one level, and all the time I know about what's happening and my place in the Change Time. I realize now how every single thing that's ever happened to me has all come together to make me the special person I am now. I've come through the flames and into the light. My dreams are poems that will come true. My mind's a magic lantern and a window to the future.

But there is no future, no past, only the Now and Forever. It's all so clear to me now. The history of the New Time is written in my dreams and in the voice of the bird and in all the Chosen. We are the Children and the Parents, and together, we are God. God is me and I am God.

The third entry, in purple, read:

I'm at Bellevue High School. I am supposed to take a science test, or I won't graduate. Then, a golden sleigh comes down from the sky. I step in and sail away, far away. Pretty soon, I am flying all by myself. I zoom over my house and then across the lake. I am skimming the water, and then I stop and dance on the water. It is night and the moon has left little dapples of light all over the surface of the lake. The dapples of light dance with me on the water, and then they turn into little silver fish. The fish are singing, and their voices are like chimes. Then, the dolphins come and circle us and they speak, and I understand them and learn that all the history of the cosmos is coming from their smiling mouths.

It figured. Linda was just the type to believe that the dolphins had the accumulated wisdom of the ages in their streamlined skulls. While Jane thought dolphins terribly appealing, with their nice lines and mouths that looked like human smiles, she had never for a moment suspected they were more intelligent than humans.

Until she'd bumped into this trite opinion, she'd actually found Linda's dreamlike prose rather seductive. But one thing stood out, however. If Linda was suicidal, why was she concerned with buying curtain material at a dollar nineteen a yard? Planning to run up new curtains and suicide just didn't mesh.

On the spiritual front, there was another disquieting

note here. It appeared that Linda had been sucked into the ultimate delusion and the gravest heresy. She thought she was God—all fuzzily connected to all of creation and in league with whoever the Chosen were—but God, nevertheless. Jane believed that thinking you were God posed a very grave danger to the soul. In Linda's case, maybe it had put her in physical danger as well.

Chapter 18

And just where the hell have you been?"

It was seven o'clock in the morning. Jane was standing on her front porch, putting her key in the lock. When she heard the man's voice, she jumped.

He stepped from the shadow of the overgrown camellia and stood next to her. She recognized the detective who'd talked to her at Richard English's Studio, but she couldn't remember his name, if indeed she'd ever known it.

"You scared me," she said sharply.

"Well you scared me, too," he said. "My main witness in a homicide investigation checks herself out of the hospital against medical advice—before I have a chance to question her—and disappears."

"I'm sorry," she said stiffly. "I wasn't thinking, I guess."

"I guess you weren't," he said, frowning, "because whatever you were doing, it wasn't as important as a homicide investigation."

"I already apologized," she said. "And there's no point in my apologizing more than once, is there?"

"I'm sorry if I snapped at you," he said. "I've been kind of irritable lately, to tell you the truth."

Jane looked at him carefully. He actually seemed to be smiling a little. She smiled back, but in a restrained fashion. "Would you like to come in?" she said.

"Yes," he said, "I would."

She felt like hell and probably looked worse. She had hoped to take a shower and change. She'd slept in her clothes, and she wanted to wash her hair. Instead, being constitutionally unable to invite another human being into her living space without offering refreshment of some kind, she made coffee, while the detective, who said his name was John Cameron, sat patiently on one of Uncle Harold's stiff sofas.

When she came back into the living room, he was staring up at the old engraving of Saint George mixing it up with the dragon. "Kind of corny, isn't it?" she said, as if she wanted to disassociate herself from Uncle Harold's ideas of art.

"I like it," said the detective. "Saint George, right? If he isn't the patron saint of police officers, he should be." He accepted the coffee she handed him.

"I've been very eager to talk to you, Miss da Silva," he began. For the first time, she really looked at him. He looked about forty. She'd remembered his brown eyes and his voice. Now she took in the planes of his face, and the way his fine dark hair sprang from a broad brow. It was a nice face with a firm mouth and a slightly cleft chin. He was tall and he was wearing a brown suit and a blue silk tie with narrow brown stripes.

"It's Mrs., actually." She didn't know why she always said that. Out of loyalty to Bernardo, perhaps.

"I see. You're married." He looked around the room, as if expecting to find a Mr. da Silva lurking in a corner.

"No. I'm a widow," she said, sitting down opposite him. "Now what is it you wanted to know? I told you everything I remember about the attack."

"Yes, and the crime scene substantiates what you've told us. What we don't understand, though, is what you were doing there in the first place."

"Well, I had an appointment with Mr. English."

He set his cup down in the saucer a little too vigorously and splashed some coffee into it. "Yes, we've been over all that. Why?"

She sighed. "It's a long story."

"No problem. I get paid by the hour." He took his cup and saucer up again and sipped, looking expectantly at her over the rim of the cup.

"Well, it's just that I thought Mr. English could help me find out—" She stopped. What did she have to tell him? Did she really want the police involved?

"Let's get one thing real straight," he said forcefully, after letting her pause hang in the air for a few seconds. "A man is dead. He was killed. A woman was beaten. That's you. It's my job to find out who did it and why. If there *is* a why, which there isn't always. I expect you and any other good citizen to help me. Which means I want you to tell me everything. I'll decide whether it's important or not.

"You seem reluctant to tell me about it. You may have your reasons. But they're not important anymore, because we're involved in a police investigation. A couple of felonies have been committed. Now let's start over again. Why were you meeting Richard English?"

She took a deep breath. "I thought he could tell me about someone he apparently knew many years ago."

"Good. Who was that?"

"Her name was Linda Donnelly. She might have used her married name, Martin; I'm not sure."

"And where is this individual now?"

"She's dead. She died sixteen years ago."

"I see. What did you want to know about her?"

"I'm helping her daughter find out about her. Linda was a member of the Fellowship of the Flame. She died—drowned—right after she'd given them all her money. I was trying to see if Leonora—that's her daughter—could get it back."

"I see. And why were you doing this for Leonora?"

"Because it's hopeless," she said. All of a sudden, she realized how bizarre everything sounded. "I'm supposed to find hopeless cases and help them," she said with exasperation. "Like Leonora. My dead uncle wants me to, and I want to, so I can send for my Jaguar and have charge accounts all over town. Oh, the whole thing's ridiculous. I should have gone to law school or something, instead of sitting here with a fat lip trying to tell you all this."

The detective's face took on an expression of veiled alarm. Jane started laughing. "I know, I know," she said. "I sound like a complete nut case, don't I?"

"Not necessarily," Cameron said warily.

"Yes I do. All right. I'll try to tell you everything."

And so she did. But she left out one detail. Until she had time to make copies of the notebooks, she didn't want to have to hand them over. She'd tell him soon enough.

After she'd finished, he leaned back in his chair and looked at her from beneath lowered lids. "So you're telling me that you're trying to be some kind of a volunteer avenger or something? Under the terms of your uncle's will?"

"That's right."

"Mrs. da Silva, please take some personal advice. Drop the whole thing." He sighed. "What you describe is a very flaky way to make a living. And what you've involved yourself in now is a very dangerous enterprise."

"So you do think that English and the Fellowship of the Flame are somehow connected?" she said.

He gave her a noncommittal look. "We'll be investigating all avenues."

She stood up. "What's that supposed to mean?" she said.

"We'll check out the Flame people, naturally, after what you've just told me. I wish you'd told me sooner," he added a little severely. "I remember them from years ago, when I was on foot patrol in the University District. We used to get a lot of noise complaints about them. They can't still be around, can they?"

"Beats me," said Jane.

He rose too. "Thank you, Mrs. da Silva. We'll be in touch." He looked down at his empty cup. "Thanks for the coffee," he added.

She saw him to the door, and he turned and looked down at her. "You live here alone?" he said.

"Yes."

"I didn't release your name or address to the news people," he said.

"I really appreciate that," she said. "I know how the press can be." After Bernardo died, she'd learned that clearly enough. Right after the accident, standing in the pits while the smoke still hung in the air, and they were still cutting him out of his car, they'd turned on her, like a pack of jackals, clicking away with their cameras, pushing and shoving and shouting to her in a dozen languages, blocking her way as she tried to find a vehicle to take her to the hospital.

Then later, at the funeral, they'd waited for her outside the church and pushed forward when she came out. She remembered thinking that if Bernardo had been there he wouldn't have let them crowd his wife like that. He'd have kept one hand on her arm, guiding her through the crowd, and using the other to push at her tormentors, lifting his chin up belligerently and calling them sons-of-bitches in Portuguese.

"Be careful," Cameron said. "And call me if anything comes up." He took out a card and wrote on the back of it. "My home number's on the back. Call anytime."

As soon as he left, she went upstairs, took off her clothes, and got into the shower. She washed her hair and scrubbed herself hard, even though the bruises and scratches hurt.

When she got out, she wrapped herself in a terry bathrobe and lay on the bed, staring at the ceiling and thinking.

She'd read all of Linda's diaries last night, and followed her spiritual development through vague, pantheistic odes to nature, through the excitement of the Fellowship of the Flame, to her final apocalyptic ramblings about the End Time. Well, she'd got that part right. For her, it was the end time.

Glimpses of her daily life seemed incredibly mundane, although there had been some nice bits about her baby daughter that might make Leonora feel better.

Taken as a whole, however, the notebooks were pretty tedious. The self-indulgent work of a pretentious, unsophisticated young woman. Still, Jane felt sorry for Linda. There was a kind of desperation in those notebooks, a mad search for meaning. And for more. The Fellowship of the Flame seemed to give Linda what she needed most. A sense of her own importance.

Jane wanted to go to sleep. Instead, she willed herself up off the bed and put on her oldest, softest jeans, a nice, faded T-shirt, and sneakers, and drove to the West Seattle ferry terminal.

Vashon Island lies in Puget Sound, about thirty-five minutes away from Seattle by ferry boat. There are no bridges to the island. When Jane was a little girl, her family had come here every year to visit some friends who owned a vacation cottage on Quartermaster Harbor. Around the edges, the island had been a summer place. In the middle, it had been a rural area with dairy farms and orchards.

Calvin Mason had given her a rundown on the island today. It combined old-fashioned farms, where the dairy cattle still grazed, with quaint roadside businesses and the odd bed-and-breakfast, some middle-aged hippies with ratty dogs and ratty trucks holed up in leaky waterfront cabins and corrugated tin outbuildings, and a determined band of commuters willing to put up with ferry lines, ferry strikes, rising ferry prices, and the occasional shutdown of the system altogether during heavy fogs or fierce winds. It was a sacrifice they were willing to make for the pleasures of country life within striking distance of a city. For a while at least. The turnover in this last group was high.

At the dock, which gleamed wet in the light morning rain and smelled of salt water and creosote, the last of the morning commuters were straggling over as Jane arrived. Volvos and Hondas and Datsuns drove off the ferry with a big clunk where the metal ramp met the dock. The walk-on passengers were wearing business suits and day packs.

The boat was half-empty going over. She parked on the car deck, then went up the metal stairs and out onto the passenger deck. The engine made an agreeable throbbing noise, and she watched the white wake from the stern and listened to the gulls.

In the distance, a container ship slid through the mist. She squinted up at the sky and the smudgy, pale disk of sun veiled by fog. She remembered how the weather worked here and knew the fog would burn off soon enough.

By the time she drove off the ferry on the Vashon side, the fog was lifting, lingering in patches among the dark limbs of the fir trees that lined the curving road.

Soon, the dark trees gave way to green pastureland and farmhouses, and occasional roadside signs. HOT TUBS. HONEY. QUILTS. U-PICK RASPBERRIES. A small cedar A-frame structure had a big plastic sign that read MAPS OF THE ISLAND. A smaller sign below it read simply REALTY. She pulled over into the gravel parking lot and went inside.

Inside, there was a sofa and a coffee table to delineate a waiting area, and, a little ways away, three desks in formation. At one of them sat a woman with wavy hair and big glasses. She was reading *Good Housekeeping* magazine and eating a tuna sandwich. Soft Muzak bounced along in the background.

The magazine and the sandwich were whisked away, and the woman rose, smiling. She smoothed her sweater down over her hips. "Can I help you?"

"This is my first trip to the island," Jane said, trying to sound a little vague. "I'm thinking of buying some country property."

The woman produced some brochures. "Here are some of our listings," she said, "and a map." She didn't sound too enthusiastic. Jane figured she was probably besieged with browsers. "Are you thinking of residential property or acreage?"

"Both, actually," she said, "I want a house and a lot of land around it. I live in Southern California. It's getting so crowded there. I thought I might sell my house down there and move up here. Everyone says you get so much more for your money up here." She flashed a disingenuous smile. "And you have enough water."

The woman pushed her glasses farther up the bridge of her nose and her face took on a pleasant animation. "Oh, really? Where in California?"

"La Jolla, actually," said Jane. "Have you heard of it?"

"Yes, yes," said the woman. Jane imagined she was mentally calculating her commission. "I suppose you'd like waterfront. Maybe something with a city view?"

"That would be nice," said Jane, strolling over to a big plat map on the wall. "You know, I've heard about this place, years ago. I had a cousin who was involved in some cult that had land over here."

"There've been several," said the woman. "But they never last long. The old Bible camp was sold to a group from the Midwest a few years back, but they busted up. You don't need to worry about any of that."

"They were called the Fellowship of the Flame," said Jane, as if just remembering. "Thank God Isabel came to her senses and got out of it. She's an investment counselor in San Diego now. Doing really well."

She stood in front of the map and traced the main roads. "Do you know where that property is? Are the Flame people gone?"

"Yes, years ago. That property's the One-Ten Institute retreat now. Very legitimate people. They do corporate training and so forth." The woman came over and pointed to the map.

"You know, I could show you some very nice homes right now. Is charm high on your priority list? We have some older homes, and then a brand-new one with a nice view over the water. And, of course, you could build too. There's some fabulous acreage available with terrific view potential. Maybe we could talk about your needs in the car. Let me just go turn on the answering machine."

She went back and rummaged around her desk, allowing Jane just enough time to reach into her bag, grab a pen, and jot down a legal description of the property the woman had pointed to from the plat map.

"Just a general overview should get us started," said the woman rather breathlessly. "I'd really like to give you the lay of the land. Island living isn't for everyone," she added, her tuna sandwich forgotten. Grabbing her hefty handbag and putting it purposefully on her arm, she gazed soulfully at Jane. "But I can tell you're an island person. It's a special life-style for special people."

"Oh, I couldn't possibly look at anything today," Jane said. "But give me your card."

"I think you should start looking right away," said the woman firmly. "When these terrific properties come up, you have to act fast."

"Oh, but I have to see about the property down in La Jolla first," she said. "I still haven't finished negotiating the divorce settlement. In fact, Harry and I aren't even sure we want to go through with it and bust up."

"I see," said the woman, putting down her handbag and narrowing her eyes.

"Well, they do say it's awfully hard on kids," said Jane apologetically.

The woman handed her the brochures and her card. She had cranked up the Muzak and was back in *Good Housekeeping* before Jane had left the premises.

Chapter 19

Jane was startled to discover how much she had enjoyed lying to the realtor. Had it been necessary? She could easily have obtained a legal description of the property from Calvin Mason without assuming the persona of a restless Californian with a cousin Isabel in San Diego and plenty of equity. Jane could even imagine the house in La Jolla. It was worth a million dollars, and there was jasmine all over it.

But she'd wanted to take a look at the farm. She wanted to see the tangible asset that might have been bought with Linda's money.

It felt strange, being a liar. She wasn't used to it, and somehow she doubted Uncle Harold would approve. She made her way down quiet country roads, two-lane blacktop lined with blackberry vines in mounds by the side of the road, past neglected orchards with gnarled old trees. Somehow, she thought, Uncle Harold probably managed to do all his good works without lying. The mere force of his quiet dignity would blast on through to a solution. Was it because her motivation wasn't as pure as his, that her tactics weren't either?

The property would have been hard to find, except for the little black-and-silver signs nailed to fenceposts along the way. They all read "110%" above an arrow, and they led

her away from the grassy orchards to back roads lined
with fir trees to the site. When she got there, a similar
sign above the gate read THE ONE-TEN INSTITUTE. About
twenty yards inside, a uniformed security guard sat in a
little booth staring out through the glass. PLEASE STOP AND
CHECK IN said a sign above his window.

Beyond, she could see a big parking lot, full of cars,
and then rolling lawns, and a long, low glass-and-wood
building surrounded by tasteful landscaping. Behind the
main building were smaller buildings in the same style,
connected by gravel paths. It looked like a small, dull
campus.

She sat there for a while, and noticed a small guardhouse at the entrance. Getting in meant more lies. She
started to toss around a few ideas, then decided it would
be better to wait until she knew just what she was looking
for. She had really just wanted to see a physical manifes-
tation of Linda's money. And here it was, looking very
banal, and nothing at all like orgy headquarters for the
Fellowship of the Flame.

With a feeling of terrible anticlimax, she turned the car
around and drove back to the ferry. This time, she sat in
her car on the way back. Her car was parked in the front
row, so she had a view of the water and the city looming
toward her.

From the landing, she drove into downtown Seattle,
and went to the King County Administration Building.
Even though Vashon Island seemed miles away, it was still
part of the county. She found what she was looking for on
the third floor. The recorder's office. She had to wait a
while, but it was all there. The land, the title of which was
held by the One-Ten Institute, had been purchased in
1979 from the Flame Foundation. The selling price had
been two hundred thousand dollars for fifty acres, a
house, and a barn.

So, the Fellowship had been around ten years ago. And

they'd made a nice profit on the land. The records showed that they'd bought it just seven years before that, in 1972, the year Linda died, for the sum of one dollar.

Which blew Jane's theories about Linda's inheritance all to hell. She'd assumed the Fellowship had spent Linda's money on the Vashon Island property. She wrote down the name of the previous owner. Claire Elizabeth Tomlinson. A gullible Flame follower, she supposed.

As she drove back home, she decided she'd get Calvin to track down the foundation people. She'd concentrate on Claire, and on finding out what she could about Richard English. On a whim, she changed her route and drove along Pine Street and past his studio.

To her surprise, there was a light on. And, through the blinds, she could see somebody inside the reception area. She stopped the car and went inside.

"Hello," Jane said, looking down at a young woman kneeling on the floor in front of a large cardboard box. She had a Wilma Flintstone ponytail of bright red hair on top of her head, and huge copper earrings. She wore a tight, short khaki dress and black stockings and shoes.

"I'm Jane da Silva," she said.

The redhead woman stood up. "Oh my God," she said. "You're the one who found Rick." She looked about twenty, with beautiful clear white skin, and wide greenish eyes. She was skinny and coltish and very chic. She also had a childish, squeaky voice. Jane pegged her as one of those stylish young women who manage to appear more sophisticated and interesting than they actually are. You ran into them in menial jobs in glamour professions. There was something rather endearing and brave about them. Eventually, Jane theorized, their substance caught up with their style.

"I'm Wendy," she said. "The receptionist?" She had a kind of L.A. Valley Girl way of making a statement sound like a question. It was as if she wanted to make sure you understood her, and was asking for confirmation that the message was received. At least, Jane found herself murmuring yes and nodding vigorously.

"I guess you can imagine I'm totally in shock. Rick's wife, Gail, asked me to come here and kind of straighten stuff out, and, like, answer the phone, you know? 'Cause people were bugging her at home. It's really horrible. Like newspaper people and all that?"

"I see," said Jane.

"Anyway, I'm pretty blown away myself by all the shit that's happened, but I couldn't say no to Gail. I mean, God, her husband was murdered. It's so incredible."

"I know it must be a terrible shock," Jane answered. "I was driving by and I saw someone was here. To tell you the truth, Wendy, I've been really curious about your boss. Ever since I came here that night." She paused. "I was beaten up. I guess you heard about that."

"Yeah, I know. I can tell." She stared frankly at Jane's face and winced sympathetically. "The police told Gail. She wanted to talk to you, but they said you were in the hospital, and that they weren't giving out your address. She wanted to know where to get in touch with you, but I couldn't find you in the Rolodex or anything."

"I'll give you my number," said Jane. "I'd like to talk to her. Maybe I can have hers, too." Jane resolved to wait a decent interval for Gail's call. The woman's husband had been murdered just two days ago. But she wanted that number just in case Gail never did call.

"How come you were here that night?" said Wendy, now busying herself with a message pad at the desk. "You're not like a client or anything? Are you?"

"No. I was seeing him about something else entirely. Something that happened years ago. But I never did get to talk to him."

"The police told us you couldn't see who did it. It was

pitch black. I know how dark it can get in that studio."
Wendy shuddered.

"That's right. I never saw him."

"I keep wondering if it's someone I know. God, wouldn't
that be terrible? The police seem to think so. 'Cause
Richard, he, like, sent me home early, even though I was
working on billings?"

"He did?"

"Yeah. I thought it was weird at the time. He didn't
have any appointments in the book. Not until seven,
when you were supposed to come. It's all blank from four
on, which is totally weird." Wendy handed over a small
piece of paper. "Here's Gail's number."

"Here, I'll write down mine," said Jane. As she wrote,
she said, "Can you imagine why anyone would kill Richard
English?"

"No way! He was so nice. He was teaching me all about
production. He was always so nice. Too nice, I sometimes
thought."

"Too nice?"

"He'd do work for people and not get paid, and he
wouldn't even get pissed off. You know?"

"So he wasn't a great businessman?"

"He was like supercreative and really good at what he
did. He was a really good artist. You should see his
mattes. They're like really gorgeous. And he was a good
businessman. I mean, he started this business from nothing. Absolutely nothing. He never acted proud of that.
He was always really low key about it, you know?" Tears
started welling up in her eyes.

Just then, Jane heard a noise from behind the door
that led into the studio. She started. Wendy caught her
look and turned over her shoulder. Jane felt a little
frisson of panic, thinking about that studio.

"That's just the cops," she said. "They've been here all
morning."

The door opened and Detective Cameron emerged. He looked at Jane thoughtfully and then back at Wendy. "You two know each other?" he said.

"We just met," said Jane.

"Oh yeah?" he said expectantly, cocking his head back a little as if she owed him some explanation.

She didn't offer him any. Instead, she smiled and handed her phone number over to Wendy. "Tell Gail, will you?" she said.

On the way home, she stopped at a deli and bought a roast beef sandwich with cheddar and plenty of horserad-ish on rye and a lemonade to go. She supposed she should go grocery shopping. Fill the refrigerator. Plan meals. Get organized. She'd do it later.

When she got home, she still didn't have enough sense of the house to know where it was most comfortable to sit. She still felt like a visitor. She ended up having her lunch in the living room, with Saint George and his dragon.

The phone rang, only heightening the feeling of strangeness in the house. The noise seemed obtrusive in the stillness. She went into the hall and answered it.

"Hold please, for Mr. Montcrieff," said a crisp female voice.

She waited a while, staring down at the baseboards and studying the trim around the doors. All the woodwork needed to be stripped. It had thick, dark varnish on it. Maybe she could do it herself. The thought of getting down to a nice rosy oak and just oiling it lightly appealed to her.

Mr. Montcrieff didn't come on the line. The old boy had probably been distracted by some fauna outside his window. But she didn't dare hang up on him. It wouldn't do to antagonize him or any trustee.

Finally, a voice came on the line. "Hi there," it said. It wasn't old Mr. Montcrieff at all. It was Bucky.

"Where have you been?" he asked, sounding slightly

agitated. "The office got a phone call from some hospital billing department. But the hospital said you'd left, and I called you at home but there was no answer. Is your machine broken?"

Jane laughed. "I don't have a machine."

"You don't?" said Bucky incredulously. "I guess you've been out of the country a long time. You have to have a machine."

"Why?"

"So people can get a hold of you. So you don't miss important calls." His voice rose with feeling.

"If it's really important, they'll call back," said Jane. "Like you just did."

"Well, what's this about the hospital?"

Jane didn't particularly want Bucky telling her uncle and the trustees that she'd managed to get herself worked over and stumbled onto a homicide scene while attempting to carry on Uncle Harold's work. It might make her seem less than competent.

"I was in the wrong place at the wrong time," she said vaguely.

"It was at that studio, wasn't it?" he said. "You told me you were going there, then I read about the murder in the paper. The mystery woman who was assaulted at the scene—that's you, isn't it?"

" 'Fraid so," she said, trying to sound casual.

"My God," he said. "What have you gotten yourself into?"

"I'm not sure yet," she said. "But I'm not quitting."

"Still after the Fellowship of the Flame?" he said.

"I'm still interested in them, yes."

"Well, listen, I have a lead for you." His voice took on a conspiratorial tone. "Keep my name out of this. There's a woman in town who was heavily into this group back in their heyday. As a personal favor to me, she'll talk to you about it. She may know something about the whereabouts of the leadership," he added.

"That's awfully nice of you," said Jane. "It's really very good of you to help me."

"I want you to succeed," he said. "I want you to have that money."

"That would be nice," said Jane. "What's the woman's name?"

"I'll tell you at dinner," said Bucky. "We were going to have dinner, remember?" His voice took on a winsome tone.

"Yes, of course," said Jane, trying to sound pleased.

"How about tomorrow night?"

"Fine," said Jane. "But why don't you go ahead and give me her name? Then I can tell you all about my progress over dinner."

"All right," said Bucky. He sounded a little wary, as if she'd stiff him once she got the name. "It's Claire Westgaard. She's in the book."

Claire wasn't that common a name. "Claire *Tomlinson* Westgaard?" said Jane.

"That's right," said Bucky. He sounded surprised, and also miffed, as if she were somehow belittling his help.

"Thank you so much," she said. "And I'm looking forward to tomorrow night, too."

"So am I, so am I," said Bucky, back to his old smooth self. "I'll pick you up at six-thirty."

Claire was home, and she said she'd be glad to talk to Jane. She had a throaty voice with a hint of amusement in it. Jane had been expecting a whiny fanatic. The two women arranged to meet at Claire's house the following morning. When she hung up, she was even more curious. Claire sounded so normal.

Chapter 20

As Jane lay on the sofa, gazing up at Uncle Harold's slightly cracked ceiling, she watched the light change slowly. The room grew dimmer, but she didn't see any point in getting up and turning on the lamps. Anyway, she knew they cast a strangled yellowish light.

She seemed incapable of any action, other than to think about Linda and Leonora, and about Richard English. Was this what her life would be like if she chose to tread the path Uncle Harold had picked for her? Frantic dashing around, interspersed with periods of brooding over what she found out in her active spurts?

She wondered how many days it would be decent to wait until she approached Richard English's widow. She also thought about going to his funeral. She assumed there'd be one, even though she'd recently read an alarming statistic in the newspaper about the number of people who were simply cremated without ceremony. Another sign that civilization was dying.

If there was a funeral, she might find someone there who knew about a connection between English and Linda. She was a little irritated with herself for thinking next about what she would wear to the funeral. She had a black dress in wool crepe, but it was a little too drapy for a funeral.

She started a little when she heard the knock on the door. Quietly, for she was feeling very wary after her assault, she walked to the door and looked through the little wrought-iron peephole. It was Detective Cameron.

"Oh," she said through the door, surprised. "Hello." She opened the door and smiled. "Come in."

"I thought I'd just check up on things," he said vaguely. "Oh?"

He followed her into the living room, gazed for a second at Saint George, and sat down opposite her.

"How's it going?" she said. "Have you found out anything? About the murder?"

"Funny," he said with a little twist of a smile. "I was going to ask you the same thing."

Jane immediately felt foolish, like some would-be Nancy Drew. "I can't just charge in and ask everyone questions the way you can," she said. "I suppose you talked to a lot of people who knew Richard English."

"Apparently, he was a hell of a nice guy," said Cameron. "Happily married, no business problems, no known enemies."

"Have you checked into the Fellowship of the Flame?" said Jane.

"Long gone," said the detective. "For a while, back in the sixties and early seventies, we kept an eye on them. Outside of a lot of noise complaints, nothing."

"I thought they had a bunch of guns."

"Yeah, but we could never get anything on them. From what I can gather, talking to some of the guys who were around back then, they were basically just a bunch of wild kids, out for a good time."

"And there wasn't any known connection between Richard English and Linda Donnelly?"

"No." He paused and cleared his throat. "Have you received any strange phone calls? Noticed anyone following you?"

"No, I haven't."

"Any idea why the killer would search your purse and car?"

"To find out who I was?"

"Maybe."

She took a deep sigh. "And there was the diary."

His eyebrows rose, "Diary?"

"Sort of a diary. A series of notebooks. Richard English wanted to see them. He thought I was going to bring them with me."

"You'd better fill me in."

Jane told him that when Richard English had asked how he'd found her, she'd lied and told him he was mentioned in Linda's notebooks.

"But you didn't bring these notebooks?"

"No. I never intended to."

"How did Richard English sound when you said you wanted to talk to him about Linda Donnelly?"

"Scared."

"I see."

Jane closed her eyes and concentrated. "But kind of relieved, too."

"Where are the diaries now?"

"I left them with a friend."

"What's the friend's name?"

"Calvin Mason."

"The lawyer? Little office over in Fremont?"

"That's the one," she said. "You know him?"

"Sure. Never handles anything but a nickel-dime case, but he gets in there and fights like a terrier for his clients. Why didn't you tell me about these notebooks earlier?"

"I meant to. I—well, to tell you the truth, I wanted to make copies first. I was afraid I'd never see them again. Linda's daughter would like to read them."

He gave her a stern look.

"Would you like a drink?" she said. "Are you off duty?"

"Thank you. Yes to both questions. That is, I'm as off duty as I ever am, which isn't much these days."

She rose and rummaged around in the liquor cabinet. She'd explored it earlier and found it well stocked. "There's scotch and gin. And vermouth."

"Scotch. And a little water."

"All right." She went into the kitchen in search of ice cubes, glad of the chance to think. It didn't take her long to decide that she'd better tell this man everything. It was a question of murder. Besides, if she talked to him, maybe he'd let something slip about his investigation. Just to help him along, she made his drink a little stiffer than she otherwise would have.

She came back with two rattling glasses.

"If you're supposed to be off duty," she said, "why are you here? Are you a workaholic?"

"I'm afraid so." He took a sip. "And I'm concerned about you. Here you are, running around doing some kind of investigation, and you nearly get killed, and you're still not smart enough to tell the police everything you know."

"I meant to tell you about the diary."

"I want it."

"First thing in the morning."

"Okay." He sounded pretty casual.

"You sound as if you don't think it's important."

"It doesn't mention Richard English, does it?"

"No, it's mostly a lot of rambling. Stuff about karma and higher consciousness."

"You mean like Shirley MacLaine?"

"That's right."

"I hate all that stuff," he said with feeling. "People are such suckers."

She laughed. "I know."

There was a slight pause, and then Jane said, "How did he die?"

"He turned his back on someone, and got his skull crushed by the base of a microphone stand. An old-fashioned cast-iron thing."

"So he probably knew his assailant."

"Probably."

"And he was probably killed by a man."

"Not necessarily."

The detective seemed to be sizing up her reaction.

"Do you think I might be involved, somehow?" she said.

"It's something I've got to think about," he said. "You show up in town, all very mysterious, make a strange after-hours appointment with the guy, and next thing you know, there are the two of you, attacked and laid out in his studio. Except you're still alive."

"He didn't think I was dead," she said, startled as a scrap of memory returned. "At least I don't think so. I think I remember him feeling for my pulse."

He set his drink down. "You do?"

"Yes, just before I passed out. I'd forgotten about it until now. You know, on the wrist. Maybe I imagined it. Got it all mixed up with the hospital."

"Interesting," he said. He leaned across the coffee table and took her wrist. "Like this?" He put his thumb on the inside of her wrist, touching the back lightly with his other fingers.

The gesture jogged her memory. Now she was certain. "No. Two fingers on the part that pulses, and the thumb on the back. I remember it now. I guess he wanted me alive."

"Interesting," he said again, releasing her wrist and settling back into his chair.

"Do you think you'll get the guy?" she said.

"I think we've got a pretty good chance. There was a certain amount of physical evidence on the premises. When we get a good suspect, we can tie him in with the scene."

"You mean fibers and hair and so forth."

"That type of thing. With today's forensics, it's almost impossible to go somewhere without leaving evidence behind. Unless the killer was a complete stranger, who just wandered in off the street, we'll find him."

"And Wendy said Richard let her go early that night. As if he was expecting someone," said Jane.

Cameron neither confirmed nor denied this. Instead he said, "Where are you from?"

"Seattle. I was born here."

"But you just got here from Europe. Your identification, it was all European."

"I've lived there for some time."

"How come?"

She shrugged. "It started with a love of travel, and then I was married to a man who made his living there."

"So why'd you stay after he died?"

"I don't know. I was used to it."

"Where'd you live over there? Some of your stuff was French and some was Dutch."

"France mostly. Holland most recently. But all different places. I liked to keep moving."

"Restless?"

"I guess so. I like going places where I have to learn the language and where everything's fresh. To tell you the truth, I never really have figured it out. But partly it's that when you're an expatriate you're observing, you're on the sidelines, you see everything differently because you're not all enmeshed in it. It's kind of exciting. Life in Paris was wonderful."

"Yeah, but the French..."

"The great thing about them," said Jane, "is they don't give a damn about what anyone else does. So Paris is full of people from all over who just want to be left alone. All these people from all over the world get together in Paris and talk to each other in French. You can live in Paris for years and just hang out with other expatriates if you want.

"Being an expatriate is a life with a style and identity all its own. Pretty soon you're loyal to that life, even though it's the kind of sidelined, marginal life of the observer, just the way people in a small town might be loyal to theirs."

The detective thought about this for a second. "In some ways it sounds like being a cop," he said.

"Is that what it's like? Do you feel apart from the action?"

"No. You feel right in the thick of it. Where most people wouldn't feel comfortable. But you have to have a certain detachment if you're any good. If you let it get to you, well..."

"I can imagine. You must have seen a lot of horrible things."

"That's right," he said. "And that sets us apart."

"You hear that about policemen," she said. "That they drink too much and get divorced more often."

He looked down at his glass. "Booze isn't a problem for me. Not yet, anyway. But my wife asked me for a divorce last month."

"I'm sorry," she said.

"It's pretty rough," he said. "I've got two kids. I'm not saying I'm the easiest guy to live with or anything, but she could have hung in there for them. Looking back on it, I guess my mother put up with a hell of a lot from the old man, but they hung in there, and now they're a couple of happy old people. And we kids had a good childhood."

"Women can leave now," she said. "They can usually take care of themselves, so they don't have to stick around when they're miserable. But fortitude went out of fashion, too. People think it's more important to be happy than to be good, I guess. Better for the grown-ups, but worse for the kids."

"My wife didn't even know she was miserable until she met this other guy. She kicked me out and now she's running around with my daughter's softball coach. Can you beat that? He's the sensitive type. She said I wasn't communicating." He sighed. "They get this stuff on Donahue and Oprah. If I 'communicated' some of the stuff I deal with, she'd have left me a lot sooner, I can tell you that."

"Maybe you should have told her anyway."

"Yeah, maybe. Anyway, I wish she'd just had an affair with this guy. Got it out of her system, you know? But no. She has to bust up everything, drag the kids into it, make a mess of everything."

He looked at her sharply, then laughed. "I guess you've heard all this before, from a million guys. How the hell did I get started on this, anyway?"

She smiled. "Yeah, I've heard it before." Men who'd been dumped often had that glazed-over look, as if they weren't sure what hit them. Cameron had it. "These are rough times for men and women. Nobody seems to know what's expected of them anymore." She sighed. "I sound like one of those bartenders who gives soothing, banal advice. Would you like another drink?"

"Why not," he said. This time he got up and followed her into the kitchen for ice. While he was there, he checked the back door. "Decent lock," he said approvingly. "Before I go I'll check the other entrances."

"I think there's something wrong with one of the basement windows," she said. "Calvin Mason let himself in one of them while I was in the hospital."

"Getting those notebooks, huh?" said Cameron. He pointed to a door. "This lead to the basement?"

She nodded. A few seconds later, she heard the sounds of vigorous hammering. He came thumping up the steps a few moments later and she handed him his second drink.

"I nailed it shut," he said, accepting his drink.

"Thank you," she said. "I really appreciate it. Now I'll feel safer."

He smiled sadly. "I'm glad you do," he said. "I like making people feel safer, but my wife's been telling me it's all some sicko male power thing."

"Men can't help it," said Jane. "I think it's too bad when they get bashed for it. The day a man and woman are lying in bed together asleep and he wakes up and says, 'I hear a funny noise, will you go check it out?' is the day I'll change my mind. If it makes you guys happy to make people feel safer, maybe it's because your brains are wired that way."

"Interesting point of view," he said. "But definitely not fashionable. In today's climate, I couldn't express it in mixed company."

"It always irritates me when people believe what they wish were true or think they should believe, instead of what they know is true," said Jane. "Have you had dinner?"

"Oh, I'll grab a sandwich or something," he said vaguely.

"That's what I had. But I'm still hungry." She opened the refrigerator and peered inside. "I could make us an omelet."

"I hate to put you to the trouble," he said unconvincingly.

"Just keep me company while I do it."

He sat down at the kitchen table and took off his jacket. She glanced over at him as she broke eggs into a bowl.

He caught her glance. "What is it?"

She laughed. "I guess I've seen too many movies. I sort of expected you to have a gun in a shoulder holster."

He reached behind him and produced a gun from the small of his back, then replaced it. "Does it give you the creeps? My wife says it gave her the creeps having a man with a gun around the house."

"Are you kidding?" said Jane. "I just got beat up and

left practically for dead. Under the circumstances, having a man with a gun in my kitchen is rather reassuring."

"How long have you been a widow?" he asked.

"Twice as long as I was married," she said. "I married him when I was twenty-two, and he died five years later." She was chopping mushrooms and onions and green peppers, and arranging them with her knife in broad stripes on the cutting board. "His car ran into a wall."

"That must have been a terrible shock," said Cameron.

"It was, but it shouldn't have been," she said. "Bernardo was a Formula One driver. No one follows Formula One racing much over here, but he was the number-two-ranked driver the year he died, and pushing to make the top spot. Little boys all over Europe knew who Bernardo da Silva was."

"Da Silva. Portuguese?"

"Brazilian." She poured the eggs into one of Uncle Harold's Revere Ware frying pans. They made a satisfying sizzle.

She turned around and looked at him. "I suppose you're thinking he was crazy to race, that it didn't serve any purpose, and that his death was pointless."

Cameron looked at her steadily. "How can anyone know a thing like that—whether his death was pointless or not? How can anyone know?"

She sighed. "I don't talk about Bernardo much because I think that's what people are thinking. That he was a fool. And that I was too, to put up with him."

"I wasn't thinking that," said Cameron.

"Well, he wasn't a fool. He was just different from other people. He needed to go fast. It was that simple. He had to go fast. I could even understand it myself. I never presumed to try and change him."

"In that respect, Bernardo was a lucky guy," said Cameron.

"I was pretty lucky myself," she said. "We had some

good years." Besides, she thought to herself with a little smile, there's no point trying to change Latin men. If you ever actually managed to, which you couldn't, they wouldn't be appealing anymore.

"There are some plates in that cupboard next to you. Would you put two on the table, and hand me one for the omelet?"

The omelet looked a little lonely. She took an orange out of the refrigerator, cut it into slices, and arranged them on the plate.

They sat down, and she divided the omelet. "You're the first guest I've had here," she said, feeling the stab of sudden, unexpected intimacy.

"I'm glad to be here, to tell you the truth. I hate eating alone."

"I don't mind it if I have a book," she said.

"I'll just have to get used to it," he said.

"A person does," she said. "But maybe you won't have to. Maybe she'll come to her senses."

He put down his fork and looked at her with a rueful smile. "I feel like a total jerk," he said. "I'm whining. I can't believe it."

"It's all right," she said, smiling back. "Actually, I kind of like it when people tell me their troubles. It's interesting, and it makes me feel good—like I'm a sympathetic person."

"Then I guess you'll enjoy carrying out your uncle's wishes," he said. "Helping the hopeless or whatever it is."

She touched her swollen lip. "So far it's had its downside," she said.

"That's the difference between listening and actually getting in there and helping," he said. "The difference between being a cop and a social worker. A fat lip."

"I don't remember Uncle Harold ever getting a fat lip. In fact, I wish I knew exactly what the old boy was really up to all those years."

"You mind if I say something?" he said, not waiting for her assent. "This is a really flaky deal you're getting into here. You're a smart lady. There's got to be a lot you can do without having to take on the world's injustices. I do it because I'm stupid, and they issue me a weapon and pay me a salary. What's your excuse?"

"The money's a lot better than what the taxpayers are willing to pay you," she said. "A lot better."

"Yeah? So that's it? The money?"

"Maybe I wouldn't do it otherwise. I don't know. I guess Uncle Harold thought that, or he wouldn't have made the terms so tempting. And right now, to tell you the truth, I haven't got anything else to do."

"Yeah?"

She shrugged apologetically. "I've been kind of drifting, I guess."

"You don't look like you've been drifting."

She laughed. "You mean I don't have all my possessions in a shopping cart?"

"No, I mean you look like you know what you want and you know how to get it. I mean you don't look wishy-washy. You know how some people have those kind of blank faces? A lot of people, in fact. You don't look like that."

"I guess I've been a determined drifter," she said. She looked over at his plate. He had practically inhaled his half of the omelet, and neatly stripped off the orange slices. "Are you still hungry?"

"No thanks. That sure hit the spot."

"Coffee?"

"Great." He settled back in his chair. In fact, he looked as if he were hunkering in for the evening. In a way, this pleased her. There was something very large and comforting about him.

Jane decided his wife was an idiot, nagging him about being more sensitive. Didn't she get it? Men weren't

necessarily subtle. If they didn't discuss their more complex emotional thoughts it was because they weren't interested enough in subtle nuances to have any complex
thoughts, or, more importantly, to listen to anybody else's
with much perception. They'd rather go down in the
basement and nail shut a window to keep out bad guys.

She made coffee and suggested they have it in the
living room. She tucked her feet up underneath her on
the sofa and shook her hair back. "I'm glad you came by,"
she said. "To tell you the truth, I've been pretty skittish
since I was assaulted. Little noises make me jump."

"Real common," he said solemnly. "To be attacked like
that, it changes your view of the world in some way. All of
a sudden, it isn't as predictable a place. But you seem to
be doing great."

Paradoxically, these encouraging, if slightly patronizing, words made her feel helpless all of a sudden. She
briefly imagined her head on his shoulder, the rough
tweed of his jacket on her cheek and his fingers in her
hair. She caught herself up short, but it was too late.

"I'll be fine," she said, in a low, confident voice, with a
wave of her hand. But she knew he'd seen that helpless
flicker in her eyes. Because now he was looking back at
her with a kind of intense, shiny-eyed look of his own,
and she saw that male protective instinct that could get all
tumbled up with sex given half a chance. The older she
got, the more she thought that beneath a veneer of
civilization, human beings hadn't changed much since
sabertooth tigers lurked outside the cave.

"I'd offer to stay," he said. "Sleep on your sofa here, if I
thought you were scared. But to tell you the truth, I've
got a van parked at the corner. You're under surveillance.
It'll be there all night."

"For my protection? Or are you just keeping an eye on
me?"

"Both," he said, with a sideways smile, sipping his coffee.

"I see."

"Those guys outside are going to wonder what's happened to me," he said, setting down his coffee cup. "I appreciate your feeding me and listening to my troubles. Like I said, you've probably heard it all before. Insensitive jerk husband who doesn't understand what women want, wondering why he got dumped. Jesus."

She walked him to the hall. He stood in front of the door for a moment, and she touched his sleeve and gave him a level gaze. "Don't apologize," she said. "This man-woman stuff can be rough. Sometimes I think we fail to communicate because we're two separate species and we only come together to mate."

"Yeah. Same old battle of the sexes."

"Thank God for the truces, though," said Jane.

"I'm kind of battle fatigued right now, but basically I agree with you," he said. He gave her a slow, appreciative smile, and reached toward her face, almost touching her mouth. "Take care of that lip," he said. "And don't forget, I want that diary."

Chapter 21

Just as Jane was leaving the house to go see Claire Westgaard, the phone rang. It was Gail English.

"Wendy told me you came by," she said in a voice that sounded more agitated than strained. "I'd like to see you. The police have been helpful, but there's more I want to know. I hope you'll come."

"Of course," said Jane. "I have an appointment right now, and I don't know how long it will take, but I'll come right afterward. All right?"

"Yes. Please. I don't understand what happened to Dick, and I want to know."

"Of course you do," said Jane. "Give me your address."

"It's right near the Pike Place Market." She gave directions to a downtown building of expensive condominiums.

In the car, driving up the shady, tree-lined streets on Queen Anne Hill, Jane tried to imagine what Claire would be like. She imagined her as a grown Linda— intense and fanatical. Or perhaps she was a different sort of cultist entirely, passive and suggestible. Maybe Claire had been a friend of Linda's. Maybe she could tell Leonora something about her mother. But if Claire was too crazy, Jane thought, it would be better that she didn't.

Claire lived in a gray-and-white cottage that appeared to be staggering under the weight of wisteria vines. The house and garden were surrounded by white lattice, similarly engulfed by jasmine and clematis. The effect was frivolous and cheerful.

Claire herself, when she answered the door, proved to be a round, rosy, pretty woman with pre-Raphaelite hair in a golden cloud around her face. She was also in an advanced state of pregnancy, but Jane could tell from her full, round arms and her ample breasts that she had always been large.

"Come in," she said in a voice full of girlish anticipation. "I'm so glad to meet you."

Inside, Claire's house looked like something from a Laura Ashley catalog, a riot of chintz print slipcovers, white baskets filled with flowers, botanical prints, ribbons and lace, and painted wicker furniture.

Claire led her outside to a small deck surrounded by roses. They sat at a table set with teacups and a teapot in a tea-cozy of glazed floral cotton trimmed with white eyelet lace. Claire herself wore a loose Victorian-looking garment in an apricot-colored floral pattern, and reminded Jane of a comfortable, slip-covered chair. Jane admired her rounded, alabaster arms as she poured them tea, her agreeable face, and the sheer volume of her red-gold hair.

"Bucky," Claire announced, "is crazy about you." She looked up at Jane for some reaction.

"He is?" said Jane, managing a pleased but slightly puzzled air. "I've only met him once."

"I know. He told me that too. But you made quite an impression." Claire sipped tea. "You see, Bucky is sort of an old boyfriend of mine, and I always like to keep track of old lovers. You know, make sure they're happy? Anyway, that's why I let him talk me into telling you about the Fellowship. I was curious about you."

Jane gazed through the french doors at the decor of the room they'd just left.

Claire laughed. "My decorator hates it," she said. "But I just tell her, look, if you want me to get someone else to order all this stuff and arrange for everything and take the commission, I will. I know what I like."

"I think it's fabulous," said Jane. "I mean, if you're going to go chintz and flowers and white wicker, why not push it to the limits. You don't want to be skimpy with this kind of country stuff. It should look rampant and abundant. Like perennial borders."

"Exactly," said Claire. "If I was going to go minimalist, I'd go really minimalist. Just a white wall and a stainless steel coffee table and one thistle in a vase or something."

"Nobody could call this minimalist," said Jane, who thought living here would be slightly claustrophobic, but that it was a nice place to visit. It smelled of roses.

"You're not like I imagined you," said Claire.

Curious to know what Bucky had to say about her, Jane said, "What did you expect?"

"Bucky didn't say you were skinny," said Claire. "But, if you don't mind my getting personal, I'm not surprised you have a chest. Bucky's crazy about tits."

Jane laughed. She had never thought of herself as skinny, but realized this was a relative term.

"They're real, aren't they?" Claire persisted. Then, as if shocked at her own impertinence, she added jokingly, "I hate it when thin, flat-chested women get implants. If they're going to be fashionably scrawny, they shouldn't be able to add on the benefits God intended for us full-figured gals."

"They're real," said Jane, who found it astonishly easy to slip into intimacy with Claire. "They're the old-fashioned kind that sort of flop to the sides when you're on your back."

"Believe me, I know," said Claire.

"You're not going to tell Bucky that, are you?" said Jane, suddenly alarmed.

"Oh, of course not," said Claire, looking deadly serious. Jane wasn't sure she believed her.

Jane felt that an afternoon discussing decorating and cosmetic surgery with Claire might be a lot of fun, but she supposed she'd better get to the matter at hand. "Bucky tells me you were a member of the Fellowship of the Flame."

"It's so embarrassing, really," she said. "But I was *very* young."

"Tell me about it," said Jane.

"Well, it was all about getting your flames glowing at the right rate. Proper balance. You were supposed to get proper balance."

"What did you do, exactly?"

"Mostly we chanted and listened to the Flamemaster. The deal was we were always on the chilly side, and he felt our flames needed to be higher. So we'd have these kind of orgiastic dances in the middle of the night. The whole thing was basically party time, with some lectures thrown in. And of course we all thought the Flamemaster was just fabulous, so spiritually in tune, so wise. He could look right into our souls and see just how our little flames were doing." She waggled her fingers in the air to represent flames.

"Definitely the charismatic type, then?"

"Oh, definitely. It's hard to figure it out. I mean, he isn't that attractive or anything. Kind of a wimpy-looking guy with thinning hair. But glowing eyes and a great voice." Claire looked thoughtful. "Voices are really important, don't you think?"

"Absolutely," said Jane.

"I mean, could you be attracted to a man with a horrible voice?"

Jane thought for a minute. "No," she said. "I don't believe I could."

Claire entwined her fingers in a nearby bit of jasmine. "Before I came to my senses and met and married my nice husband, I hung out with a lot of unsuitable guys. I specialized in screwed-up types. Borderline alcoholics, manics, that kind of thing. You know. I thought everyone else was boring."

"I know," said Jane, sighing. "Slightly crazy guys, or starving artists and musicians, or guys in dangerous professions. Why do we do it?"

"So we can enjoy the benefits of craziness without being crazy ourselves?" mused Claire.

"I think you're on to something," said Jane. "Seems unfair to all those other nice, responsible men."

"You're assuming they want some thrill-crazed woman around," said Claire. "Anyway, I finally came to my senses. As far as the Flamemaster goes, physically anyway, it was his voice that got us, I guess. All the girls, anyway. I think the guys were only there to pick over the girls after the Flamemaster had his fill."

"You mean he was—"

"We were all fucking him," Claire said matter-of-factly. "What do you expect when you get a guy who tells everyone he's God and put him together with a lot of stupid young girls? Anyway, it didn't seem like such a big deal back then because everyone was fucking everyone all the time anyway." She paused. "He was a pretty boring lay, to tell you the truth, but he always made you feel that it was some kind of a religious rite or something, and that if you were bored it was because you weren't spiritually in tune.

"We'd all be dancing around, tearing off our clothes and drinking cheap wine, and he'd kind of flit around and choose someone and slip into his room with them. It smelled of incense in there and there were a lot of draperies and things, and a big waterbed. Sort of a low-budget Hugh Hefner scene. He really got off on two girls at a time." Claire laughed.

"Do you remember Linda Donnelly?"

Claire scrunched up her face in concentration. "No, but I'm no good at names."

Jane took a photograph of Linda from her purse and slid it across the table.

"Oh, yes. I do remember her. Linda, huh?"

She stared at the picture, a plump hand sliding absentmindedly over the melonlike bulge of her pregnancy. Claire looked like a fabulous piece of ripe fruit, thought Jane.

"She was pregnant when she first came to the group. The Flamemaster was too conventional to want to nail her—in that state anyway—so I think she was kind of ignored."

"Linda had that problem a lot, I think," said Jane.

"She was kind of sullen, but very intense. A little scary." Claire looked up. "What happened to her? Let me guess. She's running her own cult now."

"She died. She was drowned. They thought it was an accident, but it was rather mysterious."

"How awful." Claire's forehead puckered up. "What happened to her baby? It was a girl I remember. She brought it around once. To be baptized by fire."

"Her father raised it. Linda had a husband. What was the baptism by fire like?" It sounded alarming.

"It was sort of a fire ceremony. We just passed the baby around and chanted some stuff about flames. The Flamemaster made it all up as he went along, I'm sure."

Jane made a mental note not to tell Leonora about the baptismal ritual. Too *Rosemary's Baby*.

"Anyway," continued Claire, "we never saw the baby much after that. And then I guess this Linda dropped out. We didn't see her around anymore."

"Did anyone talk about her?"

"For a while the Flamemaster was real down on her. That was how it worked. A sort of personality thing. You spent all your time deciding whose flame was balanced. The Flamemaster would drop these little hints and pretty soon people would be down on you and kind of freeze you out. If there was anyone he couldn't control, he'd start the whispering campaign. He'd act really sorry, like he wanted them to get it right but they just weren't cooperating. Linda was 'willful' he said. 'Willful' meant you wouldn't go with his program."

"Did she have a friend there named Robin? Apparently there was a kind of buddy sytem."

"It wasn't that organized, but the Flamemaster would sometimes assign us to spy on each other. You know, 'Keep an eye on so-and-so. I'm worried about her levels.' That kind of thing. Like we were supposed to be thermometers or something."

Claire concentrated for a moment. "There might have been a Robin," she said after a while, "but I don't remember one. Like I said, I'm not good at names."

"Linda apparently gave them some money. An inheritance. Did anyone say anything about it?"

"Really? I never heard about that. Of course, we were all supposed to turn over everything, so I'm sure she did. In fact, I do remember we were all supposed to visualize generosity for Linda. The Flamemaster said her flames were blocked because she was holding back. Of course he said that about a lot of us.

"You'd worry that everyone would freeze you out if you didn't. And of course, the more you had to give, the more you were appreciated. After I gave them my farm, I was the Queen of Sheba around there. My flame was perfect as soon as I signed the papers." Claire seemed amused at her youthful self. Jane would have thought she would still be resentful.

"At first we were supposed to all get jobs, but we were up all night chanting, and people kept calling in sick and getting fired. And then people would talk about all this flame stuff at work and scare the hell out of their coworkers and end up getting fired.

"For a while he sent us out to panhandle, and then he wanted us to run a business. Finally, he said he'd received a vision that we were to move to the country and live off the land.

"So I gave him the farm and we all moved over to Vashon and the Flamemaster was nice as pie to me. I was the anointed one, sort of his chief consort. That's what made me realize how stupid it all was. And it was pretty boring over on the island. We had to do a lot of manual labor, getting the place fixed up. People started drifting away after that."

Jane forgot momentarily about Linda. "What did you do then?" she said.

Claire laughed. "Well, it had turned into the seventies, and I'd been fooling around like a stupid hippie worrying about my flame levels and cooking dinner for a hundred people at a time in a leaky old farmhouse. I came back to town and found out everyone else was making money, so I got my real estate license. I was selling all this property and doing okay, but I got really mad I'd given away that farm. I met Bucky at some stupid networking cocktail party and we had a little fling there for a while—he was the first not totally whacked-out guy I had a relationship with as I made my re-entry into normal life—and I told him about it and he got a nice settlement out of the Flamemaster. So I had my down for an apartment building."

"So you know who the Flamemaster is? And you got your money back!" said Jane.

"That's right." Claire looked smug. "And Ben was one of my tenants. That's my husband. He's an engineer at Boeing. Anyway, then it was the eighties and everyone was finally getting around to getting married. And now, I'm finally getting around to having a baby." She sighed happily.

"We're both so excited about the baby. I can't wait to see a perfect little pink-and-white baby with golden curls tottering around the house."

Jane glanced nervously through the french doors into the living room. She'd seen how even reasonable children could systematically trash a house. She imagined a little child knocking over the ceramic geese, grinding sandbox sand into the white carpets, and rubbing half-chewed graham crackers into the white lace cloths that hung like Victorian lingerie from all the tables.

Claire seemed to be reading her thoughts. "I know," she said, somewhat defensively. "Everyone says we'll have to childproof in there a little."

"But how did you get your money back?" said Jane. "I mean, you'd signed it all over perfectly legally, hadn't you?"

"Sure, but Bucky just wailed on him. Part of the settlement was that I couldn't reveal his name, or his past." Claire paused and looked sly. "And of course Bucky couldn't either. I mean, he was the attorney of record and all that, and if it got out, well, Bucky's basically a chicken anyway. That's why he asked me to talk to you."

"But you can't tell me?" she said.

"No."

"Can you give me a hint?"

Claire giggled. "Well, let's just say he's up to his old tricks. Like me, he updated his act for the times."

"Where should I start looking for him?" said Jane.

"Forget looking for him in any records. He never used his true name on the deed. He's using his true name now. Part of it, anyway. The whole thing is too dorky to be believed. I saw it on his driver's license once."

"Is he still around? In the area?"

"Why don't you start by asking at my grandmother's farm? It's called the One-Ten Institute now. The Flame-master gave me cash. He kept the farm and sold it to them."

"I will," said Jane, puzzled.

Before she could probe further, Claire bounced back in her chair and folded her arms. "So let me tell you about Bucky," she said. "I think he's ready to get married and settle down. I really do. And he thinks you'd be perfect for him."

"He does?"

"Yes. And now that I've met you, I can see why. Bucky's a terrible snob. You look sort of elegant and you've lived abroad. He likes that. He said you were sophisticated."

And, Jane thought, he thinks I'm coming into a great deal of money. He's even trying to get Claire to help me do it.

"Of course he'd die if he knew I was telling you," Claire continued, "but what the heck. All this middle-aged court-ship is a real drag. People don't have time anymore. Besides, I believe in love at first sight. That's the way it was with Ben and me."

"I hardly know what to say," said Jane.

Claire laughed heartily. "I know. Bucky does seem like a sleaze. He is, really. But he can't help it. He's a very good lawyer. And he'd probably make a perfectly good husband. And he thinks marriage would be good for him. Help him be responsible."

Jane nodded thoughtfully, resisting the temptation to say that maybe a puppy or a paper route would do the trick as well as a wife.

"How old a man is the Flamemaster now?"

"Let's see, I'm thirty-nine." She patted her stomach. "Just getting in under the wire with this kid. And he was about ten years older. So he's pushing fifty." This seemed to startle her. "God, it's hard to believe.

"Anyway, I've said enough. I did say I'd keep it confidential, and I'd just as soon not cross him. He was a jerk, but he's kind of a psychopath too. He's always been out for himself, and I wouldn't put anything past him."

"Do you think he could kill someone?"

Claire thought for a second. "He'd never do it himself. He'd get someone to do it for him."

Chapter 22

Jane drove back down Queen Anne Hill, and stopped at a gas station in the business district at the bottom of the residential neighborhood. She was delighted to find it was full service. She hated pumping her own gas, and there seemed to be practically nowhere in town that would do it for you. While the tank was being filled, she went to a phone booth and called Calvin Mason.

"What have you been up to?" he said. "I tried to call you. A Detective Cameron was here and he asked for the diary. I'd already made the copy, so I gave it to him and got a receipt. He didn't have a warrant, but he could have got one easy enough."

"Fine," said Jane. "I was calling to tell you he'd probably be by. Also, I just finished talking to someone who knew Linda back in the old days. The Flamemaster's still around, but she won't tell me who he is. Anyway, he sold that Vashon land to the One-Ten Institute a few years back, so I thought I'd check with them and see if they know who he is or where he is or both."

"The One-Ten Institute, eh?"

"Yes. Who are they?"

"It stands for a hundred and ten percent. They sell high-priced seminars to businesses. Sales motivation stuff. Goal setting. It's a lot of crap. A friend of mine who works for the phone company had to take one of their courses. They have retreats over on Vashon, where you have to sit in the hot tub with your boss and tell him where you want to be in ten years. They really pile in the bucks with that stuff."

"Sounds hideous," said Jane. "I'll call them after I go see Gail English. Richard English's wife."

"Not an easy call to make," said Calvin Mason sympathetically.

• • •

Gail English was about forty, a tall, angular woman with heavy dark hair streaked with gray and cut short and chic. Her face was tawny and blotched with recent tears. Her greenish eyes searched Jane's face greedily.

"Thank you for coming," she said at the door to her apartment. "You've got to tell me what happened to you. I have to know what you were doing there and who you are. I can't make any sense out of any of this."

They sat on two rattan-and-stainless-steel chairs in a vast apartment with a view of the sound, an apartment as austere and spartan as Claire's house was cluttered.

Jane told her as succinctly as possible about her search for some background about Linda, about Leonora, and about how she'd come across her husband's name in a conversation with Judy Van Horne.

Gail English hugged herself with her thin arms and seemed to be rocking back and forth a little as she listened. Then Jane told her about the struggle in the dark and ended by telling how she had found Richard English's body.

Gail sighed. "I suppose I didn't really know him," she said. "None of this makes any sense. I've never heard of Linda Donnelly or the Fellowship of the Flame—although it rings a bell from the sixties. But I know Dick never mentioned them."

She turned to Jane. "We were married for seven years. And I never heard any of this. There must be some horrible mistake."

"Was your husband ever in group therapy?"

"Yes. Briefly. Before I met him. He had been unhappy. I knew that. But he always told me that after he met me he didn't worry about being happy anymore."

"I hope that can be a comfort to you," said Jane. "That you made him happy."

"This girl died? This Linda?"

"That's right. She drowned. In 1974. What was Richard—Dick—doing then?"

"That was the year he started his production business. Up until that time he'd been free-lancing around. Doing special effects. Renting equipment, scrambling around for crews, renting a crummy space on a pier that rocked every time a boat went by. Doing events and trying to get into film and into video, which was all brand new.

"He'd dropped out of film school and he'd done light shows in the sixties. Remember them? Little slides of colored water. It was supposed to look psychedelic. Projected images that went with the music. Crude stuff, but Dick was incorporating film and other techniques, and making it more sophisticated.

"When he started his business he got into computer graphics, and suddenly he was doing commercial work and postproduction. He had the best facility in town." She smiled. "He won some money on the exacta at Longacres and put it all into the best stuff around."

"Did he ever mention a woman named Robin?" Jane asked. "She was a friend of Linda's. Near the end of her life."

"Robin? I never heard of her."

"I told your husband that Linda had a diary," said

Jane, skirting around the lie she'd told. "She did, but he wasn't mentioned in it. Did he say anything about that?"

"He was very nervous the day he died," said Gail. "Very hyper. He told me he'd be home late, but he never told me about his appointment with you. Why didn't he tell me? I just thought he would be working late. He did that a lot. He was working on a claymation project."

"Dinosaurs with pizzas," said Jane.

"Yes. It sounds trivial. I know it does, but Dick made everything into art. He loved the processes, the detail, all the hard work to get the perfect effect. He loved his work. It gave meaning to his life, even if it was some stupid pizza commercial. He didn't care about that, he just wanted it to be perfect. And it always was."

"He was never involved with any cult?"

"Absolutely not. He'd been raised a Catholic and he turned against the whole thing when he was a kid. He didn't like any form of organized religion."

Gail sighed. "He still had the guilt, though. Sometimes he seemed to think he was a bad person. He told me so once. That I was too good for him, and that it was a good thing he didn't believe in sin because he was in a state of sin." She shuddered. "It frightened me."

"Did he tell you why? What he'd done?"

"He hadn't done anything," she snapped. "But he said a couple of times that if he was dying, he might ask for a priest and that I should get him one."

She began to weep softly.

"I'm sorry," Jane said rather helplessly, her own eyes beginning to sting with tears. Gail had said "if," not "when." She hadn't expected he would ever die. No one seemed ever to expect anyone to die.

Gail raised her voice, gagging on tears. "Why did you call him? Why did you? Everything was all right until you called him. What did you want from him?"

The sick feeling of guilt that had been welling up inside Jane now threatened to engulf her entirely. "I wanted to see what he knew about Linda," she whispered.

"I never expected to be alone so soon. I never expected him to die at all. And then to have him just go off one day and not come back. If I'd just been able to say good-bye." She rubbed her eyes with her fists and sniffed, then pushed her hair back from her face. "Do you have a husband? Be kind to him."

"My husband died in an accident. Ten years ago this summer."

Gail looked at her with a brief interest and her tears stopped. "Oh." She was silent for a moment before she said, "The police wouldn't tell me anything about you. They won't tell me anything at all. But someone came before you came. Someone came and killed him. Who would do such a thing? I have to know."

"I hope you will."

"Your lip is swollen," she said. "Did he do that to you?"

"Yes."

"But you didn't see him. Couldn't you see him at all?"

"No. It was dark," Jane said. "I'm sorry."

"Dick was a wonderful artist. He was always quiet, working behind the scenes. He never talked much. No one knew about his mind, about the visions he had. Why couldn't he tell me? About his demons? I loved him."

"Sometimes artists can't talk," said Jane. "That's why they're artists, maybe. Or maybe they can't talk because they're artists." She hesitated, wondering if she was saying too much, then she plunged on. "It can be hard on people who love them."

"Sometimes he had nightmares," she said. "He said he didn't remember them." Jane sensed that Gail didn't believe that.

"Is there someone staying with you?" said Jane. "I don't think you should be alone right now."

"My sister's coming out from Chicago. Dick's parents want me to stay with them. They want him to have a Catholic funeral. I don't know what to do."

"It might mean a lot to them," said Jane.

There was a strident buzz all of a sudden, and Gail walked wearily over to an intercom. "It's Wendy," said a crackling voice.

"She's been very sweet," said Gail, hitting the buzzer. "Just a kid, really. She's been handling all the clients for me. They all loved Dick."

Jane was relieved Wendy was coming. She hated to leave Gail English alone, yet she knew she couldn't help her. Her swollen lip was just a reminder that Jane had lived and her husband had died. And died, perhaps, because Jane had stirred up something from the past.

She was also glad Gail lived in such a secure building. If Jane's suspicions were correct, and the killer had wanted a look at the diaries, he might want to search here for them. Gail was easy to find.

Gail went and opened the door to the apartment, and Jane rose too, planning to leave as soon as Wendy arrived. After a moment, they heard the elevator chime. A second later, Wendy came up the hall, struggling with a huge flat parcel wrapped in brown paper. She looked dwarfed by it.

"Hello," she said, nodding at Jane. "I found one more matte," she told Gail. "I thought you'd like it. I've never seen it before."

"My husband did beautiful work," Gail said to Jane. "You know what a matte is? It's the background, then you put live figures or animation in front of it. His were beautiful."

She pulled off the brown wrapping paper. "I've never seen this one," she said.

"I found it behind that long counter on the side of the wall," said Wendy. "It's really more than a background, because the figures are painted in. I never saw it before myself."

Jane hadn't either. But in a way, she had. There was a tangerine sky, all streaked with silver clouds. Winging its way across the canvas was a flock of unicorns. Just as in Linda's diary, the unicorns were laughing.

Chapter 23

There was a connection now, a connection between Richard English and Linda Donnelly. A second one, really, because a guilt-ridden Richard English had already acknowledged the connection years ago in group therapy. But now there was a link between her mind and his art.

She twisted that concept around in her mind as she drove back to Uncle Harold's house. Had Linda seen that picture and written about it? Had he read her description and then painted the scene? How could he have read her notebooks?

She had more pieces to the puzzle now, but she felt more frustrated. The only solution, she believed, was to keep going, to pursue every lead.

Back at home, she called Judy Van Horne.

Judy answered the phone on the fourth ring. "Hello," she said in her rather dejected voice. There was a din of yapping dogs in the background.

"This is Jane da Silva. We talked about Linda Donnelly a few days ago," she said. Had it really only been a few days ago?

"I read about Richard English in the paper," said Judy. "Was it the same guy?"

"I'm afraid so."

"Oh my God."

"I didn't get a chance to talk to him," said Jane. "I wanted to ask him about Linda."

"I know."

"I wondered if you remembered anything more. Did he say how well he knew Linda?"

"No. That was the whole point. He wanted to know about her. Of course, I had just told the group"—here she broke off to scream at the dogs. "Shut up, goddammit!" Then she continued, "I'd just told the group all about Linda's rejection of me. And he listened really carefully, and he asked if it was a girl who drowned, and I said it was.

"Anyway, he said he just met her once, but he'd always felt bad about her, and he wanted to know more about her."

"He'd met her just once?"

"That's right. I remember thinking he was a really sensitive guy to have cared so much about someone he barely knew."

"I see."

"But people get like that in group. They act more caring than they are, because the shrink makes you feel cold if you don't listen to everyone else. You know? No matter how much you're hurting yourself. I think individual therapy is better, but my insurance didn't cover it."

"Does his murder...does it have anything to do with Linda?"

"I don't know," said Jane.

After she thanked Judy and hung up, she looked for the One-Ten Institute in the phone book. They had a downtown phone number—"corporate offices," and one on Vashon Island—"retreat complex." It sounded like a psychological term.

She called the corporate offices. An exuberantly friendly and sincere female voice answered. "You've reached the

One-Ten Institute," it said. "This is Cheryl. How may I help you today?"

"I have a question about some real estate," began Jane.

"Just a moment and I'll connect you with our account representative who works in that area," said the voice. "Have a terrific day."

Jane cringed, and a moment later a male voice, equally cheery, came on the line. "This is Bob," it said. "How are you today?"

"I'm fine, thank you," said Jane.

"That's great!" said the voice. "I understand you're in the real estate business. It's a really great business, that's why I enjoy working with people in it. Are you familiar with our real estate sales seminars?"

"No," said Jane. "And I'm not in the real estate business."

"Oh."

"And I don't plan to be either," she said. "And I don't want to do any seminar. I want to talk to whoever bought your Vashon retreat."

"That would be Mr. Wayne himself," said the voice. "I don't quite understand what you want."

"I'm looking for the previous owner of the property," said Jane. "Kind of an informal title search. Do you think I could talk to Mr. Wayne?"

"You could talk to someone in his office," said the man, whose cheeriness had abated somewhat.

"Thank you," said Jane.

She was put on hold for a moment, during which time she heard a mellifluous recorded male voice. "You're on hold," it said inanely. "The One-Ten Institute will handle your call promptly. Please be patient while we speak with others like yourself who choose one hundred and ten percent effectiveness. Meanwhile, keep this thought. Every day is a terrific day if you make it that way."

"Others like *you*," corrected Jane. "Not others like *yourself*. You people are idiots." Spooky New Age music of the spheres came on, and Jane wondered if it wasn't laced with some ghastly uplifting subliminal message.

An older female voice now came on the line. This woman, too, sounded as if she were on drugs of some kind. "This is Dorothy. You've reached the One-Ten Institute Executive Suite," she said happily. "How may I help you today?"

"My name is Jane da Silva. May I speak to Mr. Wayne?"

"Mr. Wayne is in Washington, D.C., conducting a personal workshop for top-level employees of the Internal Revenue Service," said the woman breathlessly. "We expect him back in the office tomorrow morning. Is he expecting your call, Jane?"

"No. He doesn't know me," said Jane. She felt like adding, "And neither do you, Dorothy, so you can call me Mrs. da Silva."

"Well, Mr. Wayne is very busy and he only takes calls from his prescreen list," Dorothy said in a whisper, as if she were embarrassed at Jane's ignorance.

"Perhaps you can help me," Jane suggested.

"Boy, I sure hope so."

"You people own some property on Vashon Island."

"Yes, we certainly do. Have you ever been there? It's just gorgeous. A really great facility."

"I'm sure it is," said Jane. "I'm looking for the previous owner."

"I don't know anything about that," Dorothy said, sounding a little flat. Jane noted with satisfaction that these people seemed to lose their iridescent personalities when they heard anything that wasn't in the script.

"Well, I wonder who does," said Jane.

"That's an excellent question," said the woman. "Can I take your name and number and have someone return the call?"

"Fine," said Jane, supplying it.

As soon as she hung up, she dialed the main number

again, bracing herself for more sweetness and light. This time, Fran wanted to know how she might help. "Give me the public relations department," Jane said.

"Just a moment please, and we'll have someone in Corporate Communications speak with you," Fran said, bubbling over with goodwill, and Jane was back on hold, with Mr. Mellow intoning and the spooky music again.

"Hi! This is Pat in the Corporate Communications Department. How may I help you today?"

"My name is Jane da Silva."

"Hi, Jane."

"Hello. I'm looking for someone and I hope you can help. Apparently, the property the Institute owns over on Vashon Island once belonged to a group called the Fellowship of the Flame."

"Oh, really?" said Pat.

"Yes. And I'm looking for the guy in charge of that group. He owned the property when you bought it. Do you have a record of that somewhere?"

"This is certainly an unusual request," said Pat. Jane thought she detected a little strain behind the voice.

"Yes, it is," agreed Jane.

"Let me put you on hold for just a moment."

Jane braced herself for another thought for the day, but she just heard clicks and buzzes this time. After a few moments, Pat came back on. "There's no one here who can help you today," she said. "Could you give me your number so I can have someone call you back?"

Jane gave Pat her number.

"I'm filling out a 'request for corporate communication' form," Pat said. "And just what is it you need to know? I need to fill that in too."

"It sounds crazy," said Jane, "but I'm looking for someone who called himself the Flamemaster. He used to own your Vashon property."

"I see," said Pat unconvincingly. "We'll see what we can do and get back to you. 'Bye now, Jane."

Exhausted from her attempts to penetrate the exuberant but not particularly efficient bureaucracy at the Institute, Jane checked her watch. Bucky would be picking her up in an hour. She sighed. She would have liked to weasel out, but thought she'd better go through with it. Unfortunately, Bucky Montcrieff was in a position to do her harm as well as good.

She thought about a nice hot bath, during which, she knew, she would wrack her brain trying to put together all she had learned so far. But the phone rang.

It was Leonora.

"How are you?" said Jane. "Is everything all right?"

"Yes. A policeman came and talked to us about my mother."

"Detective Cameron?"

"Yes. Some other guy was with him, but he asked most of the questions."

"I know. I've talked to him, too."

"Anyway, I felt better after talking to him. He wouldn't tell me whether he thought my mother had anything to do with this Richard English guy."

"The police don't tell you anything," said Jane. "They just ask questions."

"Uh-huh. He sort of made me feel better, you know? He asked how come you were involved, and I told him how you heard me play and how I talked to you and all that. I hope that's okay."

"Of course. You have to tell the police everything you know."

"Good." Leonora paused. "There's another thing."

"What?"

"My aunt called me. My half aunt, I guess."

"Susan Gilman?"

"That's right. She said after she met you she decided

she should get in touch with me. She has a little baby. My cousin."

"That's right."

"Well, I was wondering if you'd go with me. Dad doesn't want to, and to tell you the truth, I'm kind of nervous about going by myself."

"Of course I will," said Jane. "Your aunt is really very nice, and her baby is adorable. I'm glad she called you." And about time, too, she added mentally.

"Thank you," said Leonora. "I really am glad you'll come. She said day after tomorrow."

"Fine. What time?"

"Ten o'clock. She said the baby would be awake then."

"Great. I'll pick you up at nine-thirty."

Talking about Susan Gilman and Bellevue reminded Jane of Dr. Hawthorne. She had a follow-up question for him, now that she'd collected more information. He was out of the office, but his service said she could leave a message. She didn't have much hope. In her experience, doctors seldom returned phone calls. "Ask him to call Jane da Silva, please." She left the number and added, "Ask him if he remembers a friend of Linda's called Robin."

So far, no one remembered her. No one except Kenny. Yet Robin was there at the very end. And then she'd disappeared. Jane felt sure that if she found Robin she'd be halfway home.

She went upstairs and ran a hot bath. She decided she'd order a very expensive dinner. That would cheer her up. And she'd wear a very nice dress. That would cheer Bucky up. She wasn't about to alienate Bucky at this point. Nor was she about to marry him or anything in between, either. Bucky would have to be handled tactfully, which meant, she thought, her black, drapy dress.

Chapter 24

Jane's black dress was the kind of thing you could wear anywhere without looking under-, or worse yet, overdressed—even in Seattle, where, for some people, logging attire provided a workable basic wardrobe.

When Bucky arrived, looking like an amiable cad in a double-breasted silk blazer, she was pleased to see they seemed to match.

"So this is Uncle Harold's place," he said, strolling through the living room with his hands in his pockets after he'd given Jane herself his appreciative once-over. The decor seemed less to his liking. "Kind of creepy, isn't it?" he said, eyeing the mohair upholstery. "But the house is great and the neighborhood's terrific. I'd say twenty or thirty thousand and this place could look fabulous."

"Maybe more," said Jane. "If I redo the kitchen and bathroom and enclose the back porch."

"Well, it's all up to you. And the trustees." He gave her his wide, sharklike smile.

"Yes," she said demurely.

"Anyway, I have a great decorator," he continued. "She just did a great southwestern thing for my apartment. Sort of postmodern. Very spare but with some whimsical touches. It really works. I got her to kick back some of her commission, too. She was great to work with." He gazed up at Saint George and shuddered.

"I think that stays," said Jane, following the gaze. "A tribute to Uncle Harold. Of course," she added, "I don't intend to count my chickens—"

"Before they're hatched," he finished. "Come on, give me a break. You've already got that money spent—at least mentally—and you know it."

Jane laughed. "Well, maybe some of it."

"You like oysters, right?" he said.

"Crazy about 'em." Jane remembered how he'd snagged more than his share at lunch, and made a note to watch him like a hawk this time.

"Well you're in luck. Because I know where to get the best ones in town."

They drove to a waterfront restaurant. As before, in the elevator after they'd just met, Jane felt slightly overpowered by his cologne in the small confines of his vintage Porsche, which he drove fast and aggressively. Once inside, Bucky ordered a bottle of Veuve Clicquot and a dozen oysters. "Make sure they're the Chiloés," he said.

"You see," he said, beaming, "local oysters aren't at their best now in the warmer months. But in Chile, it's winter, right? These little guys are perfect. Very firm, with an incredible finish. They taste like Olympias, but better."

Jane loved food but hated food bores. She nodded politely. The oysters were, however, just as advertised. She bit into the first one and sighed happily.

"Divine," she said, counting the remaining oysters on the plate from the corner of her eye as he filled their champagne flutes.

"Mmmm," said Bucky, taking his first sip. "Now tell me how things worked out with Claire."

"She was delightful," said Jane. "And quite helpful. I really appreciate your giving me the lead. She painted quite a picture of the Fellowship of the Flame. Said you helped her get some money back from them. Just what I'm trying to do."

"Can't discuss it," Bucky said, with a gleam in his eye.

"I understand. Anyway, I'm trying to track them down through the One-Ten Institute."

Bucky clicked his tongue. "They're a real piece of work," he said. "Half the executives in this town have been through their training program, and they come back with glazed-over eyes and sign up the typing pool. Those guys are raking it in. Absolutely raking it in."

"What exactly are they selling?"

"Oh, it's all bullshit," said Bucky, "but it goes over very big. My theory is that a lot of these managers don't do anything much. I mean the regular people run the businesses, right? In some haphazard fashion.

"But, instead of going out and playing golf in the afternoons like managers in my uncle's generation did, these guys think they're supposed to be actually doing something. *Managing*. So they sign everybody up for these rah-rah workshops."

"Sounds plausible," said Jane.

"But forget about all that," said Bucky, his eyes narrowing. "You're doing more than just trying to get that money back, aren't you? I mean this Richard English character was killed. What's going on?"

"I suppose when Uncle Harold ran things, he didn't run into anything like that, did he?" Jane asked, a little nervously.

"You mean will the trustees take kindly to rough stuff? I don't know. The main thing is to conduct your part of the business respectably and discreetly. Don't break any laws. The judge is a stickler on that point. And no cheap publicity, either."

Jane nodded.

"Not that you'd ever do anything like that. You strike me as a very well-bred lady, if I may use that term." He raised an eyebrow as if bestowing a very important and perspicacious compliment.

"'Lady' is fine. But I always think 'well-bred' is a term that applies more properly to Bedlington terriers than to human beings, don't you?" said Jane. She smiled nicely, aware that she was careening just a little too close to the edge. Guys like Bucky were intrigued when you insulted them, but only to a point.

"Oh, you know what I mean. It's just that there are a lot of tacky people around these days," he said in a confidential manner. "And a single guy like me, doing well in his profession...well, I meet a lot of women. It's just refreshing to meet one like you."

She smiled warily.

"Tell me about yourself," he said.

"No," she replied, eager to seize control of the conversation. "Tell me about yourself."

Bucky looked pleased, and proceeded to launch into his résumé. "Well, I grew up here in Seattle, and I prepped at Lakeside; then I went to Stanford—Dad's old school."

And that's perhaps how you got accepted, thought Jane.

"I was in retail for a while," he confessed. "A youthful aberration. I liked the design aspects. I have a strong visual sense, but there's no future. So I went to law school. Uncle George found a place for me in the firm."

"How nice for you."

"Yes, it's worked out really well. Do you want to know more? Like those personal ads? Ever read them? They're all the same. 'Enjoy long walks on the beach, cozy fireside chats, romantic dinners, reading the Sunday *New York Times*, mountain bikes, and music from Bach to Brubeck.'"

Jane laughed and added, "'Might be ready for a commitment with a sexually uninhibited, nonsmoking, disease-free woman uninterested in marriage and children—'"

"'And not averse to being tied up and tattooed,'" finished Bucky.

"It's kind of sad, really, all those ads," said Jane.

"To be honest, lately I find being single is getting to be kind of a drag," said Bucky. His face took on a sensitive look, meant, she imagined, to convey a sincere desire for a warm, committed, intimate relationship after years of predatory dating. Probably scared to death of AIDS.

Jane took on a brisk, hearty manner. "Well," she said, "I'm sure you won't have to rely on one of those ads. The world is full of lonely women. I'm sure you could snap one up in a minute." She held up an admonishing finger. "Watch it! That's my oyster."

"We'll order some more." He summoned the waiter.

Despite Bucky's obvious shortcomings, Jane could see how Claire had succumbed to his charms. He wasn't bad-looking, he was amusing, and he was so transparently out for himself you had to admire the guy's nerve.

"When people see me," he said huskily, "they see a guy who looks like he has it all together. But underneath the tailoring, I'm sometimes a lonely guy."

"Speaking of tailoring," Jane said rather desperately, "I was admiring your sport coat."

"You like this?" said Bucky, pleased, running a hand over the lapel. "You know, this is a great shopping town. There are some fabulous stores here." He leaned over eagerly. "Shopping's a little game with me. I never pay full retail."

"Really?" said Jane.

"Why do it? I like nice things and I can get more of them if I pay less. I just picked up a fabulous Armani suit for fifty percent off." His eyes lit up, and Jane relaxed. "A very subtle tweed, kind of khaki, with a little thread of blue." After his wardrobe, she'd proceed to his decor and then perhaps where he had his hair cut. That should carry her through to dessert. And then there was his car. Bucky may have been a lonely guy, but he had lots of nice things to keep him warm. Jane just wanted to make sure she didn't become one of them.

It wasn't until much later, on Jane's porch, that Bucky summoned up the wistful expression once again. "It's been really great to talk to someone—*really* talk to them. You know?"

"Absolutely," agreed Jane. "I enjoyed it so much. Thank you." She stuck out her hand for him to shake, and Bucky looked down at it mournfully. "I'd ask you in, but I have to get up early tomorrow," she said. He took the hand and held it.

From behind the door, she heard the phone ring. Bucky released her hand and Jane opened the door and made her escape.

She heard his Porsche screaming down the road as she reached the phone. It had rung five times.

"Jane da Silva?" It was a woman's voice.

"Yes? Who's this?"

"Robin. I was Linda Donnelly's friend."

Jane tried not to sound overwhelmed. "Yes, of course."

"I've known for some time you've been looking for me."

Jane racked her brain to try to remember whom she'd asked about Robin. A lot of people. But no one had said they knew of her. No one except Kenny.

"I'd hoped we could get together," said Jane. "I'm trying to find out some things about Linda. For her daughter."

"Oh no," said Robin. "I don't want to meet you. And I won't call you again. Mostly, I want to know who you are and what you want. You can't be part of the Fellowship. Are you?" She sounded a little hysterical.

"No. What makes you think that?"

"You never know," she said. "God, it's been so many years, but I'm still frightened of them."

"Why? What did they do?"

"They're just so ruthless."

"What did they do to Linda?"

"Besides take all her money?"

"Yes. What else happened? Robin, how did she die?"

"I'll never know. I was hoping you'd tell me. What have you found out? Tell me what you know."

"Nothing. Just that she drowned and gave her money to the Fellowship shortly before."

"We were separated that night."

"What happened? What happened after you left Linda's house? She said good-bye to her husband and her baby. Then what happened?"

"I drove her over to a meeting."

"Where?"

"Oh, I don't remember."

"At the farm on Vashon? Was it there?"

"That's right. We had to take a ferry."

"Then what happened?"

"We all dropped acid. The rest of the evening was a blur. I only remembered one thing."

"And what was that?"

"Linda, she told me"—there was a sob in her voice—"she told me the Flamemaster had put her down. Said she wasn't spiritual enough. He'd thrown her out of the group and she said she didn't want to go."

"Did anyone try to stop her?"

Robin seemed to be openly weeping. The phone was silent, except for a gasp, and then she said, "I was too messed up. I should have helped her. She got a ride back to town with a couple of guys. Later, they told me they dropped her off downtown and she told them she was really miserable. That's what she told them."

"Robin, why didn't you tell anyone at the time? Why didn't those guys who gave her a ride come forward?"

"The Flamemaster told us not to. He said she'd been thrown out, and that it wasn't our problem. He said we

might be investigated. It might come out we were dropping acid. I was afraid. And besides, what good would it
have done?"

Jane wasn't sure how long Robin would stay on the line.
She wanted to nail down a few points while she had the
chance. "Let me get this straight, Robin. She gave them
the money, her inheritance."

"Yes. In cash."

"She said she didn't want to go on living."

"Yes."

"And you heard from two guys later they'd driven her
to town and she'd been despondent."

"That's right."

"I wish we could meet," said Jane. "It would mean a lot
to Linda's daughter."

"No way," said Robin. She was completely self-possessed
now, and her voice had taken on a hard quality. "I'm
happily married, I've got a couple of kids, and a career. I
don't want anyone to know I was mixed up with the
Fellowship back then. It wouldn't bring Linda back. She
killed herself, it's that simple."

"The Fellowship—are they still around?"

"Maybe."

"How do I know you're Robin?"

"You'll just have to take my word for it."

"No, I don't. I know you have a black mole. Where is it?"

There was a longish pause. "On the back of my left
leg," said Robin. "About four inches above the back of my
knee. Who told you that?"

"Who told you I was looking for you, Robin?"

"You don't want to know," said Robin. "If you're smart,
you'll drop it."

"Did you know Richard English?"

Robin hung up.

Chapter 25

She sat for a minute. Somewhere, somehow, she'd bumped into someone who knew Robin. And that someone had lied and said they didn't know her. Was that someone part of the Fellowship of the Flame? Apparently not. Because Robin seemed afraid of her old friends at the Fellowship. Presumably, whoever had told Robin about Jane was also afraid of them.

There was another possibility. Richard English could have told Robin before he died that Jane was looking for her. There could well be some connection between them. It was when Jane had asked her about Richard English that Robin had hung up.

The phone rang again. Her heart was beating faster. She hoped it was Robin calling back with second thoughts. Jane would attempt to get through to her, sell her on the idea of a meeting. She should come forward. A man was dead.

It was a male voice. "Mrs. da Silva?" he said in polite, measured tones.

"Yes."

"We know all about you," he said. "We know that you are asking about the Fellowship of the Flame. The Fellowship lives, Mrs. da Silva, forced below the surface until the time is right. We don't want to draw attention to

205

ourselves." He sounded remarkably casual about the whole thing. Somehow, that made it more chilling.

"I can understand that," she said. "But can we meet? I have some questions. I want to find the Flamemaster."

"The Flamemaster is a very important man," said the caller, rather peevishly.

"I respect his desire for privacy," said Jane. "Tell him that I'm looking for him, and that if we can meet then I won't have to keep looking, perhaps threatening your privacy."

"Threaten?" The man's voice became indignant. "You? Threatening the Flamemaster?"

"I just meant—"

"Listen, you stupid bitch," he said now, almost in a whisper, "back off. Back off now. Don't even think about trying to find us. And remember, we've already found you."

"I'll find you sooner or later," she said. "Tell the Flamemaster that."

"That's a really dumb answer," said the voice. "I guess you still don't get the point. We'll have to make it more clear. When we finish, you'll get the point all right. It's real simple. The difference between us and other people is, we're not afraid. We're not afraid to hurt people. We're not afraid to hear people scream. When we finish, you'll have so much respect for the Flamemaster you'll never dare utter his name again. You'll know that compared to him, you're nothing. Just a little speck. A dirty little speck."

"Just tell him this speck wants to talk," she said. Then, before she was hung up on for the second time that evening, she replaced the receiver.

She'd been indignant when she'd been talking, but now that she'd hung up, she had a sick feeling in her stomach. She'd brushed up against something very nasty. She was unaccustomed to blatant, arrogant rudeness, and felt there was never any excuse for it. Never. Even a declaration of war could be phrased politely. She half expected the phone to ring again. She was relieved it didn't. She had a lot to think about. They had found her.

But now what? The chances of getting Leonora's money back from someone who viewed the rest of humanity as a collection of dirty specks seemed remote.

At the same time, the group was obviously vulnerable. They were in hiding, for one thing. And nervous about it. Claire had pried some money out of them. It sounded like she'd blackmailed them, with Bucky's help. But how could they have any money? If they were underground, their opportunities for fund-raising were limited, unless they were robbing banks or something. Had they killed Richard English?

The more she thought about it, the more she decided she'd better find them first. First thing tomorrow, she'd go downtown to the One-Ten Institute and rattle their cage. She knew she should be afraid, but she wasn't. She was angry. The man who'd talked to her on the phone sounded like such a jerk.

Maybe, she thought, it's the Flamemaster himself. No, it couldn't be. Claire had said he'd had a terrific voice. This guy sounded young and whiny.

And how had he found out about her? Someone she'd talked to must have told him about her interest in the Fellowship of the Flame. Robin and Calvin Mason's anonymous friend had both sounded frightened.

Was the person who'd tipped off the Fellowship the same person who'd tipped off Robin? They weren't in the same camp at all. Jane sighed. She was missing something.

She had two links between Linda and Richard English: the picture he'd painted of her vision, and what he'd blurted out in group therapy years ago. Not a lot to go on.

And now, some person or persons had talked to Robin

and the Flamemaster about her. The disquieting thing was that someone had lied to her when they said they didn't know who or where Robin was.

Claire was the only one who'd admitted knowing about the Flamemaster. But Claire had a plausible reason not to tell what she knew, and Bucky had backed her up. Actually, it had been damn nice of Claire to help her at all.

It was hard to sleep, but Jane went through the motions, anyway. She undressed, brushed her teeth, hung up her black dress, lay in bed, stared at the ceiling, wondered who had lied and what she missed. It seemed as if her dinner with Bucky had happened in another lifetime.

Suddenly, she felt like talking to Calvin Mason. She checked the clock, decided it might be too late, then decided she didn't care if it was. The phone rang three times and his machine came on. "It's Jane da Silva," she said, lingering in case he was really there. If he was, he still wasn't picking up. It would have been nice to talk to him about what had just happened. "Call me if you get a chance," she said. "I'll be up late."

At first, when she'd started looking for Linda's past, the trail had seemed so cold and stale. It had been difficult even to conjure up a picture of Linda herself. She was long gone and not terribly missed. All she'd left behind was a big hole in Leonora's life—a hole where a mother should have been.

Now, after two anonymous phone calls, the forces that had been swirling around Linda at the time of her death seemed as if they were kicking back to life. Somewhere under a pattern of lies and secrets lay the truth. Jane had only seen flickers of that truth behind the patterns.

Some of the truth had died with Richard English. She was sure of it. Thinking of him, the sight of his body laid out on that table, the pain and anger of his widow, Jane was engulfed all of a sudden with a sense of evil. Why hadn't she felt the horror of it before? She sat up in bed, frightened. Although she knew she should be, she wasn't frightened of the physical danger in which she might find herself once again. She was frightened of the evil.

Trembling, she turned on the light at the side of her bed. Detective Cameron had told her to call him anytime. And she'd just been threatened by an anonymous phone call. It was late, but he had said to call whenever. Why did she have to do everything alone, the hard way? Perhaps because it always seemed easier. But was it?

He'd given her his card before, with his home number on the back. It was in the nightstand. She glanced at the clock. Midnight.

He answered on the first ring. She assumed he must have been in bed. There was a TV on in the background. It painted kind of a lonely picture.

"I'm so sorry to bother you at home at this hour," she said. "This is Jane da Silva."

"Is everything all right?" he asked in his calm voice.

She felt better immediately. Better than she had any right to feel, she thought to herself.

"I got a phone call. From the Fellowship of the Flame. They—they threatened me."

"Who's 'they'? Did they identify themselves?"

"No. It was a man. He said they'd hurt me if I kept looking for them. He said they knew I was looking for the Flamemaster."

"Are you?"

"Well, yes, I guess so." She ran a hand through her hair and felt foolish. "Listen, I'm sorry I called you now. I was scared I guess."

"Want me to come over?"

"I should have called you at your business number in the morning," she said. "I'm sorry to bother you. I just thought it might have some bearing on your case."

"You didn't answer me," he said. "I said, do you want me to come over?"

"It would be silly."

"That's not what I asked," he said patiently. "Do you want me to come over?" he asked for the third time.

"Yes," she said.

"I'm on my way," he said, and hung up.

Jane felt like an idiot. There wasn't anything to tell him she couldn't have told him on the phone. But she was glad he was coming. Excited almost. She got out of bed, fished in a drawer for her one nightgown, a plain white cotton which she owned primarily for calling room service in hotels, and put on her robe, a masculine navy blue wool with white piping. Then she went into the bathroom and brushed her hair. She examined her face critically in the mirror and wondered if this was one of those days she looked older or one of those days she looked younger. There were both kinds of days at her age.

She knew why she was wondering, too. It didn't please her to realize she wanted Cameron to think she was pretty. Damn. She had to make sure he didn't know. She had to keep any trace of sexuality out of her demeanor. It was humiliating, but there it was. She was lonely and frightened and he was lonely too and she wanted to collapse against him and comfort him and be comforted.

The doorbell rang.

He was wearing jeans and a sweater and he didn't look like a cop at all, except for that calm face.

"I'm sorry," she said.

"Stop apologizing. Are you going to ask me in?" His eyes flickered over her robe. She wondered if she should have dressed. She held the lapels together in a nervous gesture. "Of course."

They sat down opposite each other.

"So tell me what this caller said."

She repeated the conversation as well as she could. He nodded as she told him, interrupting only to say, "He called you a dirty little spic?"

She laughed. "No. A speck."

"I thought maybe because your name is da Silva—it might have meant he only knew your name and hadn't seen you. You're very fair complected. Go on."

She finished her narrative, and he was silent for a while. "Did you get the sense there was someone with him? You can sometimes tell."

She thought for a moment. "I couldn't tell, one way or the other."

He looked pensive again. "We'd better look into this. To tell you the truth, I thought this Flamemaster business was a little farfetched."

"Maybe it still is," she said. "Maybe whoever it is was just trying to scare me off searching."

"I wish they would," he said. "I wish you'd drop the whole thing."

"That would be the sensible thing to do," she answered.

"Something tells me sensible isn't the way you operate."

"I'm very sensible," she said, slightly miffed.

"You're shrewd and smart, but you're a flake at the same time. I know the type." Before she had a chance to sound miffed again, he smiled disarmingly. It was really rather a lovely smile, and she smiled back. They sat there looking at each other like a couple of teenagers for a few minutes, and then she coughed and said, "Well, I really appreciate your coming over. It wasn't that important."

"Listen, most women"—he corrected himself—"most people would be scared to death to get a call like that. I'm not a bit surprised you called. Usually, though, I don't go out and check it out. But this is a murder case. And besides, I was hoping you'd offer me a drink." He rose. "But it's late and you're all ready for bed, so I guess I'll run along."

"I could use a drink myself," she said, walking over to the liquor cabinet. He followed her into the kitchen when she went for ice. She wondered if she should have offered him the drink, instead of waiting for him to ask. He stood there awkwardly as she made the drinks and they went back into the living room.

"I wasn't scared. The guy on the phone didn't scare me. He just made me mad. It was something else," she said.

"Oh yeah?"

"A sense of—evil."

"A kind of sick, cold, helpless feeling in your gut?"

"Yes. And fear. Fear of the evil."

"The fear goes away. That feeling in your gut doesn't." He took a sip. "But you learn to live with it." He shrugged. In that shrug, Jane saw a sort of lonely bravery. She supposed she was projecting it onto him, imbuing him will all sorts of nobility so she could count on him emotionally.

She stared at him. She felt tears forming in her eyes, and she wasn't sure why. They could have been for her. Or because she had been touched by what he had just said. She felt giddy and on the brink.

He look alarmed, the way men often do when confronted with the sight of tears. "What?" he said.

Now the tears formed and spilled warmly onto her face. She closed her eyes and bent down her head. "I'm sorry," she said. "It's just all so overwhelming, I guess."

He put down his glass and came to her side. "It'll be okay," he said. To her shame, she felt her body collapse into a sob. He put his arms around her and she fell against him, weeping. She felt a surge of relief, warm and comfortable with his arms around her, and she let herself weep just a little longer while he patted her back. Then she disentangled herself from him and wiped her face with her fingertips, closing her eyes hard to make the tears stop. It worked. She opened her eyes again and found herself staring into his face.

"I'm sorry," she said again.

"You apologize too much," he said, pushing a strand of

wet hair from her cheek. He let his hand linger on her face.

"You must think I'm one of those hysterical women who call the cops and say they heard a prowler just so they can have a man to lean on."

He laughed. "There are plenty of those. Usually they wear slinkier bathrobes when they answer the door, though. And then the robes fall open accidentally on purpose." They both laughed and then he stopped laughing and pulled her toward him and kissed her.

It was a friendly, tentative kiss, the kind that could have just ended. But it didn't. Driven by a kind of desperation, she made it into something more. By the time she realized what was happening, he was kissing her throat and pushing aside the lapels of her scratchy wool robe and touching her breasts. She felt her body relax and her head go back, and then he stopped.

"Listen," he said thickly, one hand on either shoulder. Her hair was disheveled, her face flushed. "I gotta get out of here now. Prying myself off of you is going to be a real bitch. But I have to do it. You know why?"

"Why?" she asked, dazed.

"Because I'm trying to clear up a homicide and when I do, you just might be an important witness. It comes out you and I— Well, any halfway decent defense lawyer can get the case thrown out."

He got up and she backed away, into a corner of the sofa. "I'm sorry," she said again.

"*You're* sorry? Jesus. I'm *real* sorry." He looked her up and down longingly.

He smoothed down his sweater and she retied her bathrobe, painfully aware of her own lust.

"Besides," he said, sounding more like his old, calm self, "you might regret this. You're just feeling helpless and vulnerable right now. After this is over, you might feel differently. Not that I'd let that stop me, if it wouldn't screw up a case."

Jane gave him a level gaze. "Maybe that's why I want you," she said. "But right now it doesn't seem that way."

"I'll be around to find out, anyway," he said. Then he smiled quirkily. "You've given me a terrific incentive to wrap up this case. Don't see me out. I might not make it." He went into the hall and called out over his shoulder, "I'll give those guys in the van outside orders to shoot anyone who tries to get in. Including me."

Chapter 26

The One-Ten Institute was located on the top three floors of a black glass building a little north of the heart of downtown. The elevated monorail, left over from the Seattle World's Fair of 1962, sped by, reflected in the dark glass of the third story. Only the row of leafy green trees lining the street prevented the scene from looking like some old-fashioned vision of a high-tech future.

Jane assumed that the gung-ho staff would be in early. All that cheeriness she'd received over the phone smacked of early-morning industriousness, but she hoped they'd be less on their guard at eight-thirty. Anyway, she'd been eager to get started, and she'd figured she'd get a parking meter if it was early in the day.

The black glass doors were heavy. Inside was a dark marble lobby with a bank of brushed chrome elevator doors.

The tenth floor was a reception area. Jane was determined to get past it, and hunt down a simple answer to a simple question. She was glad to see that the young girl behind the mammoth reception desk looked young and impressionable. She had a cute little pudding face that was made up with cherry red lips and too much mascara, in an unsuccessful bid at a sophisticated appearance. She also had rather outdated big hair bristling with gel.

215

"Good morning," Jane said, unsmiling. That ought to throw her for a loop here in happyville.

"Good morning," said the receptionist, smiling through a yawn. "How may I help you?"

"Jane da Silva. I'm here to see Mr. Wayne. If he hasn't arrived yet, my instructions are to wait for him."

"He's here," she said, reaching with a plump hand over to a bank of phone buttons.

"Oh no," said Jane. "Don't call his secretary. I'm expected to come straight through."

The girl frowned, and Jane frowned back. "Weren't you briefed?" she said. "I'm very surprised. I was led to believe you people were very efficient."

"I don't understand," said the girl plaintively. "Let me call the secretary."

"She won't know about it," said Jane decisively. "She hasn't been cleared."

"She has a list," began the girl, looking genuinely confused.

"Well you won't find me on the A list," said Jane. "I'm on the double-A list."

Jane removed her wallet from her purse and flipped it open, momentarily flashing her international driver's license, and sailed past the desk. She managed a wintry little smile. "Don't worry," she said. "I won't mention you weren't briefed. This is a very high-level meeting, and I know I can count on you not to mention it."

She left the receptionist, hand poised in midair over the phone buttons, with a quizzical expression, and made her way down a carpeted hall.

A young man in horn-rimmed glasses, wearing red suspenders and gray flannel trousers, walked by, carrying a cup of coffee. "I'm lost," said Jane, flashing a smile. "I was on my way to Mr. Wayne's office."

He pointed her in the right direction and gave her directions, which led her to a cavernous reception area presided over by an older, sharper-looking woman in a poodle sweater with gray bouffant hair.

"Jane da Silva, here for our special meeting. You must be Dorothy, so you'll know Mr. Wayne expects me. I'm sorry I'm late." Jane managed to keep any trace of remorse from this last phrase.

"Does he expect you?" said Dorothy, looking flustered.

"Oh yes. I'll just go on in. I hate to keep him waiting."

"But you can't," said Dorothy, straining to look cheerful and firm at the same time.

"I know," said Jane, waggishly. "You're going to ask me 'How may I help you?' Terrific training, great attitude, a hundred and ten percent. I just love it. Well Dorothy, you can help me by letting me take care of myself. Oh, and perhaps you could bring me some coffee. Black. And no decaf."

"But Mr. Wayne's just about to leave for Vashon Island."

"I know," said Jane, trying to look as if she were masking exasperation. "That's why it's so important we meet immediately." She debated flashing the international driver's license, but this woman didn't look as stupid as the receptionist.

The phone on the woman's desk chirped. Looking warily at it and back at Jane, Dorothy held up her hand. "One moment, please," she said, reaching for the phone.

Jane smiled and waved and kept walking. She heard Dorothy say, "I know. She's here now." The pudding-faced receptionist had apparently finally decided to sound the alarm. Jane pushed open a pair of double doors in some Oriental wood.

A plump middle-aged man, bald with a fringe of gray hair, sat at a large desk. He looked up, startled. "Mr. Wayne," Jane said, in a voice brimming with enthusiasm and confidence, "I'm so happy to meet you." She came toward him, extending a hand. It was just then that she noticed another man lounging on a sofa reading a paperback book. It was a spy novel, and the book was so battered, Jane had the impression he'd been slogging through it for weeks. He stood up and looked alarmed.

"So glad I caught you," she continued, holding the hand Mr. Wayne had extended in a bemused reflex action. "Jane da Silva." Mr. Wayne's eyes flickered and he withdrew his hand. She was surprised. That flicker seemed to say he knew who she was—that his moment of surprise was over.

"I'm sorry I don't have an appointment," she said. "But it will take just a moment."

Mr. Wayne's features rearranged themselves into blandness. "I'm glad to meet you. Please sit down," he said courteously. He made a quick gesture of dismissal to the man on the sofa without taking his eyes off of Jane or changing his pleasant expression.

"Thank you," she said.

She was startled by his voice. It was absolutely gorgeous, rich and deep with texture and shading. The man with the book left, rattling the door.

A moment later, Dorothy came in. "I'm sorry, Mr. Wayne," the secretary said, almost trembling. "I didn't have a chance to—"

"It's all right, Dorothy," Mr. Wayne said benevolently. Dorothy looked pathetically grateful.

"Never mind the coffee, Dorothy," Jane said kindly.

"And what brings you here?" said Mr. Wayne.

"Your Vashon land," said Jane. "You bought it from the Flame Foundation, didn't you?"

"I'm not really sure. Some sort of a religious group. It was all handled by realtors. Why do you ask?"

"I'm looking for them," she said.

"I see. Well, I certainly can't help you. It was strictly a cash transaction. The deal was cut in a day or two. I don't remember much about it, to tell you the truth. The

Institute needed a retreat close to town, and when the property came up I grabbed it."

"I see. But there must be some record somewhere—"

"I suppose. Frankly, I don't really care. One of the important rules we teach here at the Institute is to see what you want, grab it, then forget about the details. We only concentrate on the really useful information. Information that leads us to our goals. Focus. Learning focus. Focus leads to proper goal identification; then we capture that goal, seize it, make it ours. Once I had the property I needed, I didn't think about anything else. And"—he leaned back, eyeing her benevolently, as if speaking to a charming child—"that's why I remember little or nothing of the transaction."

"Very interesting," said Jane. "But you must have records."

"Property transactions are all filed somewhere," said Wayne. "With the county or someone. Why come to me?"

"The original owners just had a post office box. I haven't been able to trace them."

"Well, I wish you luck, but as your search doesn't mesh with my own goals, I can't take the time to help you. Even if I could." He leaned forward, placing his hands on the desk. Jane noticed he wore gold cufflinks in the shape of percent symbols. "Why are you looking for these people?"

"They owe someone some money. I'm trying to collect it."

"How much money?"

"About two hundred fifty grand," said Jane, wondering if her suspicion was ridiculous. But why else would he ask? "And interest, of course."

"I see." He checked his watch. "I'm going to miss a ferry if I spend any more time with you. I'm sorry I can't help you, but if anything comes up, where can I reach you?"

"You can't," said Jane. "That is, I'm just in town temporarily."

"Good," said Mr. Wayne. Jane's eyes widened. What did that mean, exactly? He rose. "I'm sorry to be ungracious," he said, "but you'll have to leave now. I'll have someone from security escort you out."

"That won't be necessary," said Jane, marveling at the odd turn the conversation was taking. Mr. Wayne was very smooth and relaxed, but clearly wary and, she thought, angry, too.

"Oh, I insist," he said.

Outside, in the reception area, the man with the spy novel stood up. "This is Mrs. da Silva," said Mr. Wayne pleasantly. "Call one of the security people and have her seen out, won't you?"

He turned on his heel and left.

The man with the book—in his late twenties, beefy-looking with oily dark hair and shiny skin—stared at her curiously. Dorothy said, "I'll call them," and hit the phone.

Jane smiled at both of them, and decided that if they bought Mr. Wayne's gobbledygook, they were probably impressionable, unsophisticated people. Not to say downright stupid. She figured they'd believe anything.

"Mr. Wayne is so security minded. Just what we appreciate. Our subcontractors don't always understand the importance of security, but that's our business and we take it seriously."

She leaned over to Dorothy. "You won't mention my visit here, even within the Institute, will you? We haven't finished the clearances on key employees. I expect them from Washington any day now."

Dorothy looked bemused but impressed.

"And there's one more thing," said Jane, as a uniformed security guard came into the room. "I'll need Mr. Wayne's full legal name. For the contract. The CIA has to go through some of the same cumbersome procurement procedures as the IRS or anyone else in government," she added with a weary air. She was enjoying herself immensely. This was a better rush than lying to the Vashon realtor.

The man with the spy novel gasped appreciatively.

"Oh, we never give that out," said Dorothy, after a pause. "He doesn't like—"

"I must have his full legal name," said Jane severely.

"It's D. Clark Wayne," said Dorothy.

"What's the *D* stand for?" Jane asked, taking out a little notebook and standing with pencil poised.

"Dwayne," said Dorothy. "D-W-A-Y-N-E."

"Dwayne Wayne. An unusual name, all right. Thank you."

She didn't wait to get home. She called Claire from a pay phone a few blocks away as the monorail rumbled past, shaking the acid green leaves of the maples. "Claire," she said, "let me just go over some of the things you told me about the Flamemaster. Thinning hair. Undistinguished appearance. Great set of pipes. And a dopey name."

"That's right." Claire giggled.

"Maybe a name that rhymes."

"You mean like Kevin Devon or Harry Carey?"

"No. Like Dwayne Wayne."

Claire giggled again. "I never said a word," she said.

Jane said a hasty good-bye and hung up. She glanced around and decided she hadn't been followed. Dwayne Wayne was pretty stupid. Selling his own land back to himself. Running his new improved scam in Seattle, where he'd presided over the Fellowship of the Flame. The sheer arrogance of it was mind-boggling.

But then, wasn't that just the sort of thing a guy like Wayne would do? Surrounded by loyal followers, eventually believing the stuff he was dishing out himself, the man probably thought he could get away with anything. Even murder.

Jane knew she should call John Cameron. She knew

she should tell him everything she knew. But where would that leave her with the trustees? Would she have solved a hopeless case? She could say she'd brought Richard English's murderer to justice. But couldn't they say that she'd provoked his death, by going after the truth about Linda?

And what proof did she have that Dwayne Wayne was involved with either of them? None. One thing was certain: If she called the police and they crawled all over Wayne and the Institute, she would have nothing to bargain with. He'd be exposed and she could forget about getting Leonora's money out of the bastard.

Which would leave her back at square one. Maxed out on her Visa card and cast adrift in a country that didn't even have socialized medicine. They'd pitch her out of Uncle Harold's house, too. While she was looking for a job, she'd probably have to throw herself on Bucky's mercy, but deprived of her fortune, her appeal for him would probably fade fast.

She fished in her purse and found the business card of the American-Samoan Collection Agency. The police would just have to wait.

Chapter 27

There was a pay phone on the ferry dock. While she waited for Bob, she called Calvin Mason. He wasn't home again, so she left another message on his machine. "This is Jane da Silva again. It's Friday morning, and I'm on my way to the One-Ten Institute compound on Vashon Island. I have an appointment with a Mr. D. Clark Wayne. That's Dwayne Wayne. Actually, I don't have an appointment, I'm just dropping in. If you don't hear from me tonight, please call Detective John Cameron of the Seattle Police Department and tell him where I was going and whom I was going to see. Thanks."

When she got off the phone she saw a carload of Samoans pull up in an old Toyota. There seemed to be two of them in the front seat and two in the back, wedged in like balloons from the Macy's Thanksgiving Day parade. Bob Manalatu struggled out of the backseat, slammed the door, and waved good-bye to the car. He was wearing a nubby gray silk sport jacket, probably a size fifty-six, over a hot pink polo shirt and black polyester slacks with razor-sharp creases. His black slip-ons had heavy gold chains across the insteps. Fully clothed, Bob was an even more awesome sight than he'd been in his workout gear.

"I'm glad you could make it," she said, shaking his hand.

"I really like a ferry ride," he said. "The air's so clean, you know?"

"That's right."

"So what's the story here? Someone been messing with you?"

"No. But they might try to. I just want you to go along and stand next to me while I talk to someone who owes a friend of mine some money."

"Okay," said Bob. "And what do I do if he says no?"

"We'll play it by ear," said Jane.

"No marks on him, though," said Bob. "That's never a good idea."

"No marks," Jane agreed solemnly. Bob looked pleased that their business style was congruent on this point.

Jane had checked the schedule and figured that Wayne had sailed on the previous boat. That was fine with her. It might be better to let him relax a little before she faced him again.

She tried to figure out what he'd do. That phone call from the Fellowship of the Flame last night must have been from one of his people, alerted by her request that day through the PR office. She'd left her name and number. But the caller hadn't been the greasy kid with the spy novel who had the lunky look of a bodyguard, though. He'd bought right into her ridiculous CIA story, which by now, she thought with some satisfaction, had probably made its way throughout the organization. She'd made sure the security guard who'd escorted her respectfully out of the building had overheard it.

And, it wasn't Wayne's own rich voice either. She would have remembered that.

From what she'd seen, she doubted that the cult still existed. It had been updated, repackaged, repositioned, and marketed to a much broader base. A much more lucrative base.

But Wayne still scared people. He scared Calvin Mason's anonymous phone informant, and he scared Robin. She'd carried on as if the Fellowship still existed in its older, cruder, less profitable form. Maybe this was a story Wayne put out to keep his former followers silent.

From what Claire had told her, the Flamemaster's original scam had basically provided him with a harem of nubile young girls. That made sense. He'd been in his twenties when he started. Now, in his forties, he'd decided to go for the bucks, probably in addition to, rather than instead of, hassle-free sex from impressionable young women.

On the way over, Bob sat beside her in companionable silence, while she thought about Dwayne Wayne and separating him from $250 thousand. It shouldn't be too much for a guy like that, she figured. He'd want to protect his investment. All she was asking for was Linda's money back. In return, she wouldn't tell the world about his older, less polished identity.

She still hadn't figured how Wayne tied in with Richard English, though. She wouldn't even think about that. There was a good chance he didn't know she'd been in the studio that night. The police had kept her name out of the papers.

Unless of course Richard English himself had told Wayne she was expected. The police could sort that out. After she got a cashier's check. Or cash, the way Linda had turned it over in the first place.

As they drove from the ferry dock, light flickering through alders and firs, Bob talked about how much he loved the country. "I mean it," he said. "I'd like to get me some land someday. Get away from all the crap in the city, you know? Get a real big place, so no one could mess with me."

"I can't imagine anyone would ever mess with you," said Jane. "That's why I hired you."

Bob laughed. "I mean messing me with like hassles, you

know. Stupid stuff, like paperwork and all that." He gestured vaguely. She didn't burden him with the thought that paperwork and all that was an inevitable part of modern life.

"Listen, I'm not sure how easy it will be to get into this place," said Jane. "It's like a compound, you know? A guardhouse and a security guard who checks the cars."

"With a gun?"

"I don't know. I'll talk my way through." She suddenly realized how silly she'd feel if she couldn't get in, having dragged Bob all this way. But he seemed pleased enough to have an outing in the country, she rationalized.

"Okay." Bob seemed agreeable and put on a pair of mirrored sunglasses. It was a nice, menacing touch.

When they pulled up to the guardhouse, a skinny, ruddy man in a uniform like the one she'd seen on the guard back in town came up to the car and gazed curiously at them. She flashed her international driver's license once more. "Jane da Silva," she said.

"Let me check the list," he said.

"Forget the list," said Jane. "Call security back in Seattle. Tell them Jane da Silva is here. This is" —she cleared her throat self-consciously—"a special operation."

"Uh, okay," said the guard, looking nervous because he didn't know what she was talking about and she was acting as if he should. While he called, Jane tried to look bored and stared over the steering wheel.

When the guard got off the phone, he gave her a sketchy salute. "I'll just get your badges," he said, fumbling with some plastic name-tag holders and a felt pen.

Jane rolled her eyes at him. "No badges," she said impatiently, half-tempted to quote *Treasure of the Sierra Madre* and scream, "Badges? We don't need no stinking badges." She floored the accelerator and drove up to the main building.

"What the heck's a special operation?" said Bob.

"Beats the hell out of me," said Jane, setting the parking brake.

"Well, that rent-a-cop bought it," said Bob with a chuckle. "No gun on him either. What kind of place is this, anyway?"

"A place where people spend a lot of money hearing a lot of stuff about how they can be happier and more efficient if they decide to get whatever they want and screw over anyone who stands in their way."

"I know a lot of people who got to that place without spending a dime," said Bob philosophically. "Well, are we ready to kick some butt or what?"

"We're ready," said Jane, immensely grateful to have Bob at her side.

To her delight, there was no one in the main lobby. Just a black felt reader board with WELCOME TO ONE-TEN INSTITUTE in big white letters and beneath that what appeared to be a sucker list of the Institute's clients in residence: Evergreen State Association of Accounts Receivable Clerks, Laidlaw Brothers Tool and Die, and Corinthian Auto Sales.

"Accounts Receivable," said Bob, his mouth smirking beneath the mirrored glasses. "That's us, I guess." He squared his shoulders and Jane got the distinct impression Bob was a man who enjoyed his work.

"Well," she said, "I guess we just start opening doors." They went down a hall carpeted in steel gray. The first door she opened revealed a group of men and women in casual garb lying on the floor in neat rows. In front of them stood a lanky man with closed eyes, swaying from side to side. "Now," he said in a whispery voice, "you're squeezing down that narrow tunnel. It's getting narrower and narrower." Jane closed the door gently and left them to their birth trauma.

The second door revealed a classroom setting. Judging from the collection of garish sports jackets on view, these were the car salesmen. They frowned in concentration as a redhead in a purple knit dress gestured to a chart composed of circles and arrows and dotted lines. "Excuse me," said Jane, withdrawing and closing the door gently.

The next two rooms were empty. At the end of a hall was a door marked EXIT. They went outside, and Jane strolled purposefully with Bob in tow past a group of middle-aged people. Men and women were twirling around and around and looking up at the sky. Wayne seemed to have borrowed a little something from the whirling dervishes.

The next building was silent. Past a sort of lounge was a hall lined with more doors. Jane opened a few of them. Each featured twin beds and twin bureaus and had an unpleasant monastic air about them. "Looks like a minimum-security facility," said Bob.

At the very end of the hall, however, Jane found Dwayne Wayne. In a big, steamy room with no windows and a floor of cedar slats, he was sitting naked in a hot tub with two mature-looking, fleshy ladies, similarly naked. The water was still, and Wayne was lolling back, allowing his legs to float, while the two women giggled, their breasts bobbing in the water. One of them was snuggled up against him, and the other, perhaps feeling left out, was shyly stroking his thigh and working her way north toward a penis that seemed to be lacking in clear purpose at the moment.

"Hello, Mr. Wayne," Jane said pleasantly. "Please. Don't bother to get up." She paused. "No pun intended. Honest."

Wayne sat up straight with a look of panic and, in a gesture of modesty, hit the button that agitated the water. The two women screamed.

Jane was delighted. What better negotiating stance than to be fully clothed while one's adversary was stark naked? Wayne's gray chest hairs clung wetly to his rounded form, and Jane noted the bristling hairs on his shoulders, too. She reached over and selected a pair of towels from a stack. "The ladies will excuse us, I'm sure," she said, handing each of them a towel as they eyed the hulking form of Bob beside her with horrified expressions. Bob removed his shades, which were steaming up, lowered his velvety lashes, and turned around while they clambered out of the water, wrapped towels around themselves, and scampered through a door marked WOMEN.

"What the fuck do you think you're doing?" said Wayne.

"This is my associate, Mr. Manalatu," said Jane. "I'm here on behalf of the estate of Linda Donnelly. I'd like you to give back the money you took from her when you called yourself the Flamemaster."

"The two hundred fifty thousand dollars you were rambling about in my office?"

"That's right."

"Who was Linda Donnelly? I never heard of her."

"Come on. She inherited some money and she turned it over to you. In cash. I know she did. If you return it to her daughter, we'll forget all about the old Flamemaster act. It's very simple. You can continue to conduct your business, which, I gather, is very profitable."

"You're damned straight it's profitable," said Wayne angrily. "You know why? 'Cause I'm not stupid. In fact, I'm very smart. Too smart to let some stupid cunt push me around."

"Hey bro. When you talk to the lady, talk with respect," said Bob, taking a step forward. Jane raised her hand slightly, and watched with satisfaction as Wayne's eyes followed her gesture nervously. Bob stepped back a pace and put his hands behind him in a parade rest.

"You know what?" Wayne snapped. "I don't even remember Linda Donnelly."

"Dark hair. Back in the old days in the U District. An intense, high-strung girl. Had a baby. You baptized it in flame."

"Oh, her," Wayne said, sneering. "She never gave me a cent. She was just a pain in the neck. Her flames were always too high. Usually, people needed them moved up."

Jane raised her eyebrows. "So you believed all this thermostat stuff?"

"Of course," he said indignantly. "The work I did back in the sixties and early seventies has provided an important base for the philosophy of the Institute today. It was pioneering thought, and without it, we wouldn't have the system of effectiveness that's provided so many individuals and corporate entities with the tools for success and personal satisfaction in goal setting and achievement well beyond what had once been thought possible." When delivered in his melodious voice, the pitch almost sounded as if it made sense.

Bob wasn't buying it, though. "Want me to hit him?"

Jane shook her head. "Save it for the suckers," she said to Wayne. "Or maybe you do believe what you dish out. But I can't believe you'd want some of your current clients to know that the Fellowship of the Flame was basically a teenaged nookie society with you as the principal beneficiary."

"Look," said Wayne, exasperated, "maybe we could reach some kind of a settlement if I had actually received any funds from the little bitch."

"I know for a fact she handed her trust fund over to you. In cash. In a suitcase."

"Well, that sounds pretty untraceable to me," Wayne jeered. "Why are you wasting my time?"

"Because you owe Linda's child two hundred fifty thousand dollars," Jane said coldly. "Maybe you owe her a mother, too, but all I'm talking about is the cash." Jane hadn't meant to go that far. "You're good for it."

"How can I make sure the kid keeps her mouth shut after I pay her off? If I do, which I guarantee you I don't intend to do."

"You can't. You just have my word. But if you don't pay her, I'll guarantee you the word gets out."

He sighed. "Okay, years ago I screwed a few willing girls. I can work with that. It happened long ago. What you don't seem to understand is that there's no such thing as guilt anymore. We're working toward a guilt-free society. And I'm proud to say the Institute is part of that.

"Shit, no movie star can check into a rehab clinic, no Congressman can get caught with his hands in the till or up some skirt, without everyone hearing about it. What do they say? Do they say 'I was wrong'? No. They say, 'I made a mistake. My judgment was poor. I've learned from this mistake. I'm in therapy.' Then they make a million bucks on the lecture circuit. Everyone gets rehabilitated these days—even those Watergate guys. All you have to do is get caught and say you made a mistake. And you know what? The public respects you even more."

If Wayne had picked up her hint about Linda's death, he wasn't revealing it. It seemed time for the close.

"Twenty-four hours," she said. "In twenty-four hours I want a quarter of a million dollars. If it takes longer to come up with the funds, I want a note for the full amount payable in thirty days. Linda's daughter is a talented pianist and she needs the money to study seriously. Her teacher thinks she might be good enough for Juilliard. You're going to pay it back. Mr. Manalatu and I will be in touch."

She turned away from Wayne in his caldron of churning water, in hopes he wouldn't get the last word. Before she reached the door, however, it swung open. She saw the man first, the ruddy skinny guy from the guardhouse. Then she saw the gun. Or the barrel of it. She didn't know much about guns, but it looked like a shotgun. She watched it move back and forth between her and Bob as they both returned, walking backward, into the room.

Behind the guard, the two women, with damp hair and frightened faces but now fully clothed, stared at her.

"I'm sorry, Mr. Wayne," said the guard. "I shouldn't have let them in. I thought she was with the CIA."

"Where the hell did you get that gun?" demanded Wayne, taking advantage of the moment to step dripping out of the hot tub and wrap a towel around himself.

"I keep it in my pickup," said the guard. "What should I do? Call the sheriff?"

Wayne smiled. "I'm not sure." He turned to Jane. "I guess your large friend seems less comforting now. What took you so long?" he snapped, turning back to the guard.

"I came as soon as I could," he whined.

"The ladies probably waited to call him until they'd gotten dressed," said Jane. She imagined them pulling panty hose over their wet bodies in a state of panic. "I've got friends who know where I am. And so does Mr. Manalatu," she lied, counting on the fact that his friends were bound to be more worrisome.

"Well, let's see," said Wayne, narrowing his eyes as if trying to think of some kind of torture. "Maybe just a word with Mrs. da Silva will do. Close the door, will you?" He waved at the women in the hall. "Run along, girls. We've got this under control." He turned slowly to Bob. "This big slob can leave too, while we talk."

The guard had leveled his gun at her. Now he turned it back on Bob. He licked his lips nervously. Then the barrel of the gun wavered back toward her chest.

Bob took one giant step toward him, grabbed the barrel of the gun, jerked it out of the man's hand, and swung it like a club, clipping it hard against the man's ear.

He yelled, and Bob grabbed Jane and hustled her out of the room. He pushed his way past the two women and ran down the hall, holding Jane's hand in one of his huge paws and nearly dragging her along behind him. Her heart was pounding fast, and she felt a prickle of fear all over her body. As they went outside, Bob tossed the gun into some low shrubbery.

They ran around the building, slowing to a brisk walk past the whirling dervishes, who seemed too transfixed to take notice, and reached the front of the main building, where they found her car without anyone appearing to follow them.

"Let's go," he barked, and she yanked the car into gear and screeched out past the empty guardhouse.

When they'd reached the main road, Jane said, "Jesus! That was an incredible thing to do. He could have killed us."

"No way," said Bob. "That wasn't a shotgun. Notice the pump action? It was a pellet gun. Can't kill you unless you aim it at the eye or a chest in close range." He startled Jane by beginning to laugh. "Those guys aren't so tough."

"They scared me a lot," said Jane. "Do you think they'll follow us?"

"What are they going to do? Gun us down while we wait for the boat? How's that old guy in the hot tub gonna explain a nice lady like you and a big Samoan dead on the dock?" He frowned. "I don't know if you'll get your money, though. Not unless you really lean on him. But he's thinking about it. I can guarantee you that."

"I don't know," said Jane. "Maybe I better back off."

"I'm in the collection business," said Bob. "And the bigger the bucks, the more trouble it's worth to go after the creditor. Now two hundred fifty thou', that's plenty. You were doing great."

"I wasn't doing too badly, was I," said Jane, pleased. "I'm not used to talking to people like that, but I've got to admit, it all seemed to come naturally, and I enjoyed it." She smiled happily, but then her face clouded over. "Until that gun thing of course. Damn, I'm glad you were with me."

"I don't know the whole story here, what all went down about this money," said Bob. "But I think you got a chance. Call him in twenty-four hours. He's not going to mess with you while he thinks it over. He know where you live?"

"He knows my phone number."

"A guy like that, he can find out where you live from that. They got these backward directory things."

"But the police are watching my place."

"That's too bad."

"No, it's okay. They're protecting me."

"Well, it means I can't keep an eye on you there. There's a little chickenshit warrant out on me. No big deal, but I don't want to mess with the police right now. Gee, it's really too bad. I could have hung around for twenty-four hours in case they come after you with any more light artillery." Bob laughed again. "I'll bet that shit-kicking security guard has a headache for a few days." Suddenly he looked alarmed and patted the pocket of his sport coat. He looked relieved and pulled out his sunglasses. "God. I thought I left my shades back there."

"I'd hate to have to go back and get them," said Jane.

"Scared? Wish I could hang around for a day, until you hear?"

"I'll be okay," she said. "I've got another job for you, Bob. The kid I was telling him about? Linda's daughter? I want you to watch her for twenty-four hours. I'll call her when we get back to town and arrange the whole thing. If anything happens to her because of me—"

"Okay. No problem," said Bob. "I'm free until Friday night. My band plays every Friday night at the South Pacific."

"Really?"

"Yeah. Hawaiian shit. You know?"

"But you're Samoan."

"No one seems to care," said Bob with a shrug. "These haoles don't get it. Anyway, are you going to be okay?"

"Sure. The police are out in front of my house."

"Yeah. Anyway, if he comes after you, it'll probably be because you caught him with his dick hanging out, not because of the money or anything you've got on him."

Jane wished she had a lot more on Dwayne Wayne. She wished she could connect him to Linda's death, and to Richard English's murder. But she wasn't sure how it could be done. She'd have to tell Detective Cameron what she knew.

Eventually she would. She'd tell him absolutely everything. Twenty-four hours from now.

Chapter 28

When Jane went to pick up Leonora the next morning to take her over to her half aunt's house in Issaquah, Bob Manalatu was sitting in the living room, looking very much at home, watching a daytime game show with Kenny. The two men were drinking coffee.

"Do you really think we need him?" said Leonora in a whisper at the door.

"Just for a short while," said Jane. "I'm working on a deal with the Fellowship of the Flame, and I gave them twenty-four hours to think it over."

Leonora looked worried. "All right. I mean he's nice enough but I don't know how long I can go on feeding him." She went out of the room and Kenny got up, but Bob kept watching TV after giving Jane a friendly nod.

"Just what's going on?" said Kenny. "What kind of trouble are you expecting?"

"With Bob on the job, none," she said. "I found the head of the Fellowship of the Flame and I've asked him for Linda's money back. He's thinking it over. It's just that the Flamemaster tries to sound threatening once in a while. I thought it would be wise to have Bob around, just in case. They've already seen him in action."

"Wow. You really got into this, didn't you?" said Kenny. "I feel like I don't know what's going on."

"It's better that you don't," said Jane. "And it's not for too much longer."

"So how much did you ask for?"

"A quarter of a million. That ought to get Leonora through school."

"Well, if it's Linda's money it's really mine, now, isn't it?" said Kenny. "I mean of course we'd use it for Leonora's education and all that. But I've got some old debts to clear up myself."

"Let's not worry about that until we get the money," said Jane. Privately, she decided she'd make sure Leonora got the money, not her father. It was stupid of her not to have foreseen that Kenny would want some. Jane sighed. Leonora was a minor. She'd have to have it put in trust or something. She'd figure it out when and if she got the money.

If seemed a big if to her right now. She'd had time to think about the previous day's events. Wayne hadn't seemed particularly eager to hand over any funds. He acted as if he could talk his way out of any embarrassment. But if he was a killer, how could he be so cool? Either he was very stupid and believed in his own invincibility, or he had convinced himself in some mad way that he hadn't done anything wrong.

Well, the police would decide all that. Jane hoped to turn everything she knew over to them as soon as Leonora got her check. For now, she didn't want Leonora to feel any strain. Whatever happened, it was probably a good thing that Leonora was going to meet her family.

Leonora was dressed tough, in jeans, a black cotton top, and a beat-up gray jacket. Around her neck was an olive drab scarf with black blotches on it, which gave her street urchin punk look a dash of real chic. Jane guessed Leonora had dressed tough because she didn't feel tough. She was braced for the kind of rejection her mother had never handled very well.

"Nervous?" she said with a smile.

"For sure," said Leonora, looking suddenly very young and sweet.

Jane put an arm around her. "It'll be fine. Come on, let's go."

"Where are we going?" said Bob, his bulk rising from the sofa.

"Issaquah. But you can stay here."

"You said I was supposed to keep an eye on Leonora here until that guy's twenty-four hours are up," said Bob. He looked at his watch. The strap looked like a belt. "We got about five hours to go."

"Okay. Come on," said Jane, and they all went out and got in her car, Bob squeezing himself into the back.

As they were driving on the floating bridge across Lake Washington over to the Eastside, Leonora said, "When you found them, the Flame people, did they remember my mom?"

"Yes," said Jane.

"What did they say about her?"

"He, not they. I talked to the man who used to call himself the Flamemaster. He didn't say very much. I don't think he knew very much about her. He was only interested in her money."

"I guess no one cared about her. No one cared enough to remember her and tell me about her. Even Dad wouldn't."

"Maybe Susan Gilman will tell you about her," said Jane.

"If she doesn't like me that's okay," said Leonora defiantly. "She should have found me a long time ago, but she didn't bother, so if she doesn't like me now, I don't care."

"I hope you'll give her a chance," said Jane. "She was just a kid when your mother died." There really wasn't much point trying to convince her. It would be up to Leonora.

"I don't like their house," said Leonora as they pulled up to the driveway. "Too plastic."

"This was sort of like the neighborhood your mother grew up in," said Jane, wondering if Mrs. Donnelly would ever be in contact with her granddaughter Leonora. She knew one thing. Anyone who was kind to a child, generally got its affection for life. Anyone who rejected a child could forget about ingratiating herself later, no matter how hard she tried. It was that simple.

"Really," said Jane, "Susan's not that much older than you are. Just a few years."

"I'll wait out here," said Bob as they got out of the car. Jane was glad of that. She already felt awkward, herself, going along. The monolithic Bob's presence would be even more unsettling.

If the visit went well, Jane decided, she'd find an errand to do so Susan and Leonora could spend some time together. In fact, there *was* something she could do over here on the Eastside. A little niggling question had come up last night, when she'd lain in bed, going over everything, looking for lies. After all, it had to be in the lies that she'd find the truth.

Susan started off on the right foot. She handed baby Camille over to her cousin immediately, and Leonora turned out to be like most young girls: she loved babies. The two of them sat there and admired the infant, who gurgled and smiled and sucked on her fist. Then Susan said, "I only saw you once, but you were a beautiful baby. It was seeing you that made me know how wonderful babies were."

"Do I look like I did when I was a baby?" said Leonora expectantly.

"Yes. You do. You were a nice calm baby, with a smooth forehead. Smart-looking. Jane says you're smart and musical."

Susan tilted her head. "I think you look a lot like Linda. Want to see some pictures? I got them all out for you."

"Sure," said Leonora, swinging her legs like a gamine and looking pleased.

While Susan went to get the family albums, Jane leaned over to Leonora. "How about if I pick you up in about an hour? Give you some time alone?"

"Okay," said Leonora, looking momentarily frightened but eager. "Susan's all right, I guess. Isn't the baby darling?"

Jane patted her hand. "See? You didn't need me."

Leonora smiled a lopsided smile.

Outside, Jane told Bob she was going over to Bellevue. "No big deal, it's just a chance to leave them alone and follow up on something I don't understand," she said.

"You want me to stay here, keep an eye on the girl?"

"No one followed us here, did they?" said Jane.

"Not that I could see."

Jane bit her lip. She was half tempted to ask Bob along just because when she took the car he wouldn't have a place to sit. But then she noticed a cast-iron lawn bench on the front porch. It should hold him.

"No, I'll be back in an hour at the most. Why don't you sit on the porch."

Bob shrugged. "No problem," he said, rolling across the lawn like a tank. He was actually rather graceful, and Jane was getting used to the sheer mass of him.

She had a little trouble finding Dr. Hawthorne's Bellevue office. She was approaching it from the east this time, and it threw off her sense of direction. But finally she recognized the milky gray building and the Japanese landscaping.

Dr. Hawthorne's waiting room was empty. The receptionist was clacking quietly on a computer keyboard and listening to a classical music station.

"I'm afraid I don't have an appointment," said Jane.

"But I was wondering if I could see Dr. Hawthorne. My name is Jane da Silva. It will only take a few moments."

The woman's face showed no emotion. Probably very useful when dealing with unhappy people, thought Jane. "He's with a patient now," she said, checking her watch. "It will be another seventeen minutes." Jane imagined the punctual Dr. Hawthorne throwing out a patient in mid-sob.

"I'd like to wait, if you don't mind," said Jane.

"All right. But I don't know if he can see you." She checked an open black appointment book. "He's going to lunch with Mrs. Hawthorne."

The chippie he'd hooked up with while throwing over the psychologically deficient first Mrs. Hawthorne, thought Jane.

"Well, I'll see if he has a minute or two," she said, confident the woman wouldn't throw her out. She went over to one of the sofas and leafed through a magazine. She wasn't concentrating, though, and glanced up at the pre-Columbian artifacts. Today, their faces looked as blank as the receptionist's.

Precisely seventeen minutes later, she heard a door close and the sound of muffled voices. Presumably a patient had slunk out the back, according to psychiatric custom. Jane hopped up, but the receptionist got into Hawthorne's office first.

"By all means," she overheard him say. "Send her in."

He stood to greet her, shook her hand, looked at her searchingly with his keen blue eyes. "I wondered how you were doing," he said. "Still searching for Linda?" He shook his head just a fraction, as if to say her preoccupation was somehow mentally unhealthy.

"In a way," she said. He was managing to intimidate her, and make her feel foolish.

"I got your phone message," he said. "I'm so sorry I didn't get back to you sooner. If the name you'd mentioned had rung a bell, I would have. What was it again?"

"Robin."

"Robin. No. I can't recall anything about a Robin. Male or female?"

"Female."

"Sorry I can't help you. Who was this person?"

"I'm not sure," said Jane. "I've spoken to her, though."

"So you've found her. Well, that's good." He smiled benevolently. Jane felt more comfortable again, as if his approval mattered.

"There's someone else I should have asked you about," she said. "Richard English."

He tilted his head back and placed his forefinger beneath his lower lip. "Now that name sounds a little more familiar," he said, "but I'm not sure why."

Jane had a sudden inspiration. "Did you ever do groups? Back when you were seeing Linda. He may have been a patient."

"No. I don't do groups," he said with a condescending smile, as if they were somehow a little tacky. "And I don't think he was a patient."

"You may have seen his name in the paper then," said Jane. "He was killed on Capitol Hill in his studio. Murdered."

"Perhaps that's it," the doctor said, singularly unimpressed by the English murder, she thought. He frowned to concentrate. "Maybe I heard something on the news. Richard English. Hmm."

They were silent for a moment, and then he said: "Are you any more clear now as to why you are conducting this search into the past? I think you should understand your motivation, Mrs. da Silva."

Her brows rose a little. Conversation with Dr. Hawthorne had such a leaden quality, as if every remark were of deep psychological significance.

"I'm speaking as a human being, not as a therapist," he added gently.

"I didn't realize they were mutually exclusive," said Jane, smiling.

Dr. Hawthorne was not amused, but managed to produce a frosty little smile in return. "Well," he said with an air of finality, "were those the questions you were going to ask me?"

"Yes."

"Anything else?"

"Yes," she said. "Just one thing. You told me that Linda never remembered her dreams. Yet she left behind a book, a notebook, full of dreams. Very vivid dreams. This has been puzzling me."

Dr. Hawthorne's eyes narrowed a little and he looked thoughtful. He was silent, so Jane waited him out. Finally he said, "Perhaps they weren't dreams at all. Perhaps she was simply making them up. It would fit with her personality."

"But why wouldn't she make them up for you then?" said Jane. "Little Catholic children routinely make up transgressions for confession. Why would Linda write her dreams down and not try to impress you with them?"

He shrugged. "I really don't know."

After another pause, Jane rose. "Thank you," she said. "You've been very helpful." Dr. Hawthorne glided out from behind his desk, guided her by the elbow to the door, and opened it. "Leave your address and phone number with my receptionist," he said. "If anything comes to me I'll get in touch with you."

Outside, Jane saw a fortyish blonde with a salon tan, leaning on the reception desk flipping through the Yellow Pages. She was clearly not a patient, the way she made herself comfortable here in the office. This must be the second Mrs. Hawthorne, Jane thought, looking at her curiously. She was wearing a white silk blouse and a short black leather skirt with high heels. The outfit was a little young for her. She was thickening around the waist and hips, but her legs were still good. She'd probably worn short skirts like that twenty years ago, and was glad they'd come back again.

"I can't imagine how you forgot to make the reservation," she said to the receptionist irritably. Jane didn't recognize the voice at first. Not until she saw the black mole hovering right below the hemline at the back of Mrs. Hawthorne's thigh, exposed because she was leaning over the counter. And then Jane knew.

She walked up to the blonde, who eyed her out of the corner of her eye, slightly annoyed, as she ran a finger down the page of the phone book.

"You're Robin, aren't you?" she said pleasantly.

Mrs. Hawthorne spun around. Her eyes grew very wide and she didn't speak. She looked frightened.

Jane smiled. "I guess you are," she said. Mrs. Hawthorne just kept staring at her. Jane's face suddenly crumpled with anger; to her own amazement, she drew back her hand and slapped the blonde hard against the side of her face. "You bitch," she heard herself say.

Chapter 29

Mrs. Hawthorne let out a little cry and tears sprang into her eyes. The receptionist, Jane, and Robin stood in a silent tableau for a second until Dr. Hawthorne emerged.

"What's going on?" he demanded in an agitated voice.

"Nothing," Jane said. "I'm leaving."

"This woman struck Mrs. Hawthorne," said the receptionist. "She called her Robin."

Dr. Hawthorne grabbed Jane by the shoulders and, although she resisted, he managed to drag her back into his office. His wife followed.

"Let me go," shouted Jane.

"This woman is assaultive and dangerous." Dr. Hawthorne yelled over his shoulder to the receptionist. "I'll have to sedate her."

"Let go of me!" Jane shouted in as imperious a voice as she could muster.

Dr. Hawthorne drowned her out. "Be quiet!" he ordered, wrestling with her and kicking the door shut. "Help me, goddammit," he barked at his wife.

"What do you want me to do?" she said.

"Help me hold her while I prepare an injection."

Jane thrashed around in his grip and managed to escape his grasp. With both hands free for a moment, she grabbed at one of his thumbs and pulled it back as far as she could.

His face winced with pain.

"I'm sorry I slapped your wife," said Jane, still hanging on to the thumb.

"Jesus, she's pulling off my thumb," said Hawthorne.

"She called me Robin," said his wife, horror in her voice. "Is it Jane da Silva?"

Hawthorne began to kick. His foot connected hard with her shin, and Jane's hands fell away from his thumb. His face was red now, and his gray hair hung over his forehead.

"This is stupid," said Jane, panting a little and stepping back.

"Hold on to her while I get the syringe," shouted Hawthorne. Suddenly, he was behind his desk, rummaging in a drawer.

"Stick me with a needle, and you'll have a malpractice suit on your hands," said Jane. Mrs. Hawthorne came toward her, hands fluttering at her sides. Jane knew she didn't have the will to grab her.

"Damn it, don't touch me," Jane said to the woman. "Don't even think about it." She smoothed back her hair. "I'm leaving now, okay? There's no point getting into a fight like a bunch of kids."

"What'll we do?" Mrs. Hawthorne asked her husband plaintively.

"We have to stop her," he said, inverting a bottle over a needle. "We'll have to get her out of here."

"Your receptionist saw me," said Jane.

"Yes, she saw you assault my wife. You're clearly psychotic."

"But what can we do?" said his wife again.

"What do you mean, what can we do," he snapped, easing the plunger of the syringe downward. "We have to get rid of her. She'll ruin everything. She asked me about Richard English."

"No, baby, no," said Mrs. Hawthorne, running to his side. "No more."

"It's over," said Jane, stepping back another step. Hawthorne's wife was clutching at his sleeve. "She's not going to help you anymore."

"I did it all for you," Hawthorne shrieked at his wife.

"All what?" said Jane.

"I don't have to explain anything to you," he said huffily. "I don't owe you any explanations. Some misplaced maternal impulses have dragged you into my business. You're a silly woman." He reached over for her, but his wife held him back. He shook his wife loose and hit her hard with the back of his hand. She fell into a corner, her black leather skirt hiked up, her face pale and startled.

Hawthorne walked toward Jane and grabbed her wrist. She twisted it in his hand. Then she heard sirens outside the window.

"It's the police," said Jane. "I wonder what Mrs. Hawthorne will tell them."

Hawthorne looked at Jane, enraged. He released her wrist, shoved his hair back in place, and went over to his wife. He tore at the wrist of her blouse, pushed the fabric up, and plunged the needle into her forearm as she screamed. A second later, Mrs. Hawthorne slumped to one side.

He threw down the syringe and ran out into the reception area. Jane followed him.

Two patrolmen walked in. One of them was speaking into a walkie-talkie. "We're in the office now," he said.

"This woman is assaultive and dangerous," shrieked Hawthorne. "She attacked my wife and then she went after me. My wife is collapsed in the other room."

Jane held up both hands. "I'm not dangerous," she said. "Honest." She tried to make her voice sound as rational as possible. "But the doctor here is all bent out of shape. His wife is unconscious because he gave her an injection."

"Why are the police here?" demanded Hawthorne of the receptionist.

"I called them," she said, wide eyed and backing up behind the counter. "You said Mrs. da Silva was dangerous."

"We've got a two-twenty situation here," said the officer into his walkie-talkie. "We'll let you know as soon as we figure out who's crazy."

"I'll go in and check it out," said the other. "We may have to call the medics."

"No!" said Hawthorne. "It's all right. I just gave her five milligrams of lorazetam. She'll be all right. I'm a doctor."

Jane remembered suddenly that gloved hand in the dark at Richard English's studio. It was feeling for a pulse in a deft professional way. Like a doctor might.

"That is—she's been sedated," Hawthorne continued. "I was trying to subdue Mrs. da Silva here, and there was a struggle. My wife got the injection instead."

"Please," said Jane, "call Detective John Cameron of the Seattle Police Department. These people know something about a homicide he's investigating."

Hawthorne sighed and rolled his eyes. "I'll put it in layman's terms," he said. "This woman is crazy. Just get her out of my office, will you?"

The second policeman came out. "The woman in there is out cold. In some kind of a coma or something. We'd better call the aid car." He looked sharply at Hawthorne. "What the hell did you do to her?" He started barking into his walkie-talkie and went back to her side, kneeling down beside her. Everyone else trailed after him.

"She'll be all right," said Hawthorne. "It'll wear off in an hour or so. I meant to sedate Mrs. da Silva, but she got in the way."

"That's his own wife he's talking about," said Jane. "Kind of cold, isn't it?"

The two policemen stared at Hawthorne with thinly veiled disgust.

"This woman is crazy," Hawthorne repeated. "And dangerous. A danger to herself and others. Mostly others."

The two policemen stared at Jane with frank curiosity. Then they looked at each other, and appeared to be making some telepathic decision. "Let's take the two conscious ones in and sort it out later," said the first one, shrugging.

"Right," said the second, reaching for the handcuffs on his belt.

•   •   •

Later, much later, Jane sat in a Bellevue coffee shop— all orange vinyl—with John Cameron and his partner.

"Okay," Cameron said to her. "Let's hear it one more time."

"It was a cult of one. A cult designed for just one person," said Jane. "Hawthorne wanted a divorce. Probably an expensive one. You can check it out. Doctors are notoriously bad financial managers. He actually told me he was. Said his accountant couldn't understand it.

"Maybe he figured that without money, he couldn't get Robin or whatever her real name is—"

"Tammy," said Cameron's partner, a young blonde man. "Her name is Tammy."

"Anyway," Jane continued, "maybe he figured she wouldn't marry him if he was in financial trouble. Who knows. He had a patient who was very suggestible. Who was about to come into a lot of money and turn over two hundred fifty grand in cash to the Fellowship of the Flame.

"What does he do? He gets her into another cult. Something more select. Something where Linda won't feel left out. And he knows just what will appeal to her.

He's listened to her most intimate thoughts for years. He even knows what she dreams.

"She dreams a wise robin flies in her window, transforms itself into a woman, and then Tammy calls herself Robin and scrapes an aquaintance with her.

"He and Tammy put together some nonsense about the Chosen. It's in that diary. She had abandoned the Fellowship of the Flame and been lured into something more secret. She heads off with Robin for some meeting, but it isn't the Fellowship of the Flame. It's this new thing—the Chosen or whatever they call it.

"They knew all her associations and they knew just which buttons to push. A lonely kid, rejected by her family. All of a sudden she's part of the cosmic plan.

"I guess they needed to make it very special, very convincing, so they get a special effects wizard—Richard English. He left behind a painting that came out of her dreams. Who knows what kind of scene they set up, but it was all intended to make Linda feel very special and that she was somehow fated to be with these people and turn over her money to them.

"And then she drowns. I don't know how or why, but she used to dream about walking on water and she couldn't swim. Maybe they talked her into the water. Maybe she was pushed. All I know is Richard English had a workshop at the end of a pier on Lake Union."

Cameron shook his head. "What proof have you got?"

"The picture. There's a picture they found in Richard English's studio. It was one of her dream landscapes. It was part of the special effects, I just know it. They used it to con her.

"And English came into a lot of money around the time Linda drowned. He started up his business with cash. Said he won it at the track." She leaned forward. "His share for putting together a package to sell her on the new way to truth. That's how she was. Looking for signs and portents all the time. When you read the diary again it will all make sense."

"We can't possibly prove a thing," said Cameron.

"Okay, let's flash forward," said Jane. "I go looking for Linda's money. I find out a Richard English knew her. I make an appointment to see him. I tell him she kept a diary. He wants me to bring it. What's he going to do after that phone call with me?"

Cameron shrugged. "Well, if he was in it with the shrink, he calls him. He tells him you're looking into this and you have Linda's diary. Maybe there's something in there that will incriminate them both."

"That's right. I think Richard English might have been ready to get it off his chest," said Jane. "He told his wife he had some guilty burden. He never came forward, but when confronted he might have buckled."

Cameron looked skeptical. "So Hawthorne goes to wait with him. Maybe they're going to make a deal with you, depending on what the diary says. But Hawthorne kills English instead."

Jane nodded. "That's right. Maybe English is weakening. Then Hawthorne waits for me and searches me and the car for the diary. He doesn't kill me because he doesn't know how much I know—or where the diary is."

"But he'd already met you."

"That's right, but he didn't have my address or phone number. He had to waylay me at Richard English's studio, after he found out Richard English wouldn't keep the secret any longer." She paused and sipped her coffee. "I'm just guessing some of this," she said, "but it's basically true; I *know* it's true.

"Hawthorne didn't have my phone number until I called him and left a message. He didn't call back. Tammy did. Calling herself Robin again and telling me Linda was suicidal and probably killed herself. Reminding me that the Fellowship of the Flame got her money, the old cover story. Then she acts scared and tries to get me to back off, claiming the Fellowship of the Flame will get me."

"But you got a phone call from an individual representing himself as part of the Fellowship of the Flame, too," said Cameron.

"I know. That was probably Dwayne Wayne and his boys. They knew I was looking for the Flamemaster. I'd called the One-Ten Institute that morning and told them what I was looking for, and they tried to scare me off for their own reasons. They weren't covering up a murder, just the murky origins of the One-Ten Institute. That's what was so confusing. They—well Wayne, actually—had something to hide, too.

"I know I'm right," Jane said. "Why else would Hawthorne lie and say Linda didn't remember her dreams? He was trying to cover his tracks. He'd used those dreams to con her and get her money. It's true, I know it. It's the only scenario that fits."

Cameron was silent for a while. "Okay, maybe it is. If we're lucky, we'll find out soon enough."

"You will? How?"

"We got a lot of physical evidence from the English murder scene. No fingerprints, but a nice collection of hair and fibers. He struggled with you, remember? We got a lot of stuff off your clothes, and off Richard English, too. If Hawthorne was there, we can probably place him there with physical evidence. But the story is so screwy I don't know what the prosecutor can do with it. I don't even know if it's enough to go in with a search warrant and look for something linking Hawthorne with the scene."

"You haven't talked to the wife yet," said Jane.

"A wife doesn't have to testify against her husband." said Cameron.

"This wife might want to," said Jane. "Especially if it saves her from a murder charge of her own. I think the guy scares her."

"We'll check it out," said Cameron. "By ourselves. No more messing around, right? I mean it. You could mess up a conviction if you interfere."

"I promise," said Jane. Then she remembered she'd never called Dwayne Wayne back. His twenty-four hours had been up a few hours ago. She supposed she owed him an apology. She no longer believed he'd taken Linda's money. Hawthorne had worked too hard to get it for himself. Which left Jane back at square one as far as her hopeless case went.

Chapter 30

Soon after she arrived home, the phone rang.

"Hello, Mrs. da Silva," said a cheery, familiar voice. "It's Dorothy. From Mr. Wayne's office?"

"Hello, Dorothy," said Jane. "How may I help you today?" she added maliciously.

"Please stay on the line for Mr. Wayne."

Jane's heart sank just a little. Dwayne Wayne was one of the biggest sleazes she'd ever come up against, but she now believed him to be innocent of the particular act of sleaziness of which she'd accused him.

No wonder he'd been annoyed. Not only had she falsely accused him and tried to shake him down, she'd cornered him practically in flagrante delicto in a hot tub. It occurred to her again that she really did owe him an apology. She sighed and began to prepare one. "Perhaps I acted hastily," she began aloud.

Wayne came on the line. His voice was affable, brisk, and professional. And, of course, gorgeous.

"Mrs. da Silva," he said, "I've been thinking about what we discussed."

"Yes?" she said.

"You know, the One-Ten Institute prides itself on seeking out symbols of excellent effectiveness. Young people who strive and achieve. The community has been good to

254

us, and we like to turn back some of what we receive. That's why this young person you told me about, this young pianist, strikes me as a perfect recipient of a new scholarship we're planning to offer. We pay all tuition and expenses, for whatever the young lady needs. And there's some cash, too. The package comes to two hundred fifty thousand dollars."

"Really," said Jane.

"Don't worry about any paperwork or anything. We'll handle all that. All I need from you is the young lady's name and a glossy black-and-white of her for the press kit."

"Is this all legitimate?" said Jane.

"Absolutely." His tone changed a little. "There are some tax and PR advantages, of course. I have to spread it around anyway. I figure this way I can take care of two things at once. This way, I win and you win and the kid wins, and everybody's happy." He cleared his throat. "And I trust I can count on your gratitude. It's a good deal. Grab it and don't push for the interest or it's all off."

"No one need ever hear about any youthful excesses you might have had," said Jane. "I mean, nobody's perfect, and there's no reason to bring up the past. Ever. I promise."

"I'm glad to hear that," said Wayne. "I trust the young lady understands all that too, and we can count on her to stick to her piano playing and keep her mouth shut?"

"She doesn't know anything incriminating about you," said Jane. "And I'm sure she'll be very glad to be a recipient of your corporate largesse."

"Good. That's settled. Now there's another matter I'd like to bring up. That's you and your plans. You know, I could use someone like you in my organization."

"With or without my Samoan friend?" said Jane.

"This is on the level," said Wayne. "I'm always on the lookout for people who know how to handle themselves.

How to handle people. You've got it, Mrs. da Silva. The touch."

"Thank you," said Jane, "but I don't think it would work out. I appreciate your thinking of me, though."

"We're talking about a lot of money," he said. "Travel. You'd meet some fascinating people."

"I really don't think so." She decided not to mention he'd called her a stupid cunt just yesterday.

"I'm sorry to hear that. Call me if you ever change your mind. Meanwhile, let's consider that other matter taken care of. We'll make the announcement next week."

"Thank you," said Jane. When she hung up, she smiled and then she started laughing and jumping.

She called Leonora first. "We got it," she said. "A full scholarship for you. And there's plenty of cash, too."

Leonora didn't answer for a long time. Then she started screaming adolescent screams of joy.

•　　•　　•

A week later, back in her Chanel suit, she summed up. "I trust you will agree, gentlemen," she said, looking out at six silver heads in a conference room at the offices of Carlson, Throckmorton, Osgood, Stubbins, and Montcrieff, "that I have carried out Uncle Harold's wishes, and righted not just one, but three wrongs."

She sat down and sipped water.

Mr. Montcrieff frowned. "Three wrongs?"

"I arranged for Linda Donnelly's daughter to receive funds enabling her to study piano, for which she shows great promise."

Judge Potter frowned. "Yes, but you tell us the party from whom she received the funds never had them in the first place. That is, this individual"—he consulted some notes through his glasses—"Mr. Wayne, never did benefit initially from Linda Donnelly's gullibility."

"That's true," said Jane. "But he did feel a moral obligation." She squirmed a little.

"Why did he come up with the money?" said Glendinning, the banker, suspiciously.

"Sounds like you had something on him," said Commander Kincaid with a chuckle. "Let's not be so picky, Potter. The bastard would have conned the girl's mother out of that money if he could have."

"Let's avoid sloppy thinking here," said Professor Grunewald.

"Blackmail," said the bishop, shaking his head. "I don't know if we can reward blackmail."

"It wasn't exactly blackmail," said Jane.

"We'll have to think about it," said Judge Potter. "How about those other wrongs. Now, let's see, there's the initial death of Linda Donnelly. That strikes me as rather vague. Is anyone going to be prosecuted for that? Does anyone know what really happened?"

"As I explained," said Jane patiently, "Mrs. Hawthorne has chosen to testify against her husband in the murder of Richard English. She has been frank about the original conspiracy. She says Linda fell into the water at the end of the pier where Richard English kept his studio during a ceremony during which she handed over her inheritance to Mrs. Hawthorne, then Dr. Hawthorne's mistress.

"Dr. Hawthorne had been hiding in a back room. His wife says he dissuaded her from trying to save the girl. I think she was pushed, but either way, it's murder."

"How could Linda Donnelly have been so stupid?" mused Glendinning.

"Tammy—or Robin—says they'd cooked up an elaborate ritual. They'd bring Linda to English's studio and show her light shows full of her dreams and innermost thoughts. Robin would pretend to trance and tie it all together with promises that Linda would be a princess of the cosmos. It sounds amazing, but people have believed crazier things. And remember, the Hawthornes did know her innermost secrets.

"The prosecutor, as I understand it, is not going to press charges in that case, but I think we can agree that Linda was the victim of a wrongful death, and she certainly didn't kill herself.

"This information relieves her daughter and her widower of that burden. It also exposes a conspiracy."

"Well," said Montcrieff, "what about this conspiracy? Shouldn't the psychiatrist give Leonora her mother's money?"

Jane shrugged. "Everything he owns could well be swallowed up by legal fees. And I doubt he'd want to give her anything. It would look incriminating.

"Anyway," she said, "Dr. Hawthorne will stand trial for the murder of Richard English. The police tell me that with his wife's testimony as well as certain physical evidence, a conviction is likely."

The trustees were silent for a moment. "Why is his wife testifying?" said Judge Potter.

"As I understand it," said Jane, "she was terrified of going to jail. She made a deal with the prosecutor."

"But," said Glendinning, "Richard English wouldn't have died if you hadn't begun your investigation. Which was based on the spurious assumption that these Flame people got Linda's money. If you righted any wrongs, it was accidentally."

They sat there in silence for a moment. Jane didn't feel she could add much more. "I believe," she said firmly, "that Uncle Harold would have approved of the results of my endeavors."

"We'll need to discuss this further, gentlemen," said Mr. Montcrieff. "Harold's work was always more cut and dried. Mrs. da Silva seems to have cut rather a wide swath."

"I did my best, and I did it in the spirit in which Uncle Harold intended," she insisted.

"What about publicity," said the bishop. "Is there going to be any publicity?"

"I have made every attempt to keep my role anonymous," said Jane. "The scholarship to Leonora was announced without any reference to me. I may have to appear in the Hawthorne trial, but only as a concerned friend of Leonora."

"No cheap publicity," said the bishop. "You don't want to be some odious local celebrity, do you?"

"Absolutely not," said Jane. "I want to lead a quiet life, doing Uncle Harold's work." And spending Uncle Harold's money, she added to herself. In quiet good taste.

Mr. Montcrieff shook his head. "I don't know," he said. "We'll have to discuss this among ourselves. This has some twists and turns that are a trifle unorthodox."

"Before I leave," said Jane, "I'd like to add that I was badly beaten during the course of this work. It wasn't pleasant or easy. I was frightened and tired, and sometimes what I learned made me very sad. But whatever you decide, I'll know I did what my uncle wanted me to. And more. And that I'd do it again."

• • •

"It was that last speech you gave 'em that almost pushed them over the edge," said Bucky later. They were at a large table at the South Pacific, a garishly decorated bar specializing in fruity rum drinks, where Bob Manalatu's band was performing standards with a Hawaiian lilt.

"I can't believe they shafted me like that," said Jane, staring gloomily into her piña colada. "I practically got killed. What more did they want?"

"They're very literal minded. And they fear anything vulgar. Uncle Harold was much more refined about the whole thing. But cheer up. They're giving you another chance."

Jane sighed. "Three more months, and an allowance. I feel like a kid on probation. I'm tempted to just tell them to—" She stopped, realizing Bucky was Mr. Montcrieff's nephew. She supposed she should try to be discreet.

"Fuck themselves?" said Bucky, finishing her thought. "Come on. Give them a break. They'll get used to your style. Just try to get a case that's a little less byzantine next time. I mean, think about it from a legal point of view. Basically, you blackmailed someone into helping out a sweet kid."

"But what about solving that old case?"

"They're not nailing him on that old case. They're nailing him on Richard English. Who never would have been killed if you hadn't stirred things up."

Jane shivered a little. "I've thought about it a lot. I can't really be held responsible for his death. Dr. Hawthorne killed him. And English sowed those seeds years ago when he took Linda's money." She tried not to think about Richard English's widow. Why couldn't life be more straightforward? She suspected that for Uncle Harold it was. Life on the edge, where she always seemed to end up—and she realized with trepidation, where she liked it—could be messy and morally ambiguous.

"You bought yourself some time with that last speech," said Bucky. "You should be grateful. It's a holding action." A steel guitar line ran through "Some Enchanted Evening."

"They might have just sent you down the road," he continued, "if they'd heard about your pal Bob. Uncle Harold never used big Samoan thugs."

"Do I look stupid?" said Jane. "It's simply a matter of the male's superior upper body strength. I mean, you guys can open pickle jars better than we can." She looked at Bucky sharply. "How do you know I left Bob out of my spiel?"

"To tell you the truth," said Bucky, "I listened to the whole thing through the door of conference room B. I was really pulling for you, kid." He put his hand on her knee and squeezed.

"Look," said Jane, waving. "There's Calvin Mason. I did tell you I invited him too, didn't I?"

"No, you didn't," said Bucky, removing his hand and looking irked. He turned around.

Calvin came up to the table. "I want something with a paper umbrella in it," he said eyeing the decor appreciatively.

"Prom drinks," sneered Bucky. "I thought you were bringing Marcia."

Calvin ignored him and scraped his chair into place. "Rough day working those divorce cases and snooping around motel parking lots?"

"I subcontract that to you, remember?" said Bucky.

Claire Westgaard, if possible even more obviously great with child, and wearing another billowing chintz slipcover of a dress, came up to their table accompanied by a thin man with glasses.

She gave Jane and Bucky each a peck on the cheek. "So nice of you to invite us," she said. "Especially after the whole thing kind of crashed for you."

"I wanted to thank the people who helped me," Jane said.

"This is my husband," said Claire, beaming. "Ben." Jane introduced Calvin. "Great place," Claire said, peering through a fringe of plastic palm leaves out over the dance floor, where the patrons seemed to be a strange mix of the geriatric and the young and trendy.

"Your Samoan buddy's band is pretty good," said Calvin Mason. "I love these old songs."

"I know them all," said Jane, reaching for pineapple and shrimp on a toothpick.

"That's right," said Bucky. "You're a singer, aren't you?"

"Used to be," said Jane.

"Let's get a couple of drinks in her and get her to sing," said Calvin.

"No," said Jane, laughing. "No. No. No."

"Great idea," said Bucky, hailing a muumuu-clad waitress staggering under a tray of drinks. "How about 'Melancholy Baby.' You know that?"

"Of course I do," said Jane huffily. "But," she added, "I'm not going to sing it now." She glanced over at the entrance.

"So who else did you invite?" said Bucky, following her glance. "You look like you're expecting someone."

She shrugged. "Oh. John Cameron said he might drop by." She shifted her gaze to the stage where Bob, swaying over the bass, lifted his chin in greeting. He was wearing a mammoth shirt covered with tropical fish and a dozen or so pink plastic leis. The band was now performing "Take the A Train" with ukeleles. It actually worked.

The waitress arrived with the latest offerings from the blender. "Nice try," said Calvin, toasting Jane. "You almost just came into a lot of money."

"Almost," groaned Jane. "I'm sick of almost."

"Too bad you can't pay my bill," added Calvin philosophically.

"I'm sorry about that." She leaned forward. "I really am. But I've got a little left of my original stipend and I am buying you that drink."

"Don't spend it all in one place," said Bucky. "Especially if it's this place."

"Come on," said Jane "Don't be a snob. This is great." In the background a macaw screamed. "You know, this concept would really work in Europe," she said. "Garish and tropical and American."

"You're not going back there, are you?" said Bucky.

She sighed. "The world is a different place. Everything

went global. It doesn't matter where I am, really. I'll always be able to find what I want, anywhere in the world. I think I'll stay right here, close to the trustees. And look for another hopeless case."

"That finder's fee still holds, I take it," said Calvin.

Claire squeezed into Jane's side and said, sotto voce, "So how about you and Bucky? Making any progress?"

Jane wasn't about to tell Claire that Bucky wasn't her type. Claire would report it to Bucky as soon as Jane left the table to go to the ladies' room, and Jane still needed an ally with links to the trustees. "To be honest, Claire," she said, lying blatantly, "I've been too busy to think about men."

Claire looked thoughtful. "When you find the right one, you'll know." She smiled over at her husband.

"I know," said Jane. Behind her, she sensed a presence. She turned to see John Cameron, looking distinctly untropical in a brown tweed sport coat. "Thought I'd just come by and say hi," he said. Jane introduced him around, and then he asked her to dance.

"Holding up?" he said, when they were out on the floor.

She closed her eyes for just a minute, and relaxed against him a little. "Yes," she said. "They gave me another chance. I get to live in the house and I get some walking-around money."

"I still say it's a screwy way to make a living," he said.

"I know. But I think I'm good at it. Or will be. Better than I was at my last job."

"What was that?"

"I sang American ballads to jaded Europeans," she said.

"You mean like 'As Time Goes By'? Stuff like that?"

"That's right. In satin dresses. I'm getting too old for that kind of nonsense."

"No kidding? With long black satin gloves, too?"

"No," said Jane, indignant. "Nothing cheap or tacky. I had a class act."

"I'm sure you did," he said, holding her a little tighter around the waist. "They scheduled the Hawthorne trial today."

Her eyes opened wide. "Really? When?"

"August twenty-first."

"Think you'll nail him?" Silently she added, "And do you think I'll nail you, right after the trial?"

"The prosecutor thinks so."

"Good."

He cleared his throat. "And my wife called this morning," he said.

"Oh?"

"Yeah. She thinks we should try and get back together. It's what I thought I wanted, but now I'm not so sure."

Jane was silent as they danced. "But I believe it's worth a try," he went on. "For the kids. I'm crazy about those kids, and they want us back together."

"Then you should do everything you can to get back together," said Jane.

"That's what I figure." They smiled into each other's faces until Calvin Mason cut in. "You don't mind, do you?" he said to John.

It felt rather comfortable to be held by Calvin, who danced in a direct, take-charge way, after the prickliness of feeling Cameron's body next to hers. "While you were gone, Bucky went up and talked to Bob," said Calvin. "The band wants you to sing with them."

"It'll never happen," said Jane, laughing.

"Oh, come on. You better get those pipes in shape. You might have to go back to singing for your supper. Besides, I want to hear you."

Over his shoulder, she saw John leave the room. He gave her a wave and a wistful smile. It wouldn't have worked anyway, she told herself. He had been lonely. And he wouldn't be anymore. She had been scared. And she wasn't scared anymore.

"Are you listening to me?" said Calvin.

"Sure. You want me to sing. Forget it."

The song ended and they went back to their table, where Bucky, sloshing his drink a little, announced, "It's all arranged. You're on next. 'Melancholy Baby.'"

"Oh, what the hell," said Jane. "This looks like a pretty easy room to work." She plucked a plastic orchid from the centerpiece and stuck it behind her ear. Then she went up to the stage.